ELONA

PATTERNER'S PATH, BOOK 1

STEVE TURNBULL

TAU PRESS 2020 LTD

Elona (Patterner's Path #1) by Steve Turnbull.

First published March 2014. Revised edition June 2017. Second revision 2020.

Copyright © 2014, 2017, 2020 Tau Press 2020 Ltd. All rights reserved.

ISBN: 978-1-910342-81-7

This is a work of fiction. Names, characters, places, and incidents are either products of the author's imagination or used fictitiously. Any resemblance to actual events, locales, or persons, living or dead, is entirely coincidental. No part of this book shall be reproduced or transmitted in any form or by any means, electronic or mechanical, including photocopying, recording, or by any information retrieval system without permission of the publisher. The moral right of the contributors to be identified as the authors of their work has been asserted by them in accordance with the Copyright, Designs, and Patents Act 1988.

Published by Tau Press 2020 Ltd.

Cover by Jane Dixon-Smith (jdsmith-design.com).

For My Baby Sister

1

'Is Mother dead yet?'

Elona peeked at her mother's pale body on the bed, lying there as it always had, for as long as she could remember. Elona's ears were filled with discordant chanting that echoed through the high chamber. Cold draughts from the vaulted stone ceiling disturbed the torch flames, making shadows dance about her mother's thin face.

'No, dearie. Just sleeping,' said Nursey, loudly enough to make the nearby servants turn their heads.

Elona watched her mother's chest rise and fall—just like Nursey's did when she was asleep in her rocking chair. Nursey must be telling the truth this time. Other things went horrid and smelly when they were dead for a long time, but Mother had been asleep for as long as Elona could remember and she smelled of flowers.

Brilliant white light flared through the high windows, momentarily making every sharp edge bright and every shadow deepest black. Elona looked up to see, and Nursey did too, but it was gone as quick as it came.

The Sisters of Taymalin stopped singing the pattern song they used to feed Mother. The echoes died away and the room brimmed with silence. They bowed their strange, shaved heads in respect. The Revered Malea turned from the bed and led the Sisters in a line towards the hall's big door. The strong scent of incense fell from them as they passed. Their grey robes rustled and their sandalled feet slapped against the worn flagstones. Elona stood sad and solemn, the way she was supposed to, and clung to Nursey's soft hand. Father stood on the other side of the chamber and his cheeks were wet.

Elona shivered. It was summertime but always cold inside. She wished Nursey had made her put on a cloak. Nursey always told her to put more things on 'so you don't catch a chill, dearie' but today Elona had to wear a special dress instead. It wasn't a very pretty dress; it was grey like the Sisters' robes. Elona thought of the Sisters with their shaved heads and ran her fingers through her loose hair.

Father stepped up to the bed, his boots echoing on the flagstones. He leant over and kissed Mother on the lips—Elona tensed, hoping she wouldn't have to do it. She tightened her grip on Nursey's hand. Father straightened and wiped his hand across his face. He turned towards them and Elona held her breath, but he walked past them without a glance. Nursey sighed heavily and dropped Elona's hand.

There was another flash of white light; Elona looked at the windows again. The light was brighter than lightning and there wasn't any thunder. An old servant looked down at her; he smiled nicely and she smiled back.

From a small door servants bustled in with thin screens and heavy rugs. Two armsmen struggled through the door with a lit brazier between long poles. Bright embers shone through its holes. The servants stood aside as it was carried to the foot of the bed. They laid out the rugs and erected screens around her mother.

Elona hung back as Nursey walked to the side of the sleeping woman and stared down at her expressionless face.

'Should let her die, I reckon,' she said. There were nervous glances from the younger servants. 'This Dedication is for the little one's future, not for picking at old wounds. He wastes his riches making her breathe and his fief goes to pieces without a care.'

An old armsman came and stood by her side. 'You'd be a murderer then.'

'Can't murder what's already dead. If he'd let her go, he could marry again and the child could forget it all. He don't really care anyway, it's just his pride.'

'It's not for me to say 'bout that, but you weren't here before it happened. You didn't know the Lady Veona. She was a good woman.'

'Was.'

'D'y'think the healers would keep her breathing if she were really gone?'

' 'Course they would. The Sisters set their price as high as they dare and care for nothing but their purses. If your Lady hadn't been trying to satisfy both guild and husband, she'd've not been on the road when she was so heavy with child...'

'It was wolves.'

'That's what I'm saying. She wouldn't have been there. Lucky for the little one I was close by, visiting my eldest. So now he's giving the girl to the Sisters and he can forget her. I'll be out without even a thank-you.'

Elona sighed in imitation of Nursey and fiddled with her fingers. She looked from one side to another; she didn't like it in here because people talked about her when they talked about her mother and the wolves. Everyone knew wolves were magic and bad.

'Do they have to cut my hair off, Nursey?' Her high-pitched voice pierced the dark of the hall.

'All the Sisters and Brothers have to, dearie, so we remember when we was slaves to the Slissac before Taymalin rescued us.'

A bright double flash lit the room, and this time everyone looked up. 'Nearly time, best we get down to the hall. Are you nervous, dearie? Me too.' She turned back to the armsman. 'Better than watching a stupid old man wasting his own life – and ours.' Nursey crossed to where Elona stood, caught up her hand, and pulled her from the room.

~

Elona stepped into the main hall of the castle with Nursey behind, pushing her forwards. The walls were garlanded with spring blossoms, green boughs and the gathered nobility in gay colours. The patterners and guild leaders stared at her. She saw a man in a big floppy hat who smiled at her with all his face. Her cheeks went red.

Nursey made her walk to where Father stood. The flagstones were hot where the sun shone on them and cold in the shadows; she could feel their smoothness under her bare feet.

In front of the windows waited the line of Sisters, heads bare. The Revered Malea stood in front of them; she stepped forward. Father put his hand on Elona's shoulder and pushed her ahead. Elona swallowed, her mouth dry.

A long white flash from behind drowned the sun; Elona saw hers and Father's shadows clearly outlined on the stones in front of her. All the Sisters blinked when the light stopped but no one said anything.

When the Revered Malea had talked to her before, she said it was always a special thing to be dedicated to the Sisters, but for Elona it was to be done on an extra special day at an extra special time: right at the time when Mother Earth fed the moons.

One of the Sisters sounded a gong.

'Who brings a novice to the Sisters of Taymalin?' asked the Revered Malea loudly.

'I am Taniel, Lord of Corlain. I bring my daughter, Elona, to be novice to the Sisters.'

Father put his hand on her shoulder and pushed her forward until she stood right in front of Malea.

'Be welcome, Elona, novice to the Sisters of Taymalin. At the beginning of things, we were slaves and we will always remember.'

The Revered Malea unhooked a pair of shears from her belt; they glistened in the sunlight. Holding them in one hand she reached out and took hold of Elona's hair. Elona choked back a whimper and tried not to cry, but tears formed in her eyes anyway.

The hall swelled with a new brilliance that held steady for a moment, then grew stronger. The faces of the Sisters reflected whiteness and they fell to their knees. The light was so bright Elona felt like it shone right through her.

Elona couldn't turn to see because the Revered Malea still held her hair, though she too had dropped to her knees and was face to face with Elona. All around people were chanting: 'Mother Earth, feed me; Mother Earth, clothe me; as the milk of the Earth feeds her children in the sky, so feed me.' Elona said the words too but the Revered Malea didn't say anything, her eyes wide as if she saw something different.

The light winked out, and everyone sighed. The Sisters stood, blinking, and looked expectantly at Elona and the Revered Malea. Elona looked apprehensively at her but she still hadn't moved, holding on really tight to Elona's hair and her eyes wide. She stared at something above Elona's head.

The silence broke with the shears clattering to the floor.

Elona was pleased that her hair was not cut off, but she rubbed her head where some had been pulled out when they made the Revered Malea let her go. Nursey had helped and pulled her hair by accident. Father had shouted a lot but the man in a big, floppy hat talked to him and stopped the shouting. The floppy hat man had made all the important people come to sit in a room off the main hall, while all the other people talked outside.

'The child should stay, Taniel,' said the floppy hat man when her father had called for Nursey to take her out.

'As you wish, Florian. As long as she is quiet,' said Father, drinking his wine.

The Revered Malea sat in a chair, sipped from a cup, while two other Sisters stood by her. Elona wondered if she would get into trouble because she still had her hair. The Revered Malea had been like someone dreaming and only woke up when two Sisters sat her down in a chair and gave her something to drink; the two waited, hesitantly watching their leader. Elona fidgeted in the corner where Master Florian had put her; she knew she'd made it all go wrong.

'Well, Malea? You saw something?'

'War, Arch-Patterner. Shaven-headed warriors invade our land, defeating all who stand in their way: Lords, Princes and King all cut down. Then—' she lowered her voice and nodded in Elona's direction. '—her, the child, walking onto the battlefield and picking up the Dragonblade. She felled the invaders like corn and drove them back.'

'What?' Father growled, and Elona shivered.

'Be calm, my friend,' said Master Florian.

'Across the deserted battlefield the king of the invaders appeared. She battled him. She slew him,' said the Revered Malea. She looked at Elona then back at Florian. 'What meaning does the Arch-Patterner divine from this?'

'Prophecies!' snorted Father and took another drink. 'It's ridiculous! A woman cannot go to war.'

The Revered Malea nodded. 'I agree. It would be impossible for Elona to do this.'

Master Florian looked like he was thinking very hard. 'But not impossible for a son. If war were to come, and it is a war where even the King, wielding the Dragonblade, cannot prevail then perhaps, if the House of Corlain were joined to the Royal line, a son of that line can.'

'You propose she marries Drahail?' said Father. 'That decision is yet to be taken.'

The Revered Malea smiled. 'Lady Metrid of Betlain and her advocate, Lord Tanderlain, will not be pleased if it is not Hope. Metrid is desperate to re-establish her dynasty.'

'Rightfully taken from them,' said Father.

Master Florian held up his hand. 'These are deeds a hundred years gone. No one has been promised to Prince Drahail as yet, so none are entitled to be displeased. This would be a liaison with many benefits even without a prophecy. And, if your vision is true, that is so much the better, do you not think? If not, what harm that Elona should marry Drahail and not Hope?'

'Save only Metrid's annoyance? I think that is quite bearable. We cannot ignore this, I will speak with the Queen,' said Malea. 'It shall be arranged.'

Master Florian turned to Elona and smiled. 'And I think we shall arrange a teacher for you, Lady Elona, for all the wisdom we think a future queen should have.'

'Do they still want to cut my hair off?' asked Elona.

2
____

Elona ran her toes along the wooden rail at the foot of her bed—it really was too small for her now; she'd had the same bed for over ten years. She could feel the patterns cut into it to bestow good sleep. They were worn out and didn't work anymore. She sighed; she was cooler now than she had been all night, but it was still too hot for sleep. She had dozed once or twice but the sweltering air stifled and made the darkness last forever. Wide-awake, she sat up on the edge of the bed and stared blankly at the wall.

Summer air pressed in through the open, unshuttered windows, carrying with it the night sounds: scratchings of little *kikisa* creeping in the walls; screechings of a *darthrak* as it floated down on its prey from the trees; and the calls of the town's nightwatch. Out there, in the dark, was the greatest fair in the world—waiting for her. And a prince, though she was not sure how she felt about that part.

Her wrists, feet and ankles itched horribly. She examined her feet by the light of Lostimal. The flying insects had taken a liking to her; she had four bites on the left and three on the right, and one of those was a big one.

Where was little Ichen when she needed him? He liked snapping up flies almost as much as catching the *kikisa*. He was small for a *chakik* and appreciated her attentions. He made cooing noises when she stroked his scaly head and snatched tidbits from her fingers. He would hold them in his claws as he sat on his back legs and thick tail. Nursey said she wasn't supposed to feed him because it was his job to eat the pests. But there were plenty of other *chakisa* around the castle to do that.

Oh, those bites did itch! She desperately wanted to scratch them but knew it would be much worse if she did. She should have been lying under the bed sheet, but it was too hot. Besides, yesterday Savi found a huge black spider when she'd turned down the bed, making it even less appealing as a place of refuge.

She slipped onto the wooden floorboards, padding across to the jug that sat like a shadow on the largest of her clothes' chests. She relished the coolness of the floor on the soles of her feet. She took the cover off the heavy water jug and poured a drink into a wooden cup. She drank deep, then dipped her fingers in and spread the water across her face and the back of her neck.

How lovely it would be to pour the whole jug of water over her head and soak herself. She picked it up and held it for a few moments at eye level, then put it down again. Nursey would never understand.

She went to the northern window and stared out and up. The sky swarmed with bright stars and Lostimal cast its white light on the eastern slopes of the Corlain Mountains to the northeast. Colimar, the small red moon, was still below the horizon but there was a hint of its light where the hills touched the sky. The silver ribbon of the Apra Road crossed the Timalay River and wound away north. It was empty of traffic, although in several places along its length; off to one side or the other; there rose silver threads of smoke.

She stood on tiptoes and, bracing herself against vertigo, looked down at the rim of the town's outer wall and followed it to where it met in two fists at the north gate. She could just make out dark shapes patrolling its length. The roof ridges of town buildings ran in confused lines to the higher inner wall. Within that wall were the darkened outhouses and homes for the castle servants. As she stared down, a wave of dizziness swept through her. She pushed herself back from the edge and raised her eyes again to the horizon and the ridge over which the north road ran. Just over that final ridge lay the whole world.

Today she would visit it.

It had been seven years since the Great Conclave had last been held in Faerholme and longer still since it had been held in Corlain lands. She had attended smaller fairs, but Father had never permitted her to travel to foreign lands. Bejeren, her teacher, said that he thought it too dangerous for the future queen and saviour of Faerholme. In a rare moment Nursey agreed with him, then started on her usual round of horror stories of monsters that lurked behind every bush, waiting for maidens to ravish.

Elona pulled away from the tall, thin window and walked slowly back to her bed. Nursey's tales didn't scare her anymore, not even the ones of the Slissac magically stealing her away to enslave her like Taymar. Nursey took the prophecy so seriously.

Saviour of Faerholme. How many times had Nursey used that excuse to stop her from doing anything interesting? She couldn't even go sledging when the snows covered the land.

Lying back on the bed, she stared at the ceiling with hands behind her head and knees bent. She would meet the Prince properly today. Then, in three years when she was sixteen, they would be married. The Prince's likeness had been sent to her and he seemed fair, but that was not enough. She wanted to love, just like the stories. She wanted a hero to carry her off and make her queen in a far-away land.

She tried to imagine herself as Faerholme's queen but could not. It was hard enough to imagine she was a Lady of Corlain. Father hated her, Nursey was smothering and Bejeren treated her like an idiot.

Elona woke with a jump. Savi had slammed the door open as she entered, both hands occupied with the breakfast tray. The sun streamed through the east window. Savi smiled smugly; it was the smile she always wore whenever she had been with Kienan. Elona could admit that the blacksmith's son had a pleasing physique, though she was careful not to stare except when no one was looking. Marriage to a blacksmith would be a good one for a maid. Not for Elona. Not for a Lady. Not for the saviour of Faerholme, the brood mare. Still, Kienan only had eyes for Savi, and her waist-length black hair and darker skin meant that somewhere she had Kadralin ancestry—Elona had to make do with pale skin and wispy brown hair that refused to grow much longer than her shoulders.

'Good morning, Mistress,' Savi said, barely suppressing her giggles. She placed the food tray on the bed and began poking around inside one of the clothes' chests.

'What's so good about it?' Elona replied. She slipped off the bed and went to the North-facing window. She leaned forward across the deep sill—taking care to keep her eyes on the horizon—the gentlest of warm summer breezes floated in carrying the delicious smell of baking bread and the ringing of hammer on metal. In the distance she could see carts moving north on the road again; dust rose and hung in the air. 'I barely slept all night,' Elona sighed heavily.

'Not me either.'

'Oh, stop it. You're just rude.'

Savi tried to suppress her laughter and spluttered. 'Does your Ladyship wish to break her fast?'

'I'm not hungry.' Or maybe she was.

'Does your Ladyship want to choose her dress for today?'

'I don't know, Savi. Do you really think we can get away with this?' Elona picked a plum off the tray and bit into it, juices dripped from the sides of her mouth. She wiped her lips with the sleeve of her nightgown.

'Well, let me think, my Lady,' said Savi. 'You can either wear that dowdy thing Nursey thinks is perfect.' Savi looked over at the grey dress on the dummy. 'Or you can wear this.' She opened the chest at the foot of bed and pulled out a red dress.

'But I can't wear any petticoats with it.'

'I know, it's so daring, but practical too, do you really want to be so hot that you'll faint? This is the style they're wearing in Canvor. Nursey is too old and ignorant to make decisions for you anymore. The Prince mustn't think you're provincial.'

Elona shook her head. 'But I am.'

There was a piece of delicately flavoured cheese that had been brought by one of the traders from lands to the south of Faerholme. Elona had eavesdropped as the Steward bartered with the man, his skin very dark. She had only been able to understand every other word, though Kalin seemed to follow the heavy accent. Regardless of where he'd brought it from, it had a wonderful smoky flavour and was sweet with honey.

When she'd asked to study the lands beyond Faerholme, Bejeren happily brought her maps. She knew of Umran to the northeast and Tirnan to the northwest, beyond the mountains of Alba. There was Raertane to the east with Dirdin beyond. Father received ambassadors and messengers from the nearer places quite often.

But other countries further away: Tenya and Taltia, Mirriasmia, the Isle of Esternes and the far Empire of Tirnia. The lands beyond, places of wonder where people made lovely cheese. And surrounding them all, the sea. She'd only heard about the sea but there was a big lake she had seen when they had travelled to the capital, at Canvor, in the south. There had been men fishing in boats sailing the flat waters so she guessed the sea was like that.

'Oh, Savi, what if he doesn't like me?'

'Well, you could go in your nightdress ... the Prince might find you more comely in that.'

Elona spun round, scowling, and threw the remaining crust at Savi. As it bounced to the ground Ichen appeared from under her bed and raced across the floor on his strong back legs, his claws scratching on the stone and long tail straight as a poker behind. He snatched up the crust in his fore claws and came to a halt next to the wall. He moved to sit in the sun, where his scales glowed; he sat back on his tail and gnawed at the stolen bread, beady black eyes daring her to chastise him.

'I hope you weren't under my bed all night,' she said without malice and walked across to where he sat. 'I was getting eaten alive by nice, juicy insects.' She reached down and scooped him up. She stroked his head and followed the brown and green patterns with her fingers. He whistled quietly in the back of his throat then downed the last of the crust. Elona carried him to the window and looked out.

'Which one can I wear, Savi?' She leant back against the wall with her eyes downcast, rubbing Ichen under his chin.

'You have the two choices, my Lady. You wear what Goodwife Akatha wants, or you wear what you want.'

'You mean what you want. I'll get into so much trouble.'

'What trouble? Your precious Nursey might act like your mother but she isn't, she's a servant like me. She will hate it, but if you're not ready 'til your Father calls for you, she won't be able to do a thing about it.' She giggled again and Elona frowned at her. 'You can wear the veil from the other one. It's not too thick but enough to keep those little biters off. There. Everyone will be satisfied.' Elona turned back to the window and watched the lines of wagons, riders and walkers moving north through the haze of hot dust.

'Are you ready, little 'Lonie? Your Father wants you now.' Nursey called in the sing-song way she had used since Elona was a babe. She pushed through the door without knocking, carrying a bulging cloth bag. Savi was knotting the last of the ties of her dress as Elona pinned the veil in place. 'Ooh, let's see you, sweetie.'

Savi stepped away and Elona turned. Nursey's face collapsed from her baby smile to fear, as her eyes swept from the bare ankles, up the full skirt and crisscrossed bodice to the face hidden by the veil.

'No, 'Lonie. No, little one, you mustn't wear that. You look like a wanton—Savi, you stupid girl, those are the wrong clothes. She must change into her proper dress. Quickly!' She bustled round and pushed Savi away, grabbing Elona by the shoulder to turn her so she could undo the laces. But Elona stepped back to the wall and raised her chin.

'No.'

3

'I will wear it, Nursey. Would you have me passing out from the heat? Or wearing my everyday clothes? I'm not a child!' Elona braced herself for the retaliation, but Nursey turned on Savi instead.

'It's you, you slut, you've turned her into this. Always sneaking behind my back, filling her with bad thoughts! You and your dirty, filthy habits.' She raised her hand to strike as Savi backed away under the onslaught of words.

'Stop it! Stop it now!' Elona grabbed Nursey's raised hand and pulled her towards the door. 'My Father is waiting, would you provoke his anger with delay?'

'I'll deal with you,' the old woman hissed at Savi. She wrenched her hand from Elona's and stalked out.

Elona followed Nursey down the spiral staircase, who took it slower than even she needed. At each turn the sun's heat burned through the arrow-slits, lighting up the dust motes that floated in the air. Elona paused for a moment by the passage that led to where her mother lay. She had not paid her respects for a full five-day but she could talk to her tomorrow and tell her about the Prince. She knew it was silly but her mother was the only one who ever really listened.

Reaching the bottom of the stairs, they walked in silence while servants moved in and out of the rooms around them. Elona couldn't help but notice the second-glances they gave her. She was certain the younger men were grinning. Some of the older servants smiled but others did not. Embarrassment crept through her.

'Got what you wanted now?' Nursey said.

They crossed the echoing main hall and out into the sunlit courtyard where Father was mounted on Ironmane. He was leaning down in deep discussion with the Steward. He then gestured forcefully, but she could tell he was angry. Bejeren was mounted on one of the castle horses. Elona recognised his favourite from the stable, Whitestar. Her mount was a small, solid piebald she called Teaser. They had only had the horses for a five-year. Many thought that *kichesa* were better mounts, but the horses seemed to like the grassy plains of Corlain and her father's breeding herd was the envy of all the Lords of Faerholme.

The groom holding the bridle gawked at Elona's chest as she mounted from the block; then he stared at her ankles. Elona cringed in embarrassment.

A troop of twenty armsmen stood at ease a short distance away waiting to mount their *kichesa*. The animals' glossy scales had been burnished with oil until they shone in colours from dark red to dull amber. Wild *kichesa* were abundant all over Faerholme, Raertane and Mirriasmia and common even further north, but they took a lot of training—from the egg preferably—before they were suitable as mounts.

One by one the armsmen stopped talking and stared in her direction. She felt alternating waves of cold and hot rising up her arms, her scalp tingling as she shivered. Without another word Nursey went to a cart drawn by a pair of matched *kichesa* sitting back on their haunches. Helped by a footman, the old woman climbed up beside the driver. She had an unpleasant smile on her face.

Father was becoming more agitated. Only he and the Steward seemed oblivious to Elona's appearance, for which she was grateful as she settled herself into the side-saddle. She jerked in momentary fear as Father's voice barked.

'... years, Kalin, and I want it stopped.'

'Yes, my Lord.'

'And no more excuses.'

'No, my Lord.'

'Find out who it is and deal with them.'

'Yes, my Lord.'

The Lord Corlain kicked his horse and moved off at a trot towards the gate, leaving the unhappy Steward. Four *kichek*-mounted armsmen fell in behind him, then came Elona and Bejeren followed by the cart and the troop. Elona's teacher moved up beside her as they passed into the shadow of the gate.

'Goodwife Akatha seems ill-amused, my Lady.'

'She doesn't like what I'm wearing.'

'I would wager that half the castle staff would disagree.' He paused for a cruel moment as he ran his hand over his balding head, then added, 'Though the distaff may be green with envy.'

'Don't make fun of me, Bejeren. It's Savi's fault.'

They broke out into sunshine again and the horses' hooves rattled over the wooden bridge. An unpleasant smell rose from the moat water. They descended into the cobbled streets of the town and the smell changed to something only vaguely less repugnant. They clattered through the empty streets; most doors were flung wide to let air circulate. Here and there, *zatesa* lay in the doorways, soaking up the heat, watching them pass. Faces appeared at the windows and Elona could feel all the eyes staring at her.

'So Savi forced you into these clothes? Held you down, I don't doubt. Tied you to your bed perhaps? While she sewed you into your dress?'

'No.'

'She is skilled in Patterning I suspect, then. She stole patterns and rituals from the Master as he slept. And now she's bewitched you, as she has Kienan.'

Elona sighed heavily. 'No, Bejeren.'

'Say not you went willing? Like a stone-struck *darthrak* falling from its tree-lair into the arms of a starving beggar?'

'Stop it!'

The teacher smiled and was silent as they made their way through the streets to the northern gate in the outer wall. The armsmen at the gate added their gaze to all the rest and followed her as she passed. Finally the procession was out into fields with fewer eyes to stare. The crops were bleached to pale gold strips by the sun. To the east the apple orchards were already being harvested.

Two of the mounted guards trotted ahead on their *kichesa* to stop the other carts and wagons so their procession could join the Apra Road without incident, then the party splashed through Timalay Ford and headed north.

'Elona, you are a pretty young lady. That nurse of yours has kept you in children's clothes for too long. Savi is right and you are right. Goodwife Akatha is wrong.' Bejeren looked across to her and smiled. He was not old but his face was lined by so many journeys across the world and his smile deepened the creases. 'Should you not look your best for the Prince?'

Elona did not reply but felt a little happier.

'Now,' Bejeren said. 'Let us review the protocols when meeting with our sovereign.'

The procession approached the top of the ridge above the valley where the Conclave stood. Already Elona heard the sounds of music, shouting and the cries of animals and people. They came over the brow, and stretched out before them was a city of tents in bright solid colours. The sun beat down and the whole view shimmered in the heat like a dream. They plodded steadily down the long slope, as Father would not force the horses, despite the heat having no effect on the *kichesa*.

The tents and stalls of the Conclave were arranged like a cart wheel, with wide avenues for spokes running out from the central arena and other streets in wider circles out to the palisade boundary. The pavilions of the innermost ring, facing into the arena, housed the kings and queens from all the realms of the world; as well as the great Guilds. Through it all swarmed the people, like ants.

'There, Elona, you can see the Guild of Patterners, that's the one with the interlocked triangles on its pennant.' Elona had to guess which one Bejeren meant as all the flags hung limp in the breathless air. 'And beside it, to the right, is the Scribes and Scholars. On the other side, farthest from us, is the Alchemists, and next to them the Healers.' He sounded excited and she looked at his beaming face. 'You see the one across the arena from the Patterners? That is the King's Pavilion.'

'Why does he not stay in the castle with my Father?'

'It is not permitted for the King to abide elsewhere during the Conclave. All the other Kings, Princes and Lords must live in conditions that are far from the comfort of their homes. Our King must do the same. It is part of the Charter.'

Bejeren fell silent as they descended the slope, to the temporary stabling that already seemed filled to overflowing with horses and *kichesa* of all ages and qualities. A fat, sweaty man with a bushy beard stepped from a nearby tent and shouted at a group of young men lolling in the sun. They jumped up and ran to hold the horses while the riders dismounted. Nursey clambered down from the cart and came to stand with them, clutching her bag.

As Elona stood beside her mount more than one of the lads stared at her ankles, and higher up. She felt herself blush beneath the veil but tried to convince herself that it did not matter, as she would never see them again.

The *kichek*-keeper waddled over and bowed low to Elona's Father.

'My Lord, my Lady, noble Scribe,' he greeted them in a surprisingly thin and high voice. 'I am so delighted to be of service to you. Be sure your mounts, fine creatures that they are, will be cared for with the utmost diligence and protected with vigilance.' He spoke the words clearly as if to impress.

'Very good. Make sure the horses are kept well-watered in this heat and that they have shade from the sun. My man will stay with them.'

'To be sure, my Lord. I have the very spot for them with lovely trees for shade and wide troughs filled with fresh water and my lads to check on them. Do any of them require shoeing, my Lord? I have my very own smith well-versed in the shoeing of horses.'

'They do not, our own blacksmith cares for that.'

'Indeed, my Lord, of course,' he bowed again. 'Is there any other service I can fulfil, my Lord?'

'Just look after the animals,' Father replied, waving his hand to dismiss him. The keeper bowed again and retreated backwards as the boys led the three horses away, followed by half the soldiers, each leading two *kichesa*. The cart was turned and driven towards the enclosures.

Then her father turned towards her and froze.

His eyes widened and he took a half step towards her. She saw him mouth *Veona*. She nervously watched his eyes. Then he shook his head and, as suddenly as they had appeared, the emotions were gone. He turned away and spoke to the sergeant-at-arms. Elona looked round and up at Bejeren beside her. He placed his hand on her shoulder and squeezed gently.

'The resemblance to your mother is striking, though hardly surprising,' he murmured. 'It seems your father is the only one never to have noticed. Perhaps it may encourage him to see you more clearly in future.'

The sergeant ordered six men to take up station in front, to plough a way through the crowds. The Lord Corlain, Elona a step behind, then Bejeren with Nursey and her bag, walked together between them.

Encircling the great fair was a wide, deep ditch, and just inside that a palisade of pickets close enough together to stop anyone squeezing between but wide enough to allow rubbish and waste to be thrown out. Father had grumbled mightily about the stakes, as it was his forests that supplied the wood though the King paid for it. She had heard the Steward complaining how it would be years before the woods could recover from such a scything.

As they approached the southernmost of the four gates Elona

tried to hold her breath to keep out the stench that hung there. The air was alive with flies, though thankfully they were more interested in the contents of the ditch than the travellers. A ragged boy trotted out the gate, pushing a small wooden barrow piled high with some unpleasantness. He turned and went a dozen yards along the ditch before emptying the barrow's slithering load into it. Elona felt sick.

The entrance to the Conclave was built of stone, though the roughness and lack of adornment betrayed the speed of its construction. The guards at the gate were the King's own armsmen; they stood watchfully in the shade, weapons sheathed but ready. They stood to attention as the party passed through and into the heat and dust of the fair. Elona stared around in wonder as they walked along the southern avenue towards the centre. The crowds milled about them laughing, shouting and crying. The heat was terrible and the feet of the multitude churned up the dust so that it dried her throat and made her cough. It was a world away from stone walls. It was wonderful.

As they passed the streets opening off on either side, she could hear the cries of the sellers with all manner of goods: clothiers, armourers, food sellers. Elona's mouth watered as she saw limes, lemons and oranges for sale and other fruit she had never seen before, all brought by patterner's path between the ley-circles. She wished Father had permitted Savi to come so that she could have sent her off to buy something. She didn't want to ask Nursey.

At one corner they passed a juggler tossing five batons in a complex pattern. On the next, a group of three musicians playing brightly on whistles of different sizes. The music had a strange, unearthly quality and she wondered what land they were from. She would have liked to have joined the crowd that stood listening but Father pressed on.

Finally they burst through to the arena at the heart of the Conclave. She could hear the clash of steel, cheers and boos from the competitions in progress.

Under the blazing sun they stood before an enormous pavilion of blue and yellow. The sergeant ordered his men to stand to the side for them. Another armsman went to the tent flap and spoke briefly to someone inside.

They waited in the sunshine. A wasp decided that Elona was a flower and she tried to shoo it away without annoying it. Father, who had been looking toward the pavilion, suddenly turned on them: 'Goodwife Akatha, I think you would be more content to visit the fair than remain here in the sun. You will wait on our return at the stables in the mid-afternoon.'

The old woman bowed her head. 'Thank you, my Lord. You're very kind.' Then, after throwing a nasty look at Elona, she walked into the crowd.

Moments later, a young boy wearing the King's colours emerged from the pavilion and tied back the flaps. He was followed by an old, white-haired man with a thin face, who stepped from the shadows of the interior. He raised his hand against the bright sunlight and approached.

'Greetings, Lord Corlain,' he said and bowed stiffly.

'Lord Tanderlain,' replied Father, with the merest inclination of his head.

'The King awaits you.' The Lord Tanderlain gestured to the entrance and went through. Leaving the soldiers outside, Lord Corlain, Elona and Bejeren followed him.

The interior of the pavilion was as dark as the outside world had been bright, and it baked hotter than a blacksmith's forge. The floor was a tight-woven matting with intricate geometric patterns and the wood-panel walls were decorated with delicate engravings. But there was no opportunity to examine them; Lord Tanderlain hurried along the corridor with surprising speed, Father close behind.

After several turns they came to a wall with sunlight streaming in around the edges of a door flap. Another servant stood at the door and held it open to allow them through into a garden surrounded on all sides by the pavilion.

They blinked in the sunshine. A fountain with flower beds around it, splashed in the centre of the garden, and near it a white awning cast shade over a table and several chairs. Two men stood at the edge of its shadow.

4

The King was a large man with close-cropped grey hair, and a small trimmed beard with grey streaks. Slightly behind, on his left, stood the Prince Drahail, the sole heir to the Faerholme crown and her husband-to-be. With his blue trousers and a loose white shirt, he was a younger edition of his Father, but with short dark hair and without the beard or extra weight. He was staring at her. She felt her cheeks redden and averted her eyes.

They waited at the entrance while Lord Tanderlain approached the King and spoke briefly, then the King nodded and looked in their direction. Father walked forward and Elona followed, while Bejeren remained by the entrance. Lord Tanderlain withdrew with a final look that Elona could only describe as contempt. As they approached, the King stepped forward and embraced her Father. Elona suffered a moment's panic—this wasn't what Bejeren had told her to expect—but for her part she knelt on one knee with her eyes to the ground.

'Taniel, my friend! It is so good to see you.'

'My liege, I am honoured.' There was a pause. 'May I present my daughter, Elona.'

Two boots stepped into her view of the grass. 'Lady Elona, you are welcome.'

She looked up to find the King holding his right hand out to her. She lifted her veil, took his hand and kissed the ring on his middle finger. Then he pulled her to her feet, which was not in the protocols either, but she managed to keep her eyes directed downwards.

'Your manners honour your father, Lady Elona. You have a good teacher.'

He released her hand and stepped away, and she allowed herself to look up. The Prince's face was pulled into a frown and his hands were white at the knuckles as they gripped each other. What could be annoying him? Perhaps he hated the idea of marrying her. Maybe the dress offended him. Still, it hadn't offended any other man who had looked at her.

The King looked back to her father.

'She has become a woman, Taniel. And has the look of her mother, too.' Father turned his head toward her and stared. She swallowed nervously; it was the look he gave when he was going to shout at her.

'Yes, Sire, she has.'

'And this is my son,' continued the King, turning to the young man who made a curt bow in her direction. 'Drahail, I will be in council with Lord Corlain this day. Escort the Lady Elona to the fair. Enjoy yourself.' The scowl on the Prince's face deepened and he looked as if he wanted to argue. Instead, he stepped awkwardly forward and presented his arm to Elona.

She swallowed and hesitantly placed her arm through his, barely touching the cloth of his sleeve. He walked away abruptly towards the exit and she followed, stumbling in his wake. The Lord Corlain looked round and spoke loudly.

'Go with them, Bejeren, and take the guards.' Bejeren nodded as Father turned back to the King. 'As it please, Your Majesty?'

'Of course, Taniel, my armsmen will attend as well. We cannot be too careful with our future.'

As the couple passed Bejeren he winked at her despairing face and followed them. The door back into the pavilion was too narrow to allow them to pass through together, and Elona was grateful for the opportunity to disengage her arm.

As they left the pavilion both Corlain and Royal armsmen fell in around them. Bejeren took up a position forcing Elona to walk between him and the Prince.

They wandered in silence around the bustling central arena, pausing to watch acrobats performing jumps and four-man-high balancing. They stopped at one of the arenas to watch a bout between two pairs of combatants. Elona watched in fascination as they exchanged rapid blows with a ringing of steel and clashing of shields; their bright swords contrasting their dark skin.

They moved on while the sun beat down relentlessly. A fruit-seller walked past shouting her wares. Elona grabbed Bejeren's arm and, at her pleading look, he left them. After a few moments of haggling he returned with three oranges. The Prince declined the one offered to him, so Bejeren got out his knife and halved one to share it between Elona and himself. She had difficulty maintaining any dignity as she sucked at it but it relieved her parched mouth.

They came upon a roped off area, people waiting expectantly. The armsmen cleared a space so Elona and Drahail could watch comfortably. The first of the mummers entered the arena; he wore a green and black mask representing one of the monstrous lizards, this one called a Slissac. They were enacting the Salvation; it was performed at every autumn feast.

Three other mummers entered, wearing skull caps to hide their hair, and their hands tied—the tall one would be Taymar, the other two, a man and a woman, represented all humankind captured and enslaved. The Slissac whipped them and forced them to walk and work for him. Then Taymar escaped his bonds and bravely fought the Slissac and threw it to the ground. He released his friends and they ran away, with the crowd cheering them as they left the arena.

Everyone booed as the Slissac got to its feet and danced jerkily about. It muttered, then shouted, devising an evil pattern. Suddenly there was a bang—Elona jumped—a plume of green smoke erupted from the middle of the arena and there stood a figure cloaked all in black, its face hidden by a dark veil. The Slissac cried out *'Kisharuk'*. The crowd gasped as the Slissac pointed in the direction Taymar and the others had gone. The evil shadow rushed after them and the Slissac followed more slowly.

Taymar and his people appeared amongst the crowd—hiding and dodging so they would not be seen—and then crept into the centre. The Shadow appeared and chased them. It caught the second man, who fell to the floor, and the crowd groaned as the Shadow ate him, but Taymar led the woman to a boat and they sailed away.

The *Kisharuk* searched high and low, threatening the audience who booed and threw things at it. Elona laughed as it came round to her. The *Kisharuk* faced her across the rope and paused, staring at her and her laugh caught in her throat.

Then the spell broke and it ran from the arena.

Finally Taymar came back leading the woman and they landed their boat. They stepped out, embraced and kissed. The audience laughed and applauded until Taymar left the arena with the woman.

The royal party walked on, taking one of the concentric outer streets. Dust hung in the air and the grass was worn to the dirt by the passage of uncounted feet. After his long silence Elona jumped when the Prince suddenly said: 'I will have a drink.'

'An excellent idea, your Majesty,' Bejeren answered. 'The sun is nearing its height and we should certainly seek shelter. I believe I see a tavern yonder that will suit.' They found the marquee, whose walls had been removed to allow the air to circulate. The armsmen cleared a space for them near the street with chairs and a table. Elona was glad to sit down, for her feet and ankles ached with all the walking, though the lack of activity brought back the itching from the bites. A few moments later a wide-eyed lad wearing loose-fitting clothes approached with his head bowed and waited quietly for their instructions.

'On such a day as this," said Bejeren. "May I venture that it would be wise to refrain from consuming the wines or ales. In such heat it would only make one the thirstier but mixed juices of fruits would be most refreshing.'

'You are not my counsellor,' said the Prince.

Elona turned towards Bejeren and pulled a face beneath her veil. He did not react but replied smoothly.

'Your Highness is quite correct but I would be failing in my duty to the King, your Father, if I were not to mention to your Highness of these concerns such as they may occur. Our escorts, too, are parched, and though I believe they would much prefer the ale, their sobriety must be maintained in accordance with their duty.' He threw a glance at the two Sergeants. The Sergeant of the Royal Guard pushed his leather helm higher on his head.

'That's most generous, gentle Scribe. We'd be most obliged, after his Highness and your Lady, of course.'

Bejeren turned to the boy and spoke rapidly with a curious accent.

'Where does he come from?' she asked after the orders had been taken. 'What language was that?'

'These traders are from southern Mirriasmia. I did spend some time there for the Guild so I learned their dialect very well,' Bejeren replied. 'All our languages are from the ancient tongue of Taymar, we are all His children. Over such distances there are changes but it does not take one long to adapt.'

The boy returned with a small, round tray bearing a metal jug and two metal goblets. He placed the tray on the table before Elona and Drahail and withdrew with his head bowed. Out of courtesy to rank, Elona waited for the Prince to drink but he seemed to be waiting for her, so she took a cautious sip. It had the sharpness of the orange but sweet too, perhaps with honey. She smiled and nodded to the Prince. 'It's delicious,' she said. The Prince took a drink and smiled. He looked quite nice when he smiled; perhaps he was as embarrassed about the whole situation.

The boy returned with drinks for Bejeren and the guards, though only half of them drank while the others remained watchful. Elona wondered at their vigilance, as Bejeren had told her there was never any trouble at a Conclave; at least nothing involving those of rank, but then she and the Prince were supposed to produce an heir to save Faerholme. She flushed with embarrassment at the thought.

As the day became hotter the tavern area filled up with others seeking shelter from the sun. Elona looked at the faces in the crowd. Between the sweaty bodies, almost on the far side of the shaded seating area, she saw Nursey in deep conversation with a man she did not recognise; his features marked him as a man of Faerholme.

As she watched, Nursey glanced around before opening her bag, pulling a sack from it which the man took. He pulled its drawstrings apart and peered inside. After a few moments he nodded, tied the sack to his belt, and passed back a small pouch. The man stood and shouldered his bag, and then he turned and looked directly across the crowds at her. She looked away quickly and when she glanced back the people in the crowd had moved, hiding both him and Nursey from view.

The heat of the day had passed and the alleyways between the stalls were once again thronging with crowds. Elona stared at fantastical creatures shaped from blue and green glass while the prince and his men had moved past to something of more interest to him, probably weapons. Bejeren leaned over her shoulder. 'Do you want to buy something?'

'I don't have money; you know Father does not give me any.'

'I'm sure the tradesman will accept a note from the daughter of the local Lord, the Steward will deal with it.

'It's not the same; it's still not mine, is it?'

'I will speak with your father. Until then I will treat you; do you want one of these?'

'Not really.'

'What then?'

'Oh, I don't know. Something for my room, a tapestry?'

'There are limits to my wealth,' Bejeren smiled. 'Let us see what there is on the way back.'

Elona finally stopped by a tent selling woven cloths of bright colours. She was sure she could find something here within Bejeren's limits that would make a new dress for her. Perhaps one which would not arouse so much interest from every man she passed.

She fingered her way through a dozen designs without finding anything she liked. She looked up to see what else was available and saw the bearded man she had seen with Nursey standing at the entrance to the tent, in quiet discussion with the cloth-seller.

~

Elona's curiosity got the better of her and she went to the tent flap, disguising her eavesdropping by studying some bolts of velvet.

Scraps of conversation floated from the tent '...how much...' '...no more...' '...best quality...' she lost interest and studied the fabric in earnest. Suddenly the tent-flap opened and the bearded man emerged in front of her, staring down at her. He grinned but there was no humour in it. 'Hello, pretty.'

Elona froze transfixed by his hard eyes and the cloth dropped from her hands. He reached out a hand towards her but a movement behind her caught his attention and instead he said, 'Excuse me, Miss,' and brushed past her.

Bejeren arrived at her side. 'What did he say to you?'

Elona shook herself from her stupor. 'He just said ... excuse me. I-I think I was in his way.'

5

———

A fine autumn drizzle descended from the slab-grey sky and, in places, the strong cold wind drove it through the closed windows. There was a message written in Bejeren's spiky hand waiting for her on the nursery table:

Elona, Your Father wishes me to rehearse the entertainments for this evening's feast in the King's honour. No lessons today.

He had signed it and then added.

Goodwife Akatha says you should pay your respects to your mother after your lessons before the midday meal.

She looked out at the rain; she might as well do something. She sighed and took up a chalk and slate and scratched out sums, easy ones. Not that she was entirely clear why she needed to be able to do sums and write, if all she had to do was produce babies for the Prince, but Bejeren said Master Florian had ordered it.

In the two years since she had seen Drahail at the Conclave, they had exchanged letters three times—of course, Bejeren had said it was good writing practice—but there was no passion in them. Savi

33

insisted he must be desperately in love with her. Elona doubted it and she was sure she didn't want to marry him; not that she had much choice, stupid prophecy. He had been civil enough in the letters, but she feared he thought her too common and untutored. Bejeren drilled her on court etiquette until she dreamed it.

Earlier Savi had helped her into her best dress to be presented to the King later in the day, but now even she, with the birth of her child barely a ten-day away, had to help with the general cleaning. The last time Elona had seen her she had been standing precariously on a bench, dusting cobwebs.

Elona thought the cleaning was unnecessary. The royal castle at Canvor was probably no better than theirs but Father wanted it perfect even if it meant calling out all the staff, including those with child.

Bejeren said it didn't matter whether Drahail cared for her or not, as Father was one of the strongest Lords and his domain was key to the defence of Faerholme. The alliance between the families was a good one, prophecy notwithstanding. She would be wedded to the Prince and it would be soon. The Queen's failure to procure any further brothers or sisters to the Prince meant they were desperate for another generation of heirs, particularly as Faerholme had sworn to uphold Taltia's sovereignty in the face of Tirnian aggression. If there was war, the King and the Prince would be open to danger. An heir was an absolute necessity.

Bejeren couldn't see beyond the politics either; she was nothing more than a brood mare for men who played politics.

She and Savi listened to the tales of love and romance, daring knights defeating uncountable foes to rescue the maiden they loved. They would sit in the orchard and make up stories.

Elona finished her first set of sums and laid down the slate. She took a dangling lock of her brown hair and wrapped it about her finger. Nobody seemed to care what she thought. Savi said she should run away and have adventures. That was easy for her to say. What life could Elona have? Where would she run to? What could she do? Sew. And that without inspiration.

It was always the knights who had the adventures. Something

needed to carry her off, then Father would have to offer her hand in marriage for her rescue plus half his lands. But who would want her hand? Nursey said she was ugly and should be glad to have made this alliance because of some prophecy. Nursey said the Sisterhood had made it all up, conniving with the patterners to get her on the throne because they could control Father.

There had been a time when Nursey had been the centre of her world. But now she could see through her. She was always harping on about the debt of life Elona owed her, how she'd be dead if it weren't for Nursey. Ha! She'd rather be dead. And what did Nursey do now anyway? Skulk about and tell Elona what to wear whenever she could; when to go to bed; when to get up. And Father let her. So did Bejeren, though she knew he disliked the crone as well. Well, let her carp. She'd marry the Prince and be Queen in Faerholme, and then let Nursey try criticising. She picked up the slate and wiped away the calculations with harsh swipes. Just let her try.

The rain didn't stop. Elona stood and brushed the chalk dust from her skirts. It was well before the time she would normally see her mother but she didn't think it really mattered—besides, when Elona talked to her at least she listened. And she needed to talk now.

The torches had not been lit and the dark clouds kept the corridors in gloom. The servants moved like spectres through the rooms and passages. She came to the door of her mother's chamber; it stood ajar and she looked into the dark hall. The screens were pulled around the bed. The Sisters would be here in a few days to feed Mother's body.

The orange light from the brazier at the foot of the bed shone through the translucent screens, and she saw a shadow moving within them. She frowned. Was Father here? No one else ever visited except during the morbid restoration ceremonies when Father insisted she and the senior staff attend. The shadow moved again and became two.

Elona moved forward as quietly as she could across the stone flags, and the low murmur of voices came to her ears. She crept on until she could feel the heat of the brazier through the fabric of the screen.

'...more.' A wave of cold went through Elona at the sound of Nursey's voice.

'I won't give you no more than two crowns.' The second harsh voice was a man's.

'They're worth thirty.'

'Maybe they are, Mother, but you don't get that. You're lucky to get three.'

'I'm a poor woman, Krazak, give me seven.' Nursey's voice took on the irritating wheedling tone Elona recognised.

'Poor as a merchant, mother. I'll give you four. No more.'

'Treat me nice and they'll be lots more, my boy. The King's visiting you know. Plenty nice pickings. Six.'

'Make it fine cloth and you'll get a good deal. This metal stuff is harder to be rid of. Five.'

'Done.'

There was the chink of coins and a metallic rattle as the shadows behind the screen moved. 'They keep the body fresh as a daisy, don't they?' he said.

'Should've let her die, I reckon.'

'And deprive us of such a quiet meeting place?' The malicious chuckle that broke from the man's lips carried an image of such horror that Elona could not stop a cry.

There was a sudden rush from behind the swaying screens and a man with wild hair exploded from behind them, whirling at her. She flung up her arms in fear and he grabbed both her wrists in one hand, pulling her hard and spinning her round. He clamped his other hand over her mouth and the seams of his leather gloves bit into her cheek. She struggled ineffectively against his weight bearing down on her shoulders.

'Hello, pretty. You're early.'

Nursey hurried from behind the screens and gasped. 'Elona—'

'Looks the spit of the unliving bitch, eh? Well, that's a bit of a treat for me. Something with a bit of life for a change. Get out and make sure you collect some good stuff. It'll be the last; they won't be needing you round here no more.'

Nursey's face contorted and she backed towards the far door.

'You can't—'

'Don't be stupid,' he hissed. 'That's why you sent the message, that's why I'm here—you'd never be able to do it. And what's your life worth if they think you're involved? Get out and don't come back. Shut the door nicely after you, my dearest Mother, no reason I can't have a bit of fun first.'

Nursey fled through the door and pulled it closed.

Krazak dragged Elona behind the screens. He released her wrists and her arms dropped limply. The hand still clamped against her mouth pinned her to him. Before her lay her mother, a fragile statue. Suddenly his other hand came into view holding a knife.

'Cry out and I'll slit you ear to ear. Run and I'll gut you and show you your liver. Get it?' She nodded weakly. Her body numb with icy terror. 'Good.'

The hand over her mouth relaxed and she fell forward. He caught her arm and pulled her round. His grinning mouth was filled with crooked teeth. He grabbed the long hair at the back of her head and forced her face against his, his lips bruising hers. He pulled her back and chuckled. 'Come on, whore. Let's get comfortable.'

Gripping her hair he pushed her ahead of him to the side of the bed, like a puppet dangling from his hand. He shoved her mother's body so it fell to the floor with a dull thump. He forced Elona down on her back. She shut her eyes as he climbed up and kneeled with one leg each side of her waist and the weight of his body on her legs. She felt the cold blade slip inside the top of her dress. She was pulled upwards slightly as it sawed through her pretty dress.

There was the slightest whirr ending in a thump, like a fist on a door.

She felt his body stiffen. He collapsed forwards onto her. The blade lay flat and cold against her stomach. Something warm flowed across her cheek. She could barely breathe under his unmoving weight and turned her head to the side. She opened her eyes and saw an archer standing in the upper gallery. The door slammed open. Shouts echoed through the room. The screens were wrenched away and flew clattering across the floor. He was pulled from her. She was lifted up and held like a child in a pair of strong arms, cold metal links pressed into her cheek. She could hear Nursey crying and saying 'I'm sorry' over and over, but she did not know to whom.

Father appeared in the doorway. Silence flowed from him like a wave and the commotion ceased. She watched him stalk across the hall. He looked down at the dead body with the arrow shaft in his neck. He looked up at his daughter's bloodied face and shredded clothes. Four strides took him from Elona to his wife's side. Elona could feel his hot rage on her back.

'Remove the filth. Restore the screens. Fetch the healers. Replace the bed. Clean the floors. Attend Elona in her chamber.'

Savi had come, face round as a moon, eyes wide as she guided her to her rooms. Elona's violated clothes had been removed and discarded in the corner. Gently the maid had wiped the crusting blood from her face and shoulders, then washed her hair.

'What happened, Elona?'

Standing by the door, wordlessly, was Nursey. Watching. No word of comfort. Face drawn and wringing her hands. Rain teemed outside. Then Father had come asking questions of the maid. She had looked at Elona once then back and shaken her head. More insistent questions. The maid had pulled the wounded dress from the pile and shown him how far down the cut had gone. Not that far. He had looked at her once more and turned away.

'What happened, Elona?'

She had been dressed in a plain sleeping robe and placed in her bed. Ichen had sniffed at the bloody pile until Savi chased him away. She had tied up the bundle and carried it from sight. Nursey still stood by the door, small and worn. Bejeren came at last and sat by her on the bed, holding her hand. Saying nothing, until finally he asked her:

'What happened, Elona?'

'He's ... dead?'

'Yes. Goodwife Akatha fetched an armsman. He shot him. A brave shot.'

Elona stared at him. Brave?

'If that villain had known he was discovered he might have killed you, or held you hostage against his safety. Your father will reward him well.'

Elona looked away and stared at the window. It was still light. Somehow she thought it should be night. Bejeren's hand tightened its grip on hers, pulling her wandering attention back to him.

'Elona, I'm sorry but your Father has instructed me to determine what happened and to do it before the King arrives. He will be here before sundown.'

Her eyes were filled with sorrow. 'Have you rehearsed enough for the banquet? My Father will be angry if there's trouble. He is always angry with me, it's all my fault.'

'All is in hand, but how could he be angry? He loves you.'

Elona did not respond. Bejeren pressed on.

'I was not teaching, so what did you do?'

'I did some sums; I did do them, Bejeren. I did them for you.' He nodded. 'I saw the message from Nursey, to see my m-mother, so I went to ...' she stopped. Her eyes saw the horror again, how could she see it? How could she bear to see it again?

'Was he a thief?' Bejeren asked. Elona nodded.

Nursey suddenly stepped forward. 'He must have been, scribe. What with all those things he'd took, plates and stuff. He's the one that's been nicking stuff all these years. Must sneak in, take some things and sneak out. Only my little 'Lonie caught him at it. Poor dearie.' Nursey sighed. 'Least she's not been ruined.'

Elona went rigid and Bejeren leapt to his feet.

'Get out, harridan! You have the sensitivity of a *chakik* though even Ichen would provide more comfort than you. Get out! I have yet to speak with you and you may be sure I will not be gentle in my questioning. Get to your quarters and stay there. I misdoubt your innocence in this. Armsman!' Nursey's escape was blocked. 'Escort Goodwife Akatha to her quarters. Be sure she stays there until I see her.' The guard grabbed the woman roughly by the shoulder and marched her from the room.

'Elona, you must tell me the truth. Was Nursey there when you arrived?'

She stared into his eyes for a long time, and then slowly nodded.

6

———

It seemed only moments that she had lain, curled up on her bed, before Savi knocked and entered. 'Your Father says you have to dress and come down. The King has been seen on the road.' The rain outside the window had stopped and the sun seemed to be trying to push its way through the solid clouds. 'We'll have to choose something decent, with your best gone.'

The maid sat on the bed heavily. She took Elona's hand, drew her up and embraced her. Elona shook with sobs. Savi stroked her hair. When the tears subsided Savi pulled away gently. 'Come. Let us restore your beauty for the Prince.'

Savi stood and searched through the chests while Elona wiped her face. 'And I brought these,' Savi said and withdrew a small wooden case from her apron. 'The Steward's wife sent them, face powders.'

'Nursey would never let me—'

'Nursey's gone! I and everyone else would have her hung, but your Father deferred to the milk-debt. Again.' She spat the words. 'That cow's been living off that gift of milk and gets away with her life because of it. To think it was her thieving and letting that son of hers have his will with—' Savi stopped. 'Well, good riddance to the both of them.'

Elona could only stare at nothing. Nursey gone? Nursey was always there. 'But what will she do?'

'Who cares? She always was a vicious bitch. You're the only one who ever liked her.' Savi picked up the pile of clothes she'd selected and carried them to the bed.

Did people think I liked her? 'I owe her my life.'

'Oh, so she always said,' Savi replied, grabbing Elona by the shoulders and turning her about to undo the ties of her robe. 'She lied about everything else, what about that, eh? Maybe that was all lies too. I think she was too old, even then.' The robe slipped to the floor and Elona shivered. Savi pushed her around again and held a petticoat for Elona to step into.

'What do you mean?'

'Well, how many years do you think she's got? Fifty, sixty? I saw that son of hers—what a mess he made when they took his head off —he must have been in his fortieth year.' The maid yanked at the ties to punctuate her words. 'So she was ... how old would she have been then, when you were born? If she's that old now?'

Elona stepped into the light yellow summer dress.

'She'd have been at least forty. And where's the child she had then? That she could be a wet nurse?'

'She said he died.'

'Very convenient. That hag was very good at making you feel guilty, I reckon.'

'But she did nurse me.'

'Says who?'

'My Father.'

Savi pulled the ribbons tight around the bodice.

'Yes, well...'

'But I'm here.'

Savi harrumphed. 'Sit down facing the light and let's see what we can do about your face.' Savi opened the box and took out a bushy brush and patted it into one of the small pots of dark colours. Then lifted it to Elona's face.

'I still think she's lying.'

'But why?'

'Keep still, you don't want to make it worse,' Savi said as she dabbed the brush on to Elona's cheeks. 'It's obvious, so she could steal.'

Elona tried to speak without moving her lips. 'She wouldn't do that.'

'She did do that.'

'That man made her. I know she wasn't a very strong person.'

'That was her son and his head is on a pike on the town wall,' Savi said with grim satisfaction. 'Like mother like son, if you ask me.'

'You don't know that.'

'Well, it makes sense to me.' Savi put the brush back in the box. 'You're done. If we had time I'd trim your brows but you better go.'

Sunbeams pierced the cloud-covered sky as Elona stepped out into the courtyard. She hurried past Bejeren and down to stand a few steps behind Father just as the King's retinue entered the courtyard. Many of his mounted troops had already arrived; she had never seen so many horses in one place. Father had ordered temporary stabling constructed—the King's *kichesa*-mounted troops would be billeted in the town.

The King wore a rich green cloak, oiled against the rain with the hood thrown back; a short distance behind was the Lord Tanderlain, followed closely by Drahail, accompanied beside him by a young woman also on mount. They both still had their hoods over their heads. An older woman followed close behind, her head bare. Elona did not recognise her but her hair was cut in a widow's bob. The horses' hooves clattered on the cobbles, occasionally slipping on the wet surface. Behind came covered, *kichesa*-drawn carriages, which turned to the left and halted just inside the gate.

As they drew closer around the edge of the courtyard Elona could see the Prince and his riding companion looking around at the soaking flags and dripping bunting stretched between the main tower and the gate and around the walls. The young woman leaned over and spoke to the Prince, laughing at her own humour. He smiled in return. Elona felt a strange indignation and anger piercing her numbed feelings.

The horses clattered to a halt before them. Father dropped to his knee with bowed head before the mounted King and Elona followed suit. She was still breathing deeply from hurrying but hoped it would be hidden by her courtesy. She saw the feet of a groom rush up to hold the King's mount. His mud-splashed boots dropped into view.

'Greetings, my friend.' His voice lacked the warmth she had heard two years before.

'My daughter.' She rose at her father's word and stood, head bowed, before her King. He acknowledged her wearily. At a signal other grooms moved forward to take the bridles of the remaining horses and the King's party dismounted. The Prince stepped forward to be presented. She kept her gaze down. At that moment spots of rain began to fall.

'Let us continue inside,' said the King, mounting the steps towards the hall with Father beside him. The Prince walked beside Elona as they climbed the flight to the door and into the main hall, which echoed to their shod feet.

'You know Lord Tanderlain and Lady Metrid,' the King was saying. 'This is her daughter Hope. They have been travelling with us.'

The Lady Metrid's face carried lines of care and her hair was streaked with silver. She had been a handsome woman but her right cheek was disfigured by a scar that ran in a gentle curve from her eye to her upper lip. Her daughter Hope had a pleasant round face and her straight, light brown hair was pulled back in a pair of braids. Her large eyes gave the impression she was perpetually startled.

'Elona, escort the ladies to their chambers and be their guide until they are familiar with our home.'

Elona felt the world closing off once again as they walked in silence to a suite of rooms in the east of the main tower. It had two bedrooms joined by a common antechamber, three flights from the ground. Their baggage had already been moved, which seemed to please the Lady Metrid, and her maids were unpacking.

'I will change into the emerald velvet dress,' Metrid said to her maid. 'Hope, you should wear the blue. Go now and change.'

'Yes, Mother.' The younger woman curtsied and went to the other room. Elona stood self-consciously in the centre of the bustle, her hands clasped before her. Metrid dismissed the servants.

'My dear, I am so happy to see you,' she exclaimed, and embracing and kissing Elona. She felt enveloped by warmth and the scent of lavender. 'Sit down, dear.' Metrid went to the bed and sat, patting the place next to her. As Elona sat Metrid caught up her hand. 'I know what has happened. You poor child. It is terrible. And your father—to find his wife so.' She shook her head as if trying to dislodge an unpleasant thought. Elona's eyes were drawn to the scar that twisted in her face. 'If you would rather go to your chambers I will not be offended. You have suffered and should no doubt rest. Perhaps you should call your Nurse?'

'M-my Nurse is dismissed, Lady Metrid,' Elona said. 'I am well enough. My Father would be angry if I deserted you.'

'Pah, such nonsense. But your Nurse dismissed? That is not good, no one to give you the care you need. Men have no heart. I know. You see this? My ornament? My dear husband gave me this. He was a good man or so it seemed. It is true he was well-mannered in the beginning. Yet within him he had his demon and he did me ill.

'And my foolish son chose to interfere. Now I wear my hair in a widow's bob while Jaymis has fled the executioner's axe and is outlaw and the land that was mine is given in stewardship to my brother-in-law.' The woman's grip on Elona's hand tightened to the point of pain. 'But we bring it on ourselves, we trust them and they betray us—do not trust men, Elona. They seem amiable and charming but you know they will hurt you. Hold your freedom as long as you may.'

Elona felt confused; she was sure it was her fault but Bejeren had said it wasn't, but how would he know, he was just a man—Lady Metrid understood better.

A knock came at the door. Metrid released her hand and stood abruptly. 'Yes.' Hope entered wearing a blue velvet gown that seemed to overwhelm her pale features.

'You are not changing, Mother?'

'Presently, my dear, I was renewing my acquaintance with Elona. Let me change, Elona. Wait with Hope and we will pay our respects to your mother.'

The three women stood outside the screens in Mother's chamber. Elona shuddered as a shadow moved within but she could hear the chanting of a healer. Metrid and Hope moved forward but Elona felt she had become rooted.

The chanting stopped and a shaven-headed woman emerged, her eyes widened with surprise when she saw the older woman.

'Metrid.'

'Malea.'

Elona saw Hope clench her delicate hands into pretty fists.

'Your presence is a surprise.'

'I travel with the King.'

The Healer's gaze flicked at Hope for a moment. Her gaze softened as she looked on Elona, then returned to their glinting severity as she looked back at Metrid.

'You have not lost your delicacy, bringing her here.'

'He did not hurt her spirit.'

They fell silent. Then the Healer smiled a thin humourless smile. 'I have completed my patterning. You may pay your respects to the Lady.' She turned, became a shadow behind the screen, then faded from view. Elona could hear her footsteps receding on the other side.

Metrid and Hope stepped forward and entered the enclosure. Elona waited outside while the dark and the silence closed in around her. There was no sound except a murmuring from behind the screens. Her thoughts drifted and the images of what might have been played over in her mind. She jumped when mother and daughter reappeared. It looked as if Metrid had been crying. Hope approached until Elona could smell the freshness of the girl's perfumes and see the powdered smoothness of her skin.

'My mother would like to know what entertainments have been prepared,' Hope said.

'My teacher knows, I will send to find him,' Elona replied. 'Perhaps if you descend to the main hall presently, he can meet you there?' Hope inclined her head and Elona hurried away towards the door, glad to escape. And ran into the Prince just beyond it. Elona looked up in surprise and then dropped to her knee.

7

'Please get up, Lady Elona, there's no need for that.' He took her hand and raised her. He was several inches taller than her now and his features had matured to the point where the youth was almost gone.

'I'm sorry; I was to send for my teacher.'

'The scribe? I saw him barely a moment ago. Let us find him together.' He offered his arm to her and smiled. 'Perhaps you will not be so eager to lose my arm as the last time I offered it?'

Elona averted her face but slid her arm through his. 'I was ... I'm sorry ... I was very rude.'

The Prince laughed. 'And I was a paragon of knightly honour? I think not. We were both children.' He smiled at her. 'And now, we are not.'

They walked in silence and Elona slipped back into the protection of her mute pain. There was a strange comfort in holding him. Perhaps this is what Savi meant. Could this be love? Her face twisted into a sad smile at her own innocence and shook her head. No, not love. Just someone willing to hold her.

He looked at her. 'Did you say something, Elona?'

'Oh no.' She searched for something to divert his attention. 'The

Queen, your Mother. She does not travel with you?' She felt his arm tense but he did not pull away.

'She is unwell and does not favour a Progress.'

'Is she ill? I had not heard.'

He sighed. 'Not with any disease the healers can mend. She fears there will be war and it preys upon her.'

'Then my prophecy would come true.'

'And my father will be slain, and perhaps me too.' He paused. 'But if there were any way I could raise my mother up, give her life again, I would do it. I swear I would stand against the *Kisharuk* itself.'

Elona shivered at the naming of the Slissac evil. 'It is not good to say such things, my Lord. Bejeren says the World's Pattern will hear such an oath and make it true.'

'Then he is a good scribe. Yet the common people utter that name a dozen times a day and no terrible fate befalls them.'

'Do you know that? Have you seen one who says the name and then followed him to the end of his days to see his fate? I haven't and I would not excuse a loose tongue that way. Taymar wrote "A man's fate is the mirror of his life."'

The Prince slowed to a stopped and turned to face her. 'You are not my counsellor,' he said with a smile.

Elona winced and dropped her gaze to the floor. 'I just meant that if you live a mean life, your fate may also be. But you are a prince and you move the world. One day you will be King in Faerholme and if it is as Taymar says, would you bring that fate down upon your land? On your people? On me?' And suddenly, in her mind's eye, she saw the gate of the town with Krazak's head on a spike above the wall; it seemed he was laughing at her, asking what did you do to bring this fate on you? She pulled away from the Prince and turned to the wall to hide the tears that fell from her eyes.

She felt the Prince's hands on her shoulders and his voice spoke beside her ear so that she could feel his breath on her cheek. 'It's alright. I wasn't angry.'

'I'm sorry.' She broke free and rushed down the passage. She could hear his heavier footsteps catching up with her as she came to a halt at the door to the main hall; there were voices from within. The Prince caught her arm and twisted her around. She would not look at him. 'My mother has always counselled my Father with wisdom, knowledge and compassion that a man cannot know. I would not consider it a bad—'

'Please forgive this intrusion, my Lord Prince,' called the Lady Metrid, hurrying down the stairs behind them with Hope in her wake. 'I asked Elona to find her scribe. Is he found?' The Prince dropped his arms and Elona felt as if she were spinning away from him like a leaf in a stream. She backed away until she reached the wall and dabbed at her damp cheeks with her sleeve. Lady Metrid glanced at her for a moment, then filled the space between them.

Through the doorway Elona could see Bejeren talking to the Steward. She slipped into the room and walked quickly across to him. The Steward saw her approach and deferred to her. Bejeren studied her face but she spoke before he could say anything.

'Lady Metrid and the Prince want to know what entertainments have been arranged for their visit. I—' she took a deep breath. '—I am feeling unwell and must retire to my chambers.' She left before Bejeren could see her tears.

'I hope you are feeling better this morning,' said Lady Metrid. They were on horseback, following the party of nobles and senior guildsmen down a windswept lane, bordered on one side by woods and fields on the other. They had passed a cart on the lane heading back to town, driven by two men and laden with cut reeds.

The wall of the Corlain Mountains stood before them only a day's travel away. Beyond the mountains lay the East March of Faerholme, then the land of Raertane, and finally Dirdin. Elona wished she were there and not here. Anywhere but here.

'Thank you for your concern, my Lady. I am feeling better.'

'That is well. It would not do for you to miss these distractions that have been prepared for us all,' Metrid paused. 'Your teacher has indeed given much thought to keeping the men amused.'

'Yes, Lady Metrid.'

'Though I suggest he has given less thought to the entertainment of the ladies.'

Elona hesitated. The Lady Metrid continued. 'We are expected simply to watch and admire the exploits of the men-folk it seems. Still, a wolf-hunt is not an every-day occurrence.'

'No, Lady Metrid. I ... I understand that the pack has been causing a great deal of trouble among the *kichek* herds, even killed two herdsmen.'

The Lady Metrid stared ahead dreamily for a while and then spoke again, but almost to herself. 'They are poor lost souls in a world that threatens them. They bite at anything in the hope that they can regain the world they once knew.' She sighed. 'Instead we will destroy them. One by one, fast and slow. Until but one remains. And that last, alone, bereft without its brothers, sisters or cousins. That one, without its pack, will be driven to the insanity of loneliness and will die.'

Elona stared at her. It seemed the Lady Metrid came to herself again and shook the mood from her. She turned to look at Elona and smiled but it was a smile without warmth.

'But do not be afraid, little Elona. You have your family yet.'

Elona turned to face forward and watched the bobbing head of her mount for a few moments. 'My apologies, Lady Metrid, I wish to enquire of Bejeren.' She urged her horse into a trot.

The wind blew hard along the valley where the party had stopped in preparation for the hunt. The course of the slow and reedy river they had been following formed an almost complete loop about them. They made their camp on the mound within the circle of water. The Lords stood at the neck of the river's loop preparing their spears, and recounting hunting tales that grew in their telling. Twenty armsmen with bows stood nearby ready to bring down any wolf that broke the cordon. Beyond them open land rose up gently to a wood, on the other side of which the beaters were now waiting for the signal to advance. The horses had been withdrawn to the far side of the mound. away from the wood and hidden from view.

'The wolves are within the trees,' Bejeren told her. 'The beaters will drive them out, along the line of the stream we crossed down-river, to where the Lords will be ranged. As the beasts come forth the King will have his sport and the farmers will be made safe. You will be able to see it clearly from here.'

'Won't they fight? What if there are many?' She had asked.

'It is not their way. By their nature, if they are fleeing they will only flee. If they are hunting they will only hunt. They act with a single mind, it as if they have but a single thought between them and they never utter a sound; it is their pattern and their weakness. But what sport would there be if there were no danger? It is the last wolf that is most dangerous, for with the rest of the pack dead it is utterly alone, driven mad by the pain of its fellows; it cannot be predicted. It may lie down and die, or it may attack in frenzy.'

Elona stood at the river's edge staring at the woods. How many wolves would there be? She did not like it here. It was cold and the sky threatened rain. No matter how slight, she did not find the danger tempting. She looked at the cut reeds. Each stalk with its angled cut just above the surface of the water pointed into the air like a dagger.

She was distracted from her reverie as calls went up and the hunting party moved off. They went to the left to take up position on either bank of the stream that emerged from the wood. As they approached their stations a horn was winded that blew loud through the trees. Moments later, in answer, a distant cacophony broke out as the beaters set up their cry to drive the creatures out.

The Lady Metrid and Hope appeared at Elona's side and the three stood staring across the sluggish water. Cold moments passed. The only sounds were the distant beaters and the hissing of the wind through the cut reeds. Finally Lady Metrid whispered: 'They come.'

Moments later a cry went up among the line of hunters they could see on the nearer bank of the stream. The men adjusted their footing and raised their weapons in readiness. A heartbeat later silent grey and brown forms flowed from trees and poured towards the hunters.

In less time than a single breath, the first of the wolves crashed against the front rank. Elona saw the Prince deal the first blow, thrusting at the neck of one of the leading beasts on his side. He pulled his spear free and blood gushed from the wound. The animal took another few paces before tumbling silently to the ground. The others flowed over it like an uncaring river.

The King and her Father lashed out on the other side and felled two more of the beasts. The Prince missed the killing blow on his second wolf, scoring only a long gash down its side before the spear was torn from his hand. The animal did not stop. The Prince grabbed another spear from his servant but the wolves were past and the second rank was striking at them. More fell. All without a cry.

Elona watched, hypnotised by the spilling blood, as the creatures fell. The hunters shouted and the beaters still raised their clamour but from the wolves there was nothing. They died in silence.

A shout of warning went up close to her and servants screamed. Elona turned suddenly as a single wolf appeared at the entrance to their refuge and pounded directly towards her. She looked wildly about; Lady Metrid and Hope were twenty paces away on the hillock. She stood alone.

8

———

She backed up two steps to the river's edge. The wolf bounded towards her. Terror froze her. As the wolf leapt her foot slipped on the muddy bank and she fell back. She felt the wolf's heat and heard its breath as it passed over her.

She felt a hundred reeds break her fall, piercing in a dozen places. Then freezing water closed over her head and seeped with frightening speed through her clothes, pulling her deeper. Something struck her head hard and scratched across her scalp. The silence of the water took her. She tried to push herself up but the weight of her clothes held her down. Numbing cold spread around her and her breath burned in her chest.

Then there were hands on her and reluctantly the river and the reeds gave her up. She breathed in, the air scraping through her throat. They laid her down. She rolled over and choked into the grass.

She opened her eyes and the Prince stood above her. The upside-down face of Bejeren appeared at her other side. Both wore a look of concern. The Prince knelt, his face stained with red and brown splatters. He took her hand in his and with the other brushed the hair from her face, and she saw his hand came away bloodied

55

bright red. The Prince looked up at Bejeren. 'Fetch the Lady Metrid, she's a healer.'

'She has collapsed. Her daughter attends her.'

Elona found something to say. 'I'm ... I think I'm alright.' Her voice was thin and uncertain. They helped her into a sitting position and Bejeren examined her head.

'Three deep scratches, from its hind leg I would guess.'

Elona turned to look at the water. 'Is it dead?' Her answer lay in the score of bloody reeds piercing through the body of the wolf. The water was red.

'Do you hurt anywhere else, Elona?' Bejeren asked.

She concentrated on the rest of her body, though the throbbing of her head demanded her attention. 'My back and legs hurt but my head aches the worst.'

While the others remained to fly hawks before the evening feast, Elona returned to the castle with Bejeren, Lady Metrid (somewhat recovered) and Hope. They spoke little on the journey; Elona felt she was in a dream, playing and replaying the image of the lone wolf leaping at her and the stifling silence of the water that would not release her.

Her bedroom seemed empty when she got there, missing the filling presence of Nursey. No one to fuss, to chatter, or even to disapprove. Savi was sent for. They had not been expected back so soon. A manservant stoked the fire back to life and its heat drove the chill from the room.

'Attacked by a wolf?' Savi studied the scratches on Elona's head. 'Lady Metrid sent this salve. She said it will aid the healing and she will attend later if more is needed.'

'Please get me out of these wet things,' Elona said and sneezed.

Savi studied the knots drawn tight with wetness. 'I shall have to use a knife—not that it matters; these clothes have been shredded by those reeds.' She cut Elona from her clothes. 'Taymar's teeth. Look at you!'

'What?'

'Bruises. You're covered with them, all down your back, your arms, your neck—everywhere.'

Elona strained to look but winced as she stretched the skin.

'It's a miracle you weren't pinned out. Let's get you cleaned up, you can take a rest and be ready for the banquet.'

'I don't want to go to the banquet. I want to stay in my room. Why don't they just leave me alone?' Elona lay face down on the bed and sneezed into the pillow.

'You have to go. The Prince would be insulted.'

'I don't care. I want to stay here.'

'That's silly. You're going to be queen.'

'I don't like him.'

Savi laughed. 'All men are dull. That's why we have the advantage; we decide what they're to do with their lives. It's not what he's like that's important, it's what he is. And he's the heir to the throne. Anyway, he was kind to you, wasn't he? He helped you?'

'Yes, but so did Bejeren.'

'Oh well, we don't want to think about that. But the Prince, you see, he's your knight.'

'He didn't do anything knightly. He was busy killing wolves but they missed that one. Nobody bothered protecting me.'

Elona rolled on to her back using the pain to fuel her anger. No one cared about her, no one thought about her feelings. She saw a large spider crawling along one of the beams. Life is like that spider. It crawls and creeps, snares and catches. It never stands in the open and to show itself clearly. It's all secrecy and lies. And it doesn't care.

'It's not like this in the stories.'

'No, and the princesses are never with child either.'

'I'm not a princess and I'm not the one with child,' Elona sighed. 'Lady Metrid said all men are bad and I should try to delay the wedding.'

'But Drahail isn't just a man. Don't worry, I'll make sure you look your best. Being attacked by a wolf makes you special.'

Elona sneezed again. Her eyes ached and she felt very tired. 'Who would love someone that special?'

Elona lay in her bed sweating and sneezing; the fire had been piled high and roared in the grate. She had not attended the feast; Lady Metrid had ordered she stay in her rooms.

'The best thing for a cold is bed-rest, plenty of food and warmth. We can't have you wandering around in draughts. Keep to your bed and you'll soon be well. And don't forget to take the herbal drink I have prepared for you.' The drink was bitter despite the honey but Elona drank dutifully.

~

Father visited her on that first day. He was gruff and it was clear he was uncomfortable. 'Do what Metrid tells you, daughter, she has had more experience than I with sick children.'

'I am not that ill, Father, Lady Metrid is kind and is making me well.' She smiled nervously and slowly reached out to touch his hand.

He looked distracted. 'I have not been the best father to you. When I saw the wolf attack yesterday I—' He sighed heavily and his face relaxed into someone she had not seen before. 'Daughter, Metrid is a good woman but your Mother was a jewel. In these long years, I have never ceased to love her.' She did not know what to say to this stranger, but then Father returned wearing the armour of ill-temper. 'Do as Metrid says and you'll soon be about again.' Then he was gone.

She sat up again, plumped up the pillows, picked up her embroidery and stitched. She wished Savi could be there but Metrid had insisted on quiet and that, it seemed, meant no tittle-tattle from the castle. Metrid herself usually sat with her for an hour or so each day and they talked about nothing.

Ichen popped up from beneath the bed and bumped his head against her hand until she stroked him. At least Lady Metrid couldn't stop Ichen from visiting, though it wasn't for love that he came.

Without Savi's rumours how would she know what was happening? It bothered her now that she did not know. She could feel a distant threat in her very bones.

After a five-day Lady Metrid declared Elona fit for human company. Elona was more than grateful; she felt if she had to stay a prisoner one more day she might indulge her fear of heights and throw herself from the window just to feel the wind once more. Yet even now Metrid had her wrapped in winter clothes, and insisted she drink the carefully prepared brews before they ventured into the castle's walled garden.

With Metrid at her side to ward off all interference, Elona walked slowly between the beds. Most of the flowers were finished and the leaves were falling, yet the air was not too cold. The heavy winter dress and wraps made her shoulders and neck ache.

'Lady Metrid, may I not discard the cloak? This dress has a high neck and I am stifling beneath it.'

'Elona, you may feel that my ministrations are overdone but how many children have you birthed or raised? Do you have younger brothers or sisters? You do not. So please forebear from suggesting your knowledge may be superior to mine.' The sharp edge of warning in Metrid's voice brooked no response.

They trudged through the autumn garden coming finally to a stone bench in a sheltered corner. The afternoon sun was pleasant though it did not give much heat and there they sat awhile in silence.

Finally Metrid spoke. 'Elona, you are a good child and have borne my cures with a kind heart. My herbs are potent but they are not pleasant.' Elona protested but Metrid laughed. 'Do not begin to deny it. You were like a wild *kichek* in a cage, ready to break itself against the bars to be free. But you are here now, nearly well. I shall be journeying on with the King when he leaves tomorrow.

'It is good enough. The King chooses to winter at my brother-in-law's seat that was my home before my husband died. It was my family that once wielded the Dragonblade until it was stolen from us.' Elona saw the shadow pass across Metrid's face and shrank back in fearful anticipation but it passed quickly. Metrid smiled. 'I must apologise, perhaps, for preventing your mixing with the Court?'

Elona looked down at her hands clasped in her lap. 'No, my Lady. I am unused to courtly ways, I am awkward and I know I make a fool of myself with every word. I was grateful to be in my room— though I would have liked a little more company.'

Metrid turned towards her and grasped her cold hands; Elona looked up into her face again. The scar stood out white, yet seemed less significant now. 'Elona, your body is full-grown, you have a pleasant comeliness, yet you are still a child. Because of that foolish prophecy you are entangled in the plots and machinations of the Court and politics before you have truly lived. This prophecy they made for you is a trap if you listen to it.'

Metrid reached into her purse. 'Here, I have two keepsakes for you; the necklace is of silver and is a gift from Hope.' The necklace was a chain of overlapping plates, each with its own individual inscribed design. 'And from me, for your protection, take care. This is no toy.' She handed her a plain sheath over a dagger with a three-inch blade covered in a delicate patterning. Elona thanked her then turned away and watched a gardener rake up the fallen leaves. A wind blew upward, dislodging more from the trees and stirred the ones he had already collected. The cold breeze chilled her and she pulled the hood over her hair. She wondered at the plots of the Court and a strange suspicion came to her.

'Lady Metrid?' She enquired quietly. 'Has my Father been out of favour with the King?'

For a while, as the wind whipped the leaves from the trees, there was no answer, then: 'It is said that the house of Corlain is closest to the King's heart. They say your Father is a good and noble man, that he deals well with his people. Why do you ask, my dear?'

Elona did not reply immediately, she wanted to say "because I must" yet she knew that would not be right. She felt that her thoughts were close to heresy, or a crime against the King, so she found a reason that would not arouse suspicion. 'It has been years since he last visited us.'

'That is simply answered. The King has not been on a Progress in that time—there has been no need. With the surrounding lands dealing peaceably with us, the King has had no need of threats or reminders of the power of the Dragonblade, nor has there been a need for additional levies.

'More than that, why should he antagonise his Lords by forcing them to spend their gold on him? No, there has been no need.'

'But he is here now? There is war?'

'I will answer you truthfully, little one. We are not at war, no, at least not yet. But Tirnia still spreads its dominion beyond its traditional borders. When the King signed a treaty to assist in the protection of Taltia, the Empire chose not to invade that land.

'But rumours from the Court say that there have been messengers from far Tirnia whose demeanour has been dour. Though the messages they bring are secret to the King and his closest councillors, these messengers are not made welcome and are sent away unsatisfied. While the ambassadors of Taltia and Raertane are received with kindness.' She sighed. 'And now the King makes a Progress and takes council from his Lords.

'But we women should not trouble ourselves with the deeds of men. They will have their tourneys and fighting and duels and wars. We remain at the hearth while they decide who will die next. Perhaps if Tirnia ruled all there would be no need of war.'

At that moment the warning bell rang out from the high tower. The castle, so quiet a moment before, seemed to explode with armsmen and servants rushing hither and yon. Elona scanned the skies for *tekrasa* but it should be too late in the season for those marauding plants. Lady Metrid rose as the tower armsman cried out, pointing north towards the ley-circle.

'Come, child. Let us return to the hall. An attack here in the heart of Faerholme is unlikely; your father guards the Wellspring diligently but if armsmen have breached his defences we must get inside. I think perhaps it is just a messenger with his escort. Still, we'd best learn what we may.' She rose to her feet and bustled Elona towards the tower door.

9

―――――

Elona could not quell the curiosity excited by Lady Metrid's words. Secrets? Secrets in her father's house? Elona climbed to her tower room and, defying her fears, leant out to see the arrivals. A huge troop of horses, perhaps fifty strong, clattered into the courtyard; more than a hundred armsmen and archers stood on the walls above, arrows nocked though not drawn.

Who had so many horses that they had no need of *kichesa*? None in Faerholme to be sure. And for the garrison to be so surprised by them they must have walked a patterner's path to the Wellspring close by. They were led by one in rich cloths; an outfit of fine frippery that was not the custom in Faerholme.

Elona crept from her room and stole through the passages; she had to know what this man would say to the King. The musician's gallery would be the best place to hide; she found the door and opened it. Closing it carefully she took up a position behind a tapestry above the Great Hall, peeping around its edge.

The King was seated in Father's chair while Father stood at the King's right hand. The Prince stood slightly back on the left, shifting his weight from one foot to another. He was not as handsome as she first thought. To the left of the King stood his personal sorcerer, the Patterner Liggel; a Scribe in Master's robes sat at a desk with a pen and parchment

63

to hand. High-ranking Lords who accompanied the King's Progress stood to the sides and were flanked by two score of the King's armsmen.

The tall candelabra had been lit to their full complement as the autumn sun, shining weakly through the windows, brought little light to the room.

Elona heard the main doors opening below the balcony and the sound of metal-shod feet crashed on the stone flags, breaking the expectant silence. The back of a black-plumed helmet come into view along with a cloak of red and black stripes with the black *tikak* of Tirnia enclosed in a circle on the back. The messenger was followed by half a dozen armsmen carrying pikes topped with red and black pennants.

The main entourage stopped just inside the door while the messenger continued forward to position fifteen feet from the King. He bowed his head slightly. From within his cloak he withdrew a parchment and offered it to the King.

The King nodded to the scribe and patterner. They stepped forward; the scribe took the scroll and examined the seal carefully. Satisfied, he passed it to the Patterner, who slowly ran his hand along it, muttering beneath his breath. Finally he turned to the King and nodded before handing the parchment back to the messenger, who snatched it with indecent speed, broke the seal, and unravelled it.

'To Kendil Oslain of the Dragonblade, King of Faerholme and Protector of the Silver Isle. From Emperor Myrlask of the Empire of Tirnia, Warder of Esternes, Taltia and the Eastern lands, Protector of Umran...' At the sound of these titles a murmur of anger went through the Lords present. Elona noted the strange way the messenger spoke the words, as if they did not come easily to his tongue.

'...Greetings to your Great Majesty. Let it be known that the Lord Nahdiril of Telsuka is my ambassador for the negotiation of tariffs and charges for the import of goods to the Kingdom of Faerholme and that he is empowered to sign in my name any treaty so negotiated. Myrlask, Emperor.'

Nahdiril lowered the scroll and re-rolled it, handing it once more to the scribe, who stepped back and studied the words.

The King spoke. 'Lord Nahdiril, your journey has been quite unnecessary.'

'Your Majesty?'

'There is no need for negotiation; we find the existing terms to be quite equitable.'

Nahdiril stiffened. 'The Emperor feels that the tariffs could be lowered so that your land may be enriched by the delightful wares of Tirnia. We have so much to offer.'

'I am well aware of what Tirnia offers. As does the Kingdom of Taltia. I was not aware that Tirnia had succeeded in subjugating the Isle of Esternes, nor that Umran had agreed to accept your protectorship. The Umran ambassador is quite adamant they do not bow to Myrlask's tyranny.'

From her position Elona could not see the Lord Nahdiril's face but she imagined he was not pleased.

'Lord King, the Empire provides stability and peace; the wild men of Esternes need our peace and they shall receive it. But returning to the matter at hand, shall we not adjourn to a more comfortable and private place to continue our negotiations?'

'I think not, Lord Nahdiril. There are no negotiations to make. Your Emperor will have to accept the terms as they exist now; there will be no reduction in tariffs. Your people will have to pay highly if they want to offer their Tirnian goods here, or my people will have to do without.

'I would offer you the hospitality of Lord Corlain but we already occupy it. Unless you are swift it will be dark before you reach the Wellspring, and your patterners may have difficulty weaving the path for your return.' The King took a step forward and the armsmen became more alert.

'Majesty, the Imperial Patterners are weary. They could not possibly make a new road before tomorrow.'

'You, your soldiers and your Imperial Patterners will leave the soil of Faerholme before midnight. Otherwise the Wellspring will be closed to you and you will find that you will be riding back to Tirnia through the lands you claim to hold. You are dismissed.'

As Elona watched it seemed that Lord Nahdiril paused overlong; then he spun around and stormed out with his entourage in tow. The doors clanged in finality behind him. The King turned to Elona's Father.

'Taniel, the Wellspring is your responsibility. With such power within it, both a blessing and a curse, we cannot fortify it with stone so we must strengthen it with the flesh and bone—your arm must hold it. I doubt even the Empire has sufficient Patterners to weave a road an entire army could walk but they may try an incursion or two to test our mettle.'

'My King, whatever they try will be crushed. I will despatch troops to escort Lord Nahdiril from our lands. And call up additional armsmen to increase the watch.'

Together they went to the west door and left the hall. Elona wanted to hear more of their plans but it was impossible. Carefully she crept from her hiding place as the noise in the hall increased with chatter from the Court.

The King departed the following day, without pomp or ceremony. Elona watched them ride away, the lords and ladies on horseback or in carriages, the soldiers on foot or astride their *kichesa*. She had barely spoken a word to the Prince since that first day; he rode beside Hope as they clattered out of the Keep's main gates. He had made no effort to see her though they were to be married. Lady Metrid was right; men were not worth a thought. She felt her heart sag; the talk throughout the castle was of the coming war, which meant nothing to her but servitude and the bearing of children.

Over the following days the weather became bitterly cold and the last of the leaves were driven from the trees. The Lord Corlain arranged for an additional corp of armsmen to be stationed at the Wellspring at all times in addition to the usual detachment. The majority were peasants but, with harvest passed, it provided an opportunity for training should they be needed in earnest later.

Elona's nights became troubled with dreams. She saw an evil magic seeping from the Wellspring, spreading through the land and spilling into the castle, consuming everyone and leaving her screaming in her room. But when she awoke crying in the dark, there was no one to comfort her.

The morning after Savi gave birth to a son, Elona was at her lessons with Bejeren in his study. The walls had embroidered maps of Faerholme and the surrounding countries. Father had a large collection of books and many of them were stacked on the shelves of Bejeren's rooms. His desk under the window was splattered with inks, much of which she had spilled herself in her early efforts to master the quill.

The talk of war had resulted in a history lesson about Taymar rescuing the Taymalin from the Slissac and their *Kisharuk* demon, then sailing across the sea to Karane. How he had led the people across great mountains, freezing deserts and down to the lands where at last they found comfort and peace. Over centuries the Taymalin had spread west through what was now Tirnia, Taltia, Dirdin, Raertane and Faerholme to the sea. Now they were expanding south through Mirriasmia ultimately to populate the entire world, as was their right and their duty.

'But what about the wild men of Esternes? And the Kadralin?' Asked Elona.

'What of them?'

'They are not Taymalin.'

'No, of course not. They did not suffer the horror.'

'But they look like us; I mean they're not Slissac. They are people.'

'Taymar says that we were purified by the horror, as the impurities of a metal are removed from its surface when it is molten. We were the ones who survived, we are the Taymalin. Some of the Kadralin realised this when Taymar came to the land, and hailed him as a god. Others did not, and they are no more.'

Elona nodded. She'd heard it in stories but somehow it didn't seem quite right.

'But Taymar is not a god, is he?'

'There are those that say he is, not all the Taymalin agree on that but it doesn't really matter. He did save us and that's what's important. We all agree on that.' Bejeren stood up. 'That's enough history for today. I think we'll do some more arithmetic.'

Elona sighed; every time she felt she was close to understanding, Bejeren would change the subject, as if he were trying to hide the truth. It seemed more and more that there were things that he kept from her. As she searched around for the slate there was a knock at the door. Bejeren opened it and the visitor spoke to him in a low voice. Bejeren glanced over at Elona.

'I will be a moment.' Then he stepped out and pulled the door almost closed behind him. Elona jumped up, why did he not want to her to hear? She pretended to search through the shelves near the door and managed to peep through the crack between door and frame. The visitor was a woman wearing the robes of a Patterner. Elona strained to catch Bejeren's words as she pretended to search.

'...not well,' said Bejeren.

'She has been ill,' said a woman's voice she did not recognise.

'It's more than that, she has become ... troubled.'

'That's to be expected, considering what's happened to her recently. No one could be unchanged by such things.'

'When the Master recruited me, he said I should make sure she knows her histories and geography, writing and arithmetic, everything that I could teach her. He didn't say anything about any change in her very nature—she has begun to pry, and seems suspicious of everything.'

'We cannot help that. We have cast our lot with the Master, you cannot change mount in the middle of a stream. Like it or not you must do as the Master says.'

'I don't like it.'

'It matters not, Bejeren. The Master has ordained it, will you defy him?'

Bejeren didn't answer.

'You won't do anything stupid.'

There was a long pause then: 'I will obey his command.'

'Be sure you do. He has not planned this long to have one replaceable scribe get in his way.'

Bejeren returned and closed the door. Elona looked through another shelf.

'Who was that?' She asked with as much innocence as she could muster. Bejeren moved round to his desk.

'Just a maid enquiring for the cook; whether I would suggest some courses for the solstice feast.'

It was as if a cold knife had sliced through Elona's heart. She almost cried but hid it with a cough; tears trickled from her eyes and she wiped them with her sleeve, sniffing.

'Are you alright?'

'I–I think my cold may have come back.' She turned away from him and stood up straight. 'I think I would like to go to my room.'

'Of course. You go and get warm. We'll carry on tomorrow.'

In tight control of her emotions, she went to the door, walked carefully out and shut it tight behind her. Then the tears burst like a flood and she ran as fast as she dared to her mother's chamber and crept behind the screens. She knelt by her shoulder and took the cold hand in hers.

'They want to kill me, Mother.' Tears fell from her eyes onto the sheets and she rubbed her mother's hand against her cheek. 'I know it's my fault you're here.'

She squeezed the limp hand. 'Please wake up. Tell me what should I do?'

Her mother's tranquil face remained silent.

'If I could get proof, if I could show Father, he'd believe me.'

She stood and placed a kiss on her mother's cheek, then gently laid her hand on the sheet. 'Thank you, Mother.'

She hurried back to her chamber. The door to her room could not be locked and it wasn't safe to leave it like that. They would be searching her room; they might try to kill her as she slept now that she knew of the conspiracy. She must persuade Kienan to fit locks.

10

Returning from the town blacksmith carrying her heavy bag, Elona passed the midwife-healer at the castle gate. She had probably woven another restorative pattern to ease Savi's aches and pains after the birth. It was so easy for them. Why hadn't there been a healer when her mother had birthed her?

The sun was hanging above the western castle walls, and the courtyard was in shadow and cold as Elona crossed the cobbles. When she opened the door to the smithy, a flood of heat poured out, though the fires were not stoked and no one was working. She went to the back of the workshop and placed her bag in a shadowy corner beneath the stairs. She climbed the solid wooden steps to the door of the private rooms and knocked loudly.

Kienan's father, a man with huge shoulders and skin blistered into permanent redness by the furnace heat, opened the door. He stepped back and, with a smile, gestured for her to enter. The small room was crowded and Savi's parents were visiting. They all rose and greeted her politely.

'My Lady, have you come to pay your respects to the baby?' asked Kienan's Mother.

'I have, Goodwife. If Savi doesn't mind.'

The women smiled indulgently.

'She has been awaiting your visit since she birthed, Lady Elona. Please go through.' She went to a door on the other side of the room and knocked.

'Daughter, it's the Lady Elona come to pay her respects.' Then she opened the door and gestured for Elona to go through. The little room that had been Kienan's bedroom all his life seemed tinier with the larger bed and the cot at its side. There was barely room to walk round the sides. Both bed and cot were covered with heavy quilts. In the bed lay Savi, her hair combed straight. She looked well and held a small bundle in her arms.

By the bed stood Kienan, his eyes filled with wonder and confusion. Savi looked at him and smiled.

'Kienan, please go and find some refreshment for Lady Elona.'

He nodded and squeezed past Elona, almost pushing her on to the bed; he muttered an apology and left. The door was closed behind him.

'Come and sit by me, my Lady, please.'

Elona did so and Savi pulled back the clothes that hid the baby's face. He was asleep, his little pink wrinkly face relaxed and at peace.

'Isn't he beautiful?' Savi's attention totally absorbed by the child.

'What was it like?' Elona hadn't meant to ask but the words just happened; she bit her lip in embarrassment, but Savi sighed.

'Well, it did hurt, even with Healer Canvorin's help. She said she couldn't really stop it all, and it wouldn't be right to anyway. And it was really hard work—I'll never complain about cleaning tapestries again. But now, look at him, Elona, isn't he beautiful?'

Elona looked down at the baby again and smiled.

'And you're alright too, Savi?'

'Oh yes, Healer Canvorin took away the pain straight after, and even helped Manvord—we're calling him Manvord—so he was alright too. I'm so glad we're in the town, my Lady. Think what it must be like for people without a healer to help ... oh.'

Elona pulled back and turned away abruptly. They sat in silence for a few moments, then Manvord stirred, and from beyond the door there were sounds of talking and the clattering of utensils. The courtyard outside echoed with the changing of the guard. Elona stared at the babe, feeling strange, and for a moment it seemed as if the child were stealing her spirit, drawing her in yet betraying her as well. But she shook her head violently to push it away; this was a newborn babe, what did it know of betrayal?

Elona took a deep breath and stood up. 'I have to go.'

'Yes, of course.'

'When will you return to my service?'

'Healer Ca ... I believe I will be able to in two or three five-days, my Lady.'

'I will see you then.' She stumbled in the tiny space and stopped at the door. 'My good wishes to the babe.'

'Thank you, my Lady. And to you.'

Elona let herself out and, after brief words of farewell to the parents, Kienan escorted Elona to the door. As she began down the steps she heard a fragment of conversation drift out '...sad, strange girl...' They clattered down the steps and, at the bottom, she retrieved her bag and thrust it at Kienan.

'You must do something for me, Kienan. Here are locks and bolts. Put them on the door to my room.'

'But, my Lady, all fixings are arranged by the Steward.'

'Kienan, you must.' She stared intensely up at his face glowing red in the furnace light. 'I'm scared, Kienan. You know what's been done to me. I can't sleep, Nursey's gone, you're the only one I can trust. It won't take you very long to fit them. It's so I can sleep at night. Would you do less for Savi if she were scared?'

Kienan's resolve crumbled. 'I'll do it, my Lady. Tomorrow.'

'Tonight!' She said, then calmed herself. 'It must be tonight, Kienan. I can't spend another night awake and alone in that room.'

'Tonight then,' he agreed.

'Soon ... please,' she pleaded.

'I'll come before sundown, my Lady.'

She reached up on tiptoe and put her hand at the back of his neck and pulled him down kissing him on the lips. 'I'll take these and I'll be waiting for you. But you mustn't tell anybody.' She smiled inwardly at the pathetic look of astonishment on his face.

As she stepped out from the heat of the smithy into the cold her eyes were stung with tears. Sad, strange girl. What did they know? She stumbled into the keep with sobs threatening to burst from her heart. The guards turned as she ran for the stairs. Sad, strange girl. Was she strange? Of course, who else carried a prophecy like hers? But how could she know? Perhaps she was different, perhaps everyone knew except her? Sad, strange girl. What did they know in the smithy? Perhaps she was not really her Father's daughter.

Tears welled up within her and she felt as if she were losing what little family she had. Lying on the table at her bedside was the dagger that Metrid had given her. She picked it up and laid it in her palm. Its comforting weight rested in her hand, reaching from her fingertips to her wrist. She slipped the blade from its little sheath. She ran her finger along the edge of the blade; it sliced sharp and deep. Blood dripped from the cut and she sucked her finger. The taste of her life—and the taste of death.

What did she have to live for? Deceit in those around her, a Father who hated her and a future bearing the heirs of a doomed dynasty. How hard would it be to take this little blade and make herself bleed until no life remained? She pulled her finger from her mouth and stared at her wrist, bringing the knife to hover above the veins.

But what if Mother should wake? What if she should wake and not find her daughter waiting for her? Elona blinked as if waking herself. If she was threatened then so was Mother; how could she desert her?

Elona took a deep breath and retrieved the sheath. She slipped the blade home and dropped it into the pouch that hung at her waist. She had some power for now, and the first step was to keep Bejeren and his conspirators out of her room.

Elona slammed the door to her room and slid the bolt home with a solid metallic thud. Kienan had fitted it well, and no one had commented on it in the passing of a moon. She was safe for the present. The window shutters were closed against the wintry air and against spies in the guise of birds.

She fumbled the large key from the chain around her neck and slid it into the keyhole; it turned smoothly. She went to her bed, knelt down, and pulled out the chest from under it. She paused with both arms resting on its top, then lifted the lid to reveal the papers she had been collecting, proof of the changes happening to the people in the castle and town. Many of the parchments were burnt but she'd managed to scavenge them from the fires. And there was her diary too; she scanned over what she found so far—precious little, just the lies of Bejeren and his Patterner.

The evil she had seen seeping from the Wellspring in her dream had become a presence in her every waking hour and infested the castle. She could feel it in the stones now if she touched them with her bare hand. Luckily the weather had turned cold so it was easy to wear gloves without drawing comment. Even Father was not immune to its effect. It was true that he'd never been warm to her but now, as winter deepened, he became more withdrawn. At those meals where they were both present, or at the restoration of Mother, he would give her sidelong glances. She guessed that the conspirators were feeding him with lies; how could she persuade him now, even with her evidence?

She dropped the most recent parchment fragment that she had rescued into the box. It was badly scorched from the fire but the evidence was clear enough. There were words on it, though they were hidden by the soot. Soon she would have the proof she needed and would be able to seek out the King so that he could save them from this nameless menace.

A five-day later there came a knocking at the door. Elona quickly piled the papers she had spread on the bed back into the box and closed it. She was sure she had nearly solved the puzzle the burnt papers presented, though they tried hard to hide it from her; she slid it into its space and pulled back the bed. The knocking came again, louder.

'What do you want?'

'It is Savi, my Lady. Your Father would like to see you … in his chambers.'

'Why?'

'I … I don't know, my Lady.'

Liar. 'Very well.'

Elona stood and brushed the dust from her heavy winter dress. She unlocked and unbolted the door, stepped through, and then re-locked it. Savi's eyes seemed to flick from one place to another, never looking directly at her. The candlestick she held shook—a sure sign of guilt. Elona smiled, then took the candlestick from her and walked ahead.

'How is your little one, Savi?'

'He is well, my Lady. Growing stronger each day.'

'Of course, I'm sure he'll become a fine blacksmith, like his father and grandfather. Motherhood becomes you and improves your prospects for attracting men.'

'My Lady?'

'Of course. You don't expect Kienan to stay with you, do you?'

Savi did not reply.

'Of course not. Did he not disappear the very day I visited? Can you not recall?'

'I don't know, my Lady.'

'Well, I think you should know that when he took me to the door of the smithy, he kissed me.' Elona laughed to herself. 'Why don't you ask him? And then ask him where he went afterwards. You think he is good and trustworthy? No man is. He came to lie with me that evening. And it was very satisfying.'

She heard the maid sob quietly behind her and smiled without humour. *That goes some way to repay her for all the pain she has caused me.*

As they approached the door to Father's chambers the two armsmen on guard stood to attention. Elona made to hand the candlestick back to Savi, deliberately misjudged the distance, and the candle tilted abruptly. A splash of hot wax landed on Savi's hand and she cried out with the sudden pain; the candlestick clattered to the floor.

'You really should be more careful,' Elona said as she went through the door.

Elona stopped in the antechamber. The door was closed behind her and she heard muffled voices ahead. Behind her Savi was now crying loudly; how could she listen at the other door? She pressed her ear to it.

'Come in, Elona.'

She cursed under her breath; the stupid guards and Savi had made too much noise. She turned the handle and went in. Her father's study was windowless apart from a shuttered skylight, and doors led off to a larger sitting room and the bedrooms. The room was lit by four candelabra placed around the walls.

With Father was another man she did not recognise. He was thin and wore the robes of a Patterner, with broad white stripes down each side at the front indicating his Master status. He had heavy black eyebrows that made his eyes sinister and dark. Bejeren stood at one side, looking unhappy. Father's hands gripped the chair arms and his knuckles were white.

'You wanted to see me, Father?' she said lightly.

'I have been informed that you have had locks and bolts fitted to your bedroom door.' His voice was tense with barely restrained anger.

Elona lifted her chin. 'I am no child. I will not be denied privacy when I desire it.'

The Lord Corlain took a deep breath.

'You have been seen scrabbling around in fires. Can you explain that?' The final word thundered and Elona shrank back to the door; she had been so careful. She glared at Bejeren, who was looking at his hands.

'Father...' She wanted to tell the truth but these conspirators would have already warned him against her. 'Father...' she repeated, torn between the need to protect her secret and desire to tell some-one, anyone who would listen and believe. Then she grew angry. Bejeren had done this, he had poisoned Father against her. Even if he were not her true Father, he had loved her in his way. Now Bejeren, the one she had loved as a father, was conspiring against her, against Corlain, against beautiful Faerholme to bring it under the sway of demons.

She felt a heavy weight about her waist as if the little dagger were pulling at her, reminding her that it was there, waiting to be used. This was the meaning of the prophecy, this was where she took the sword and cut down her enemy. She looked at Father steadily.

'I have something I need to show you.' She took a few steps towards the desk, which brought her within arm's reach of Bejeren; she lifted the pouch and pulled apart its mouth; carefully she reached in and grasped the hilt of the little blade, holding the sheath through the cloth. In a sudden movement she yanked the dagger from the pouch, turned swiftly to the side and plunged it into Bejeren's stomach. There was only the slightest resistance as the blade slid to the hilt into him.

His face showed only surprise as the pain hit him, and she stabbed again and again. Then there were arms around her shoulders and shouting in her ears. Bejeren collapsed to the floor and the other man crouched over him beginning to chant and move his hands in a Patterning.

Elona looked at her right hand; bright red blood covered it and the dagger glinted in the candlelight. The strong arms about her shoulders and upper arms squeezed tighter. And finally she heard the words being shouted into her ear.

'Drop the knife, Elona!' She did as her father demanded. He relaxed his grip, moving to hold her arms and dragging her away from the body. Elona went where she was pulled.

'Don't you see, Father? He was the leader of the conspiracy? Bejeren. Now I've killed him and everything will be alright. Now you can believe me, you don't have to listen to his lies anymore.' She turned her head and smiled up at his face, only to feel the tears that fell from his eyes. She reached up to brush them away, leaving a trail of red. 'It's alright, Father, you don't need to cry. It's over now, you're safe now, the castle is safe, we're all safe. The conspiracy will die with him.'

11

———

Two eyes peered in at her through the rough square hole cut in her door. Elona glared at them before lying back on the bed, idly stroking Ichen's little head. It was afternoon and late afternoon sunlight slashed through the barred and shuttered windows, casting grid patterns on the opposite wall. The bolts slid back and the door opened.

An armsman stepped into the room and stood by the door; Savi followed and placed a tray of food on the chest at the end of the bed. Elona sat up abruptly; the maid flinched and the armsman took a step further in.

'How's Kienan, Savi?'

The maid stood waiting, her eyes filling with tears.

'Who else has he slept with then? Did I tell you how good he was? And how he preferred my body to yours?'

The armsman took another step and pointed at the window. Elona looked away from them and walked across to the shuttered window. She traced the pattern of the stones with her fingers and listened as Savi replaced the chamber pot.

Savi's wavering voice floated across the room. 'Why do you say these things? We were friends.'

Elona turned slowly. 'Because you are my friend and what I say is true, of course.'

'But it's not. You kissed him, because he agreed to do what you wanted. He came here to fit the bolts, he didn't lay with you.'

'You can believe what you want.'

'I believe my husband and my eyes. Why would I believe someone who stabbed her own friend and teacher?'

'You wouldn't understand.'

Savi stretched out a hand. 'I'm your friend. I always have been. Don't you remember all the good times we had together?'

Elona turned away. 'You know why they bolted the windows from the outside? So I can't throw myself out! They say I'm mad; they say there's something inside; something eating me inside.

'But they're lying. They're hiding me here because they want to hide the truth. This castle's been infected with evil. All of you – him, you, my father, all of them. You're all in it together. They dare not kill me to release my spirit or I would wreak my vengeance as a demon and they fear that. The prophecy will be fulfilled one way or another. No, they keep me here. Imprison me to hide their crimes.' She hit the shutters with her fist and cried. 'They won't let me have a fire, so I freeze in this tower. Are they fair? Are they good? Are they decent? Tell me that!

'If I could see the King. If I could tell him ... but we're lost. It's the men, you can't trust them, you can't trust any of them. Don't you see, Savi? Women are stronger but that's how they get to us. You lay with them or they force themselves on you and you are infected with their betrayal. That's why I can still see, they've never touched me. I'm still free of them.'

The brooding evil within the stones around her continued to intensify as the days passed. It was so bad that she no longer needed to touch them to feel the throbbing horror that oozed from them. The freezing winter days were bad, but the icy nights were worse. The evil that slithered through the stones invaded her dreams and filled her with such dread that she feared sleep itself. She wrapped herself in her blankets to keep out the biting cold and sat awake through every endless night.

She stopped caring for herself; the very food they brought to her was like poison and she barely ate, becoming drawn and haggard. Feigning concern, Bejeren would visit and tease and cajole her to eat, hardening her resolve to resist. She cursed the patterner that had saved him; next time she would cut deeper and slice his heart from his chest, then see what Patterner could restore him.

Two moon-turns passed and there came the midwinter feast. With four armsmen in the room, but averting their eyes, Elona was washed and dressed by two maids. Limp to the gentle care, she allowed herself to be manipulated. Her clothes now hung loose about her and she shrank away whenever their skin touched hers.

She was half-carried down to the Great Hall where the tables were laid out for the sacred feast and the yeomanry; smiths and guildsmen stood by their tables. She was led out behind Father and sat listlessly near him. He did not look at her but others did, fearful and wondering.

Three bells chimed, their distinct sound attracting her attention. She saw the Master of Feasts holding the baton in his hand and declaring them 'well come' to the feast of the Salvation. The irony was not lost to her; those who were not yet under the sway of the brooding evil would eat the contaminated food and fall.

The Bread Master dealt out the bread trenchers, all of it coloured red, like scabs of blood, and the first course was served while chill midwinter music filled the hall. Eyes frequently glanced at her, as if she were a ghost, a spectre of doom, a horrific phantom whose presence was death. There was little laughter and little appetite, and though the wines and ales were consumed the carefully prepared courses were not. Elona's bread plate was piled high with food; she would not eat it and no one dared take any away.

She could feel the malignant power bleed from the walls,

infesting the food and drink with its malice. Though the others ate sparingly she could see them filling up with evil until the horror of it spilled from their mouth.

As evening crept towards the hour of death she felt the evil building within the hall, so slowly that she did not see when it arrived; a baleful creature took shape in the circle of tables, and with the fire at its heart it blazed with darkness. It fed from the crusted loathing that spilled from the mouths of the feasters. It had the shape of a wolf but its shoulders were broader. Its feet were the talons of a hunting bird and it had the leather wings of a *sikechak*. The face was a man's but the mouth was filled with arrowhead teeth.

She watched, detached. When it was fully formed it shook its head as if coming awake and showers of dark flame flowed from its back. It looked straight at her, its eyes the blue of cold crystal without heart. It drew itself back into the fire and gathered itself on its haunches. It gave a howling wail of a thousand souls in torment and leapt at her.

Elona screamed and threw herself from the chair; it crashed behind her and she lay on bruised elbows and knees. She heard it scrabbling at the table between them and leapt to her feet with sudden speed. Armsmen reached for her, to present her for the sacrifice, missed their hold and fell behind. Elona saw the light at the kitchen door, and she ran for it with the hot breath of the demon scorching her neck. Blindly she ran through, knocking aside cooks and helpers, screaming like a banshee into the freezing night beyond.

Frost crackled and bit at her bare feet as she raced across the flags. She could hear the breath of the creature behind her. A wall loomed up and she slammed into a door, fumbled at the latch, and fell through into blazing heat. Her fear told her to hide but she knew nowhere was safe. There were stairs, and there she hid beneath them cowering in the heat and the dark, praying it would not find her. She heard its paws scraping on the stone floor as she cowered beneath the steps. It hissed her name and one clawed talon descended on her shoulder.

Elona lashed out and felt her arm crash into the beast, throwing it back. She sprang to her feet with a snarl and saw it lying on the floor flailing its claws. She leapt onto it, throwing her hands around its thin neck, squeezing with all the might she could muster. She plunged her fingers into the soft throat, her eyes shut tight. The beast fought desperately; she felt it clawing at her but she held on, gripping tighter.

Its efforts became weaker and she allowed herself a grim smile when, without warning, the monster stopped struggling. She held on a little longer until she felt hands pulling at her, forcing her arms apart, prying her fingers from the creature's neck. She stood weakly and then collapsed into someone's arms.

'I killed it,' she said, almost happily, as she was led stumbling away.

In the distance someone wailed.

12

―――――――

Elona woke to the slow tolling of the castle bell. Frost covered the floor of her room and her breath froze as she exhaled. She gathered up the blankets around herself, ignoring the daggers of cold cutting into the soles of her feet, and stumbled to the window that overlooked the courtyard. With one hand she awkwardly pulled back the heavy curtain and tugged at the rod that turned the shutters. Winter sunshine poured in and she pulled a fold of blanket over her head. The morning was well advanced and no one had brought her breakfast.

She adjusted the angle of the shutters, braced herself, and squinted down into the courtyard. A group of people, wrapped up against the cold, waited in silence by the smithy entrance. The large door of the workshop, seldom opened in winter, folded back and four men shuffled from the smithy each at a corner of a coffin. She recognised the bearers: her father, the blacksmith, Kienan and the Steward. A baby cried.

Her stomach turned over with vertigo; she closed the shutters and the spasm passed. A smile crossed her face; that was one less traitor to worry about. It didn't matter who it was or how he'd died. One less to worry about.

No one came that day.

85

She lay on her bed, trying to keep warm. She listened to the evidences of their treachery shouted up to her window. By evening she was very hungry, but she would not shout and would not beg. Their tainted food was worse than nothing; better she starved to death than eat their poison. Ichen visited but she would not stroke him and there was no food. She did not notice when he left.

She slept poorly, waking at every screech and scratch, and the sound of someone screaming for her death echoing in her mind. When she slept again her dreams were filled with monsters that devoured her flesh one slow bite at a time.

She was jerked awake by a great commotion of crashes and bangs coming up the stairs. It made the new day as loud as the previous one had been quiet. The bolts to her room were thrown back and four armsmen clattered into the room. Two stood inside the door while the others grabbed her by the arms, pulling her roughly from the bed. They dragged her to the side of the room still dressed only in a shift.

Kienan and his father entered, their faces black storms. Between them they carried a portable furnace, many of their tools, and chains ending in manacles. Kienan lit and stoked the furnace, puffing the bellows with a vicious energy. His father began chipping into the wall behind Elona's bed with chisel and mallet.

'What's this?' Elona croaked, her mouth dry. No one replied.

A maid entered and tidied round the room; she fetched wood and kindling and laid a fire in the grate. At first the fire would not draw and the air in the room became smoky; with the hammering and the heat from the fiercely pumped brazier, it was like the smithy itself.

Elona giggled hoarsely. 'Who's to fetch the horses all the way up here for shoeing?'

Kienan looked over at Elona's captors and nodded. They dragged her roughly to the bed and held her down while Kienan wrapped thick bandages around her wrists and ankles. They were thoroughly wetted and the manacles clamped over them. The other armsmen added their hands to suppress Elona's weak struggles. Using heavy tongs Kienan lifted a steaming crucible from the furnace. With extreme care he poured molten metal into the manacles, and then sluiced it with a pitcher of water making great clouds of steam. One by one each of the four shackles was sealed. Even through the layers of bandages the heat from the cooling iron burned Elona's flesh. She bit her lip to hold back the pain. Finally a belt of iron was placed round her waist and sealed at the back.

The older smith had finished chipping the hole; from his bag he pulled a metal-headed mallet and an iron stake. The stake was solid for more than half its length and had a loop, the tip looked as if it were made of many strands of metal loosely woven. The smith fitted it into the hole, raised the mallet and drove it deeper with resounding crashes. It went in easily for most of its length then resisted, Kienan's father increased the power of his blows and the stake screeched as it went in a final fingers-breadth. The older man hooked a rope through the loop and tested its strength.

Kienan left the room and returned with a length of chain. They measured out a section enough to reach the window and the bed, but short of the fire. At a sign from Kienan, Elona was moved off the bed and put face down on the floor. Hot metal links were drawn from the forge and the chain was joined to the wall stake and the iron belt. A short length was arranged as a hobble from ankle to ankle, while a third was strung from wrist to wrist through a loop on the belt.

Without another word the men packed their tools and withdrew, carefully carrying the hot forge between them. The armsmen left, closing and bolting the door behind them. She was alone in silence again.

Later that day, after she had been given food, her father visited. He stood at the door staring at her through bloodshot eyes.

'You are satisfied now, Father?' Her words crusted in mockery.

'You are lost.' His voice broke as the words forced their way past his lips.

'No, it's you and this Keep that has been eaten by the beast. But I killed it!'

'You killed no beast, only an innocent maid and left a child motherless.'

'You are blinded by lies and fear and evil. Only I have the strength to see.'

Father stepped forwards and she was powerless to prevent him taking her hands gently in his. The chains slid and rattled in their loops.

'What has happened to you, Elona?' He stared into her eyes until she turned away.

'Why won't you see? It isn't me, it's you and them. Kill all the others and you'll see I'm right. I'm right. You all pretend to believe in the prophecy but you don't, you fight it. And you pretend to care now, try to make me a traitor. But I'm not fooled, you never loved me before, you don't love me now. You are not my father! It's a trick.' She tried to pull her hands from his but she was weak and helpless before his strength. 'If you loved me, would you do this?' She rattled the chains again.

'I can protect you from the Law, daughter; I am sending the blacksmith's son away to Corlain where he will cause no trouble and I have paid their blood-money. I can't lose you as well. I lost her, I won't lose you too.' He fell to his knees. 'I cannot let you die; but I cannot let you be free.' His hands released hers and she turned away, pulling her clattering chains to the bed.

'It's warmer here now,' she said quietly, then spun around. 'But shall I lie as if in a dungeon, soiling my shift like a common criminal?' She rattled the chains at him. He stood, his face spilling its grief. 'Will you dare to unchain me?' She took a step towards him. 'Or will they cut my garments from my body as I sleep for fear I'll turn on them?' She took three more steps and reached out for him, the chains brought her to a sudden halt. Father turned and walked slowly away. The door shut behind him and a few moments later, as if an afterthought, the bolts were drawn across in slow, deliberate scrapes.

Elona dragged her chains back to the bed and sat down. Ichen, his brown and green scales fading to grey, popped his head from under the bed and leapt up onto it. Absently she scratched under his chin and he made contented noises.

The moons waxed and waned. Winter turned colder. Snow covered the castle and surrounds, blizzards whipped through her room despite the glass, the shutters and curtains. Though the fire was kept lit, the chains prevented her from getting close to it when its warmth was most needed.

In the days after she had felled the demon Elona had felt more confident, but now, as the moons passed, her certainty faded again. Scars formed at her wrists and ankles from the manacles and they weighed down her spirit. The chill evil that infested the castle walls crept along them and trickled into her soul, trying to freeze her heart.

Bejeren had come unexpectedly one day offering to continue her education. He had come too close and she had lashed out with the chain, driving him away, screaming and laughing at his bleeding face. He did not come again.

One evening, a ten-day later, after her fire had been rebuilt, armsmen entered, pulled her from the bed and pinned her to the wall. Maids quickly stripped the bedclothes and replaced them, then her clothes were cut from her. Her muscles contracted as the cold iron of the belt touched her.

Without modesty she laughed at their pathetic attempts to reclothe her, the unyielding chains preventing all attempts. A knife was taken to her clothes, slitting them along seams and thongs added to each. She was fitted into clean clothes and the seams tied up. Finally, she was thrown back at the bed and the pack of demons retreated, leaving her to lick her wounds in silence and loneliness.

Once every ten-day now, her bedclothes were replaced and clothes, now carefully remade to suit her chains, were put about her, though they hung loose on her emaciated form.

In the time of her confinement her greatest sorrow was the loss of Ichen. It had become his custom to visit her at night to curl up with her warmth in the bed. Then on a night following a day of blizzards he did not come, nor the next, nor ever again. He had lived to a good age for a *chakik* but the thought of his cold frame buried in the snow waiting to rot in the thaw made her weep.

~

Winter melted. The Timalay unfroze and roared in torrents to the maelstrom of its joining with the Halat in the west where it became the River Cormark. From there it flowed in an ever-widening stream towards the south passing the town of Revor, which served as river-port to Canvor, the capital of Faerholme. Then for league upon league it swept southwards to the great sea-port of Hort, the Thousand Mouths and the sea.

In the night Elona watched as Lostimal and Colimar drew closer together in the sky, as they did once every three-year though not always over Faerholme. The dripping evil of the keep's stonework faded against the tension that grew in the north as the Wellspring swelled with pregnant energy in response to the coalescing moons. Pilgrims to the great ley-circle poured into Corlain. The town choked with their numbers and the noise of them rose every night.

As the first warm nights of the reborn year spread their comfort through the air, white sheets of light shot skywards, heralding the explosion of the Lifespring's power. As each night passed greater numbers of people stood on the walls of the castle and of the town. They stared to the North hoping to see the pillar of blazing light pouring into the sky.

Elona lay on her bed staring at the dark ceiling of her room, and every now and then the fire crackled in the hearth. The shutters were pulled back and the windows wide open, letting in the continuous murmurings of the townsfolk and pilgrims. Suddenly the southern wall of her room was lit with a bright white light, and moments later a rising tide of voices gushed through the windows. Elona leapt up to see a torrent of white cascade into the sky from the Wellspring beyond the farthest ridge. It poured into the night sky to the twin moons that stood one behind the other directly above.

Thousands of voices called the jumbled words of blessing that filtered through the light-filled night and Elona repeated them too.

'Mother Earth, feed me; Mother Earth, clothe me; As the milk of the Earth feeds her children in the sky, so feed me.'

She could see the whole world with absolute clarity as the light filled the night. She felt its cleansing power flowing through her, washing her spirit, feeding her, like a mother's milk and comfort. She felt it washing away the vile filth that lay like dung in every pore of the skin. The light shone through all the people who stood shouting and cheering to the great power that illuminated them.

Then darkness fell like an axe, a death shroud over the world, but the shouts of the people went on; the laughing, the screams of joy. Elona knew what followed. The drunken orgy of the Kadralin, joined with the feasting of the Taymalin who attributed the burst of power to Taymar's goodness. What did it matter? The people were happy as they debauched themselves, infused with the mother's milk. The milk that Elona had never sucked.

The accursed Bejeren had said that other ley-circles went through the rite of Mother Earth as well, at different times but always when Lostimal and Colimar were as one above. He told her the Kadralin called them Mother Earth's nipples—Elona had been embarrassed. It was clear now he had only said it to insult her, to remind her of her motherless heritage, to drive her to despair. But she was stronger and would never submit.

13

S pring passed into summer. The huge soaring *sikechasa* ranged far from the mountains and swept across the skies above the castle; sometimes they were close enough to see the leathery skin stretched between their bony fingers, then soaring up and away without the slightest movement of their wings to become nothing but a dark spot against the sky.

Archers on the castle walls took pot shots at them, occasionally piercing a wing whereupon the *sikechak* would veer and dive away at high speed. Or the creature would see the arrow approaching, snap it from the air, crunch it to splinters with its teeth and contemptuously spit it out. Once in a while, though, they would be brought down, and white *sikechak* meat would be served for a meal. They tasted good, though Elona made sure she ate the bare minimum to keep the corruption from her.

The days became hot and the nights hotter, the manacles about her wrists and ankles irritating her skin. At night insects came to sup on her blood. They sent healers to her yet she would not suffer them. She screamed at them, threatened them with her chains if they dared approach her. So they left salves and balms for her to use. Elona tried one but it burnt her skin, so she tossed them all from the window, cursing their tainted thoughts and minds. The cleansing of the Wellspring and the feeding of the moons had failed to alleviate the evil that grew across the land. She became afraid the moons too had been infected by poisoned milk. But they rose and set, waxed and waned without harm, so she yet had hope.

For the summer feast she was left in the tower, chains still hung about her, and a meagre meal was brought. She did not eat it. On the following day there was a commotion below; squinting against the sun, she peered down through the shutters as a messenger and three armsmen in the King's colours rode into the courtyard on horseback.

After the noon meal their horses were brought forth and they rode away again in haste. Shortly after she saw them on the north road crossing the Timalay and kicking into a gallop, raising dust until they disappeared from view. In the courtyard it did not become quiet; carriages were pulled into the courtyard and buckets of water brought forth to clean them. Horses and *kichesa* were unstabled, the horses rubbed down and combed while the *kichesa* were oiled. Father must be travelling on a long journey and with so much activity a good portion of the household was going too.

Then a clattering at her own door broke her reverie. Armsmen entered and grabbed her—her skin crawled at their touch—a chair was brought and she was forced into it. A smith she did not recognise entered, and broke the chain that bound her to the wall leaving three arm-lengths attached to her belt. Two maids entered with travelling boxes and searched through her clothes chests, removing some items.

'Where are we going?' She demanded. The two maids glanced at one another but said nothing. 'You sluts, tell me where we're going? Why does the King demand my Father's presence? Why does he want me?'

No one replied, but the understanding that she too was to go made her wonder. Why would they want her? The taint that infected the land came from the Wellspring. It infected and spread from there and possessed the traitors that succumbed to its power.

But perhaps the King was free of it? He may not know what had passed here, though it would be certain that they had lied to him.

Would he demand her as well if he were overcome by the corruption that originated here? No. It must be the prophecy. She had a chance, she could reveal the truth to him, explain how his subjects had been corrupted, about Bejeren the traitor. Yes. If she was to go she would be presented to him and they would not be able to stop her revealing the truth. And she would marry the Prince and be Queen in Faerholme, the Queen Elona. And all would be safe, and she could be at peace with Mother. She would command the Patterners to heal the Wellspring and the taint would be gone. All would be well again and the prophecy fulfilled. She smiled. They made it all so simple for her.

She was brought down by back stairs and dusty passages to an old ceremonial carriage with newly boarded windows. She was pushed inside, her chain padlocked through a heavy metal loop and the doors slammed shut. The interior was dark as night and very hot, and there were few air holes. She tried the handles in vain. She bumped about as the carriage was pulled by hand across the cobbles to the main entrance with the rest of the company. She heard a pair of grumbling *kichesa* as they were coaxed into the yoke.

There was the sound of many hooves moving restlessly on the stones and some voices spoke in lowered tones. There was none of the laughing and merriment that would have been heard before the corruption infected the castle. She heard Father's voice speaking gruffly and a reply from the lighter voice of the Steward. Father's voice called for the off; dozens of hooves and claws clattered on the stones and her carriage was kicked into motion too.

Peering through a small hole she watched as the procession clattered through the castle gate and down into the town, winding through the streets. She could see faces staring at her carriage. None smiled, none laughed; one or two dabbed their eyes but she scorned their false pity. They left the town by the west gate and picked up to a gentle trot. If Father pushed them they might make it in three days, but the horses would not like that much haste in this heat.

Father would no doubt be concerned that she would attempt to escape now that she was free of the stone walls. She smiled, let him worry, let him take precautions, he could not imagine her true intentions. No doubt he would have preferred to have walked a patterner's path between ley-circles and be resting in the Royal castle by this very evening. But that was the secret of Canvor, the great ley-circle that lay at the heart of Faerholme was deep below the surface of the lake and, though power might be drawn from it, no patterner could walk a path to it without drowning. Canvor could only be approached by land.

~

They stopped for a short time in the early afternoon. The wagons and carriages were pulled up on a grassy stretch beside the road. She could see servants erecting an awning as shelter from the sun, while others lit a fire and prepared food. The door to Elona's carriage was opened and an armsman beckoned her out; at the end of her tether she stood two paces from the carriage. Another armsman climbed in and released the lock. Holding tight to the chain he clambered back out and, with a maid in attendance, she was allowed to stretch her legs.

Light woodland surrounded them with a minimum of undergrowth. It seemed a pleasant place and Elona liked it the more for being free of the poisoned walls that had held her for nearly a year. The main body of armsmen had taken up positions in pairs around the perimeter. They chatted to one another and rested against the trees.

Elona could not see Father and Bejeren; they were no doubt staying away from her. That was well, as she did not wish to see their treasonous faces except to convince her more of her duty to her King. As she thought of him, the Lady Metrid's face swam beside it reminding her that he was but a man, flawed and foolish when not a danger. She cried out and fell to her knees as Krazak suddenly loomed above her, the knife in his hand cutting the clothes from her body. The armsman yanked her chain and pulled her face down in the grass. She breathed deeply, smelling its freshness and feeling its spiky softness on her face and the palms of her hands. But the vision had passed and she pushed herself up again into a sitting position.

96

The armsman that held her chain frowned at her. She allowed her gaze to slide from him in contempt, then looked back at him with a malicious smile:

'I need to relieve myself,' she croaked.

The man sighed and pursed his lips in annoyance, he beckoned over a maid and together the trio moved off to the edge of the woods. The man twisted another two loops of chain tightly around his gauntleted hand and stood with his back to a large tree while Elona and the maid went to the other side. When Elona emerged, she could see the nearby guards grinning at her armsman and was satisfied at his discomfort.

The food was adequate though simple, and Elona ate a little. She felt safer now that they were out of the castle. She needed only to survive to reach the King and she would be safe to eat again. The sun had reached the top of the trees when she was chained back in the carriage, and the procession set off once more through the woods. They travelled on through the gathering dusk, interspersing a walking pace with short periods of trotting. Elona wondered if Father intended to keep this up through the night. But the animals would never stand it.

It was almost dark when they came to a stop. There were shouts and sounds of tents being erected. Presently the noises died away and through the holes she could see a number of small fires had been lit. Her carriage was not opened, so she made herself as comfortable as possible on the old leather bench.

She was roused from a parched stupor by the cart splashing across a deep river. They had been travelling a good portion of the day under the blazing sun. They came to an abrupt halt and outside she could see the animals being watered. There was some seepage at the bottom of one door; she leaned down and lapped at it to quench her thirst a little. The land on the other side of the wide river ford was not wooded; instead, a range of low bare hills blocked her view. She guessed they had crossed the River Cormark, which now wandered to the north and west through deep valleys before heading south for Canvor. They travelled southwest, crossing the river again at Revor before the final stretch to the capital.

On either side of the ford stood clusters of small houses and huts; poorly dressed women and children watched as the animals were watered. Elona watched them pass as the carriages were moved across the river and up towards the hills. They were part-Kadralin and seemed to be untouched by the taint that she could still feel in the armsmen and servants and even in the water. The pollution was too diluted to harm her anymore; she had grown able to withstand the full flood of evil, and this slight stain merely confirmed her suspicions. It would serve well when she saw the King, for his Patterners would be able to perceive it too and would confirm the truth.

As the day progressed the terrain flattened out. The road ran along a river that tumbled in its over-large riverbed down from the eastern mountains to join the Cormark. Once more the road passed through woods. Here and there were villages of charcoal burners and hunters, with a few fields and orchards. But everywhere people lay down their tools to watch them ride by and children chased after them, laughing and shouting.

The sun was setting as they reached the confluence of the Cormark and the river they had been following. A small, walled town stood in the land between and a stone keep was raised at its heart. The Corlain party did not enter the town but turned off to a level area near a large inn that stood outside the walls. Several houses stood around it as if it had become a new centre.

There was the usual bustling about and preparations but Elona was not released from her confinement immediately. The light was almost completely gone when a squad of armsmen and the maid arrived. The door was unbolted and her chain unlocked. With the armsmen standing close about her she was guided across the close-cropped grass to a side door of the inn and hurried inside. There was warmth and light inside; the low ceilings, the glow of friendly fires and a beery smell made it feel homely.

Elona was pushed upstairs and into a small, simple room lit by many candles, the centrepiece a large four-posted bed draped with embroidered curtains.

The chain was looped around a bedpost and locked so she could barely move two paces from the bed, and the maid assisted her in undressing and washed her. The girl stared at the sores and scars where the iron belt had cut into her skin. The night was hot and Elona slept above the sheets, while the maid slept on a pallet on the far side of the room near the door. Elona sniffed; clearly the girl had been told not to come close, and that little throat would have succumbed easily even to Elona's weakened fingers.

14

The creature was there. She knew from her studies it was a Shocalin, half her height, covered in fur with large whiskers, and it was lithe with sharp claws. It gestured for her to sit and she did so, on the dark, blood-red cushions; food appeared on the table between them and they ate in silence. It looked sad, its mournful eyes watching her every move. They finished their food and she was full, the feeling of satiated hunger feeling strange after the fasting. The table vanished and the creature stood before her; it leaned forward but Elona was not afraid. It put its snout near her ear and its whiskers tickled her cheek. 'The time has come for you to wake up. But remember this always: *Aeshtas ulchris tahlya.*'

It was the last day of the journey; she was dressed in clean clothes and guided secretly from the inn. They travelled around the town and down to the banks of the Cormark. This far downstream the river was too strong and wide to be forded, but great ropes were strung from bank to bank and a huge raft hung between the two thickest. Capstans twice the diameter of a cartwheel, as tall as a man and turned by four *kichesa,* wound the ropes fixed to the raft, drawing it from one side to the other.

The ferry was big but the Corlain party needed two trips to get across. Ferrymen on the other bank whipped their *kichesa* into action and the giant capstans turned. Heavy ratchets on the near bank clacked as the ponderous craft floated out. At alarming speed the strength of the current pushed the raft downstream while the ropes creaked ominously and stretched. The raft crept across the foaming river and, after an age, reached the far side and was unloaded. The raft made the return journey carrying only a few travellers on foot and *kichek*-back.

It was Elona's turn. The carriage swayed unpleasantly as the raft was cast off and instantly Elona felt she was being dragged down-river out of control. She cried out in fear; if the raft toppled she would surely drown. But though it drifted and the ropes groaned in pain, they made steady progress towards the other side. Elona could see the capstan ahead turning, and when she looked back there was already a wide expanse of water between her and the eastern bank. The other side drew closer until finally the raft shuddered and ran aground on submerged logs.

With the party assembled on the other side they set off again directly towards Canvor on the final leg of the journey. The sun rose higher but clouds were drifting in from the West, obscuring it occasionally. The land they now travelled was full of people. They passed through villages frequently surrounded by the same strip fields and orchards as Corlain but there were so many more of them. Here the people working in the fields did no more than glance at the passing carriages and the children did not chase them.

They climbed slowly into a low range of hills until, as the sun was turning to afternoon, they reached the final ridge and Canvor appeared in the distance. The great capital of Faerholme was built of white stone that shimmered in the sunlight and heat. Beyond it the deep blue circle of the lake by which the city stood made it look as if the capital was a diamond in a ring of sapphire.

As they drew closer the great wall could be seen as separate from the main buildings behind, which rose up in tiers to the palace at the summit. The mound itself had been built in ancient times by the Kadralin for their own castles. When the Taymalin brought them wisdom the old building had been broken up to make the mound taller. The new castle had been raised above it all. Over the years the palace had been added to, and the city expanded in rings so that the outer wall was now nearly a league in circumference.

Their approach was announced by great fanfare, and the outer walls were decked with flowers. They passed across the first bridge and under the main gate, wide enough for three carts to go side by side. The chief thoroughfare was crammed with happy, cheering people. More flowers covered the walls and outlined the windows, and bunting was strung from side to side. Elona couldn't believe it; the city was decorated for a wedding. She peered out at the shouting people and there were some who looked her way, but crossed their palms in front of their eyes to avert evil.

A fear rose within her. She looked at the bright, white stone to see within it. As she did she saw huge globs of festering red flowing down the walls, like blood, like poison. She cried out loud though there were none to hear her above the hubbub. It was here, it was here too! She was too late, they were all corrupted, and they cheered for a wedding. Whose wedding? Who would wed? A royal wedding, it had to be, why else would they be summoned? To her? To Elona, yes, that would be it. She was betrothed to the Prince and now they meant to fulfil it. They had tried to corrupt her in all the ways they could but had failed. She alone had stood for Faerholme and until she was vanquished they could not defeat it; Faerholme stood strong in her heart. So they planned to marry her to the corrupted royalty, and when she lay with that accursed Drahail she would be impregnated with evil and it would grow within her. Their plan was so easy to see, so plain that she laughed.

Yes, she would marry the corruption and she would cut its throat as it tried to lie with her. She would be Queen in Faerholme and she would put it to rights, driving out the evil. She was the strength; she had Faerholme in her heart and they could not drive it out. They would never defeat her, for she had the prophecy that would save her.

The procession passed through the three defensive walls, each one older and with more repairs than the previous. The third had been completely rebuilt in many places, a sign of the battles it had seen in older days. The edges of the statue over the main gate were rounded with age, but showed the triumphant Taymar standing over a fallen Slissac.

Elona's carriage trundled beneath it on a stone road rutted with the passage of uncountable wheels, coming to rest before the palace. The glistening white walls and corner towers rose the height of a dozen men and were topped with highly embellished crenellations. High and low they were pierced by many windows, most of them with glass; the higher windows had balconies on which people now stood looking down on the arrived nobility.

The whole courtyard seemed to be covered in flowers, and from the heights petals floated down on them. Armsmen in the King's colours stood to attention around the perimeter, and brightly garbed grooms and footmen rushed to horse and carriage. The immense double doors that led into the palace were pulled back and the majestic presence of the King emerged, his Queen at his left and the Prince to his right. The King and the Prince were smiling, but Elona could see the Queen looking towards her carriage, her face filled with pain and sorrow. Could the Queen still be free of the corruption? Yes, perhaps she was; she might be an ally in this den of betrayal.

Father, with Bejeren a few paces behind, stepped up to the King. They knelt and the Lord Corlain kissed the King's ring. The King then raised him up and hugged him. Elona could not hear anything of what was said, though everyone tried to remain quiet despite still so much noise and commotion in the courtyard. Corlain was presented to the Queen and Prince then two women emerged from the darkness of the palace interior to greet him, Lady Metrid and Hope. At the sight of them Elona twisted in confusion. She did not cry out, nor did she attack the bars of her cage, but as Hope took the Prince's arm her blood chilled. The group turned and entered the palace walls, leaving her alone.

Elona's palms hurt; she looked at them and found four small

bloody curves on each matching her bloodied fingernails. Outside the carriage she could hear subdued discussions that went on for some time. Finally, the carriage moved again, moving around the main building and stopping beside a small door. One of the King's household stood waiting, eyeing the boarded-up windows nervously shifting from foot to foot while rubbing his hands as if he were cold.

Elona's maid and two Corlain armsmen appeared at the door; it was unlocked. Elona climbed out, allowing herself to be helped though she felt the itching irritation of evil from the skin that touched hers. The King's under-butler stared at her with contempt, so she spat at him. He leapt back but his surcoat was splattered. She laughed. He backed into the doorway.

'Bring the halfwit this way.'

'She's the Lady Elona of Corlain and you'll call her that. Or you'll feel the flat of my blade,' the sergeant-at-arms replied.

'She's a murderer, she's insane, and she spat on me—one of the King's personal staff. I was appointed by Lord Tanderlain himself. And it is not for the likes of you to instruct me.'

The armsman rested his hand on his sword hilt. 'If you had manners I wouldn't have to.' He took a step towards the servant. 'So what do you want, manners or a lesson?'

The retainer did not reply but turned and stalked into the darkness. The maid followed in front of Elona, with one armsman holding her chain and the sergeant behind.

'Sorry about his rudeness, my Lady,' he said quietly.

Elona ignored him.

They passed through the door and into the dark interior; her eyes adjusted quickly and saw that even these backwater passages were lined with good quality tapestries. The flagged floor had been smoothed to gentle humps by generations of feet and the stone steps they climbed were worn in the middle. Ornate iron stair-rods supported wooden banisters that curved delicately, polished by a million hands. Finally they came to wider passages, and at the end of one corridor they reached a door. Their guide pulled a key from a pouch and unlocked it. He then handed the key to the maid and addressed the armsmen.

'There you are. That's her room. Keep it locked, food will be brought for her and you. Keep her chained up; if she gets loose it'll be your heads, not mine. The wedding is in three days, she's not invited to any of the feasts, only the wedding. Is that clear?'

'Perfectly. Just take yourself and your bad manners away from here.'

'With pleasure.' He edged past the group and walked swiftly away. Elona watched him escape round the corner with a contemptuous grin. As she turned back she saw her three captors smiling as well, and she dropped her face into a frown. They were not her allies.

The room they entered was bright with intense sunlight that flooded through huge windows that had been thrown wide. The walls were covered in white plaster and decorated with blue-painted relief figures of both real and mythical characters, entwined in a dance that led around the room a little above head height. The high ceiling had ornate carvings painted in realistic colours, birds, dragons, *sikechasa*, *tekrasa* and other flying creatures she couldn't name, all swooping and intertwining about central candelabra.

There was only the one room, no antechamber, though there was a small door in the left wall near the window. There was a chest of drawers with a basin and jug of water on top of it. The bed stood at one side of the room, a massive four-poster with a mattress that was high off the floor. The frame and statues of dragons that comprised the four posts were of iron and the sheets were of the finest cotton woven to a beautiful gloss. Around the room were several wooden chairs, their padded backs embroidered with the King's crest; near the bed were two well-upholstered recliners and a low table. Four exquisitely painted glass screens in wooden frames stood along one wall.

'Typical,' said the maid. 'Giving us a sun-facing room in the height of summer.'

One of the armsmen wrestled a glass screen towards the window to block the sun. The other pulled Elona to the bed, muttered an apology, looped a length of chain around a bedpost and padlocked it in place, then went to help with the screens. They moved two in front of the window and two others created an area around the bed so Elona could have her privacy and dignity. The maid investigated the smaller door and found a wardrobe; she stepped through the open window and out on to the balcony.

She called back into the room. 'Do you want to see out, my Lady? It's really nice.'

Elona did not answer. She had seen well enough when they entered that they were high above the ground in the tower, never mind the height of the hill on which the tower stood. She had no wish to see how it looked. The thought of dumping the contents of her stomach over the balcony and onto the petal-covered flagstones below pleased her momentarily, but it was not worth the unpleasantness.

The maid returned, apparently unconcerned by her mistress's failure to respond. 'You can see all the city, the mountains, the lake with lots of pretty boats on it and the river going off. And you can see all the way to Revor.' One of the armsmen went to look. 'I suppose I better see about the rest of your clothes, my Lady. I'll be back soon.'

'Morag,' said the older armsman. 'Can you get another two of our blokes up here? We'll need to arrange a proper schedule. We can get a couple of chairs outside the door and lock it, if that's what the King wants.'

Elona heard the door being opened. 'More like what that butler wants, or his precious Lord Tanderlain,' the girl replied, making a spitting sound. They all laughed. The armsmen carried two chairs outside and left Elona alone. She heard the finality of the lock sealing her in.

15

Elona found her imprisonment at the palace to be little different from that at Corlain. A cage no matter how gilded was still a cage, and the pretty veneer did not hide the poison that flowed through the stones. She had no visitors, her food was brought and cleared; she found the fish more palatable than the rest, for it seemed less tainted with corruption. And when they found she ate more of that, that was what she was given.

Preparations for the wedding seemed undeveloped; she had expected a visit from a Brother or Sister of Taymar. But none came; undoubtedly they feared her purity as they had been unable to taint it with their devilry. And she expected a fitting for a wedding dress, though the maid had done some adjustments to her higher quality dresses so that they could be fitted on her without removing the chains. And yet, no new clothes had been brought, not even a wedding dress.

It bothered her, as had the sight of Hope on the Prince's arm. She knew they would not release her until the time of the wedding—that was understood—they did not trust her and rightly so. She would as soon kill them all as marry the corruption that inhabited the body of the Prince; but if that was what it took to start the deaths and purify Faerholme then she would do it. Hope was clearly his harlot. Such corruption could not refrain from corrupting all about it, and what better way than through the poisoning of the flesh? How many others had it defiled with its attentions?

No, the marriage was to be a wicked parody of the contract between Father and the King before they were corrupted. She would go along with it, she would accept the attentions of the incarnate evil until it tried to bring her to its side; then she would strike it down, destroy it. And with that one gone, her crusade would be started and finished. The others would fall easily to the strength she gained from each success. She needed that first one to bring them all down.

Though summer was beginning to turn to autumn, the weather remained hot, and on the third day the sun blazed white as ever. From her bed Elona could see the entire world shimmering beyond the window. Her chamber was in shadow, but the sun turned in the sky and soon it would fire a furnace in the room. Morag always supplied plenty of water and Elona had decided that she would kill the maid quickly when the time for revenge came, in gratitude to her simple-mindedness.

Elona dozed, turning over in her mind her plans to kill the Prince. She wondered whether it would be better to do it before the assemblage when the ceremony was complete or to wait until he bedded her. The former was more dramatic and would show the rest their time was soon to come as she fell on them. But the latter had much to commend it; after all, to kill him in the moment that he assumed his victory was complete would afford her much humour. She could imagine his face as he felt his triumph melt to horror as she slit his throat.

She came awake abruptly as the door opened. Morag entered carrying a sewing box; one of the armsmen stepped in and stood by the door. They set about the preparations with Elona being unusually cooperative. All her clothes were removed and she was washed in water that smelt of petals. As she dried, Morag brushed her long hair, then plaited and coiled it. The brush caught occasionally on the silver necklace Lady Metrid had given her. Morag brought out the clothes she had selected from Elona's limited wardrobe, including an autumnal dress in greens and golds with wide sleeves.

She helped Elona into a shift that had been split down each side. She tucked it inside the iron belt and then quickly sewed it up in wide stitches. Then she took several lengths of thick cord from her box and sewed the middle of each to the shift around Elona's body at the height of her lower ribs.

'Jonty, come and unlock this chain will you?' The armsman stepped up to the bed and unlocked it. 'Now wind it up into a ball and tie it off with this so it won't unravel.' She handed him a piece of cord and he did as she instructed. 'Now tie it to the back of the belt.' He did so.

'Alright, now, my Lady, try to keep still while we do this bit. Jonty, lift the belt so it's up here, will you?' She proceeded to tie the lengths of string around the belt so that the shift held it higher and supported its weight. 'It's a good thing you lost some weight, Mistress. Or we couldn't do this. There. You should have a bit more movement in your arms now.' Elona stretched and found that it was so, she could stretch one arm straight out and stretch the other half its length. 'And it means you can wear the dress properly, since we don't have to cut it at all. Slip it over your head.'

Elona ducked into the voluminous skirts and managed to get her arms into the sleeves; first one hand, then the other emerged. The frills at the ends hiding the manacles Morag laced up the back. The stupid maid had forgotten something. Elona shifted her feet. The chain hobble around her ankles clanked. The maid grinned.

'It's alright, Mistress. I made this.' She reached into the box and pulled out what looked like a long, thin quilt. 'If you'll sit I'll put this on the chain.' She wrapped the cloth around the chain and sewed it up, ensuring it wouldn't slip one way or the other. 'Now try walking around.'

Elona stood and the chain barely made a sound as it hit the ground, she moved around the room. In the quiet it could be heard, but not if there were any other sounds. Morag smiled. 'It worked, I'm so glad. Now let's get some stockings and shoes on you.'

Elona sat obediently.

～

The grand banqueting hall of the palace, more than twice the size of the Corlain grand hall, was overflowing with nobility and guild masters, and the two tiers of balconies were packed with faithful retainers. It was a wonder that the columns that seemed so delicate and slender could support such a weight. Elona entered escorted by her two armsmen. She walked slowly and with small steps so that the restriction of her silent hobble appeared to be dignity. She amused herself by imagining the painful crushing deaths that would result when she made the columns collapse.

Bejeren was leading her by the arm; she had to clench her teeth against his touch. She did not wish to betray her plans and could not afford to disrupt anything. The marriage must be completed. Her revenge would come at the attempt to consummate it and, for now, she would bear anything to reach her goal.

When he had come to fetch her, he had seemed pleased. He had congratulated Morag the simpleton, explaining that Elona had been made presentable enough to stand with her father. When she had begun to walk, he had stopped immediately and pulled up her dress to check she was still hobbled. His familiarity made her seethe and she swore that he would die slowly and miserably, hung from his hands and bled each day until he shrivelled to death.

They walked up the central aisle between the ranks of noble lords and ladies; she did not recognise any. But it seemed they recognised her, for their raucous yapping died away as she passed, replaced by whispered comments and hands held to mouths. Some sounded angry, others afraid. Soon they would all be afraid. The sound swelled again after she had passed.

Finally, she and Bejeren reached the front rank where Father stood alone. His face was like stone when he looked at her. He turned away. Nearby, on the other side of the hall, stood the Lady Metrid, and beside her was Hope wearing the plainest of dresses, the colour of straw. Metrid looked at Elona and smiled, but she looked like a wolf ready to devour her prey. Elona smiled back with similar venom, for she alone knew the outcome of the day.

At the front of the hall was a great dais flanked by two pairs of double doors. On the dais stood the royal thrones, four plain and simple chairs, though one was significantly larger than the others. They were carved from the same rock as the rest of the palace, to symbolise the oneness of the crown with the land. A massive tapestry was hung behind depicting the Taymalin victory in battle against the Slissac. Taymar stood as the central figure bestriding the fallen bodies of the lizard people. Suddenly a great fanfare rang out as a dozen trumpets heralded the coming ceremony.

From the doors on each side emerged two columns of the Brothers and Sisters of Taymar, dressed in their ceremonial robes of grey with black and white stripes. The Brothers carried swords at their sides while the Sisters each wore a bow and had a quiver of arrows at the hip, they formed an arc facing outwards, alternating man and woman, to protect the ritual. Then an Elder Brother stepped out and up on to the dais, placing himself in front of the larger throne.

The trumpets rang out again. From the back of the hall a procession entered with the Prince, dressed in a rich imitation of poor clothing, at its head. Following him were the King and Queen, dressed in the most elaborate costumes, and behind an honour guard of armsmen. Attached to the Prince's clothes were numerous loose rags, and as he walked up the centre aisle nobles would reach out and pull one from him. Each represented a year that the Taymalin spent searching for their new home. Finally the procession reached the dais and the wall of protectors parted to allow the Prince alone to pass through.

He knelt before the officiating Brother, who blessed him in Taymar's name and asked the formulaic questions of his reason and purpose in coming to this place. Elona allowed a caustic smile to cross her face; listening to their lies was enough to make her retch. Then the Brother stepped back and Elona knew her time had come as she heard the voice call out:

'Who has come to wed this man?'

And she shouted in reply. 'I will marry him.' And her words were echoed from the other side of the hall, gasps hissed from the lips of those who stood near Elona. She saw Hope looking round like a frightened rabbit and stepping forward quickly, moving between the lines of Brothers and Sisters to stand by the Prince. 'I have come to wed him,' Hope repeated. Elona stared at her and saw the Lady Metrid looking back at her, with triumph on her face.

A cold shiver ran through Elona as she tried to move forward herself, but a hand landed on her shoulder and held her back. She twisted violently out from under it but stumbled and fell forward.

'No, it's me! It's not her! It's me! I'm to marry the Prince. Can't you see? She's corrupt, they're all corrupt! You need me! It has to be me, it's the prophecy!' Then someone knelt by her head and pushed a kerchief into her mouth; she tried to scream, tried to push it out with her tongue. Desperately she struggled and kicked and screamed as she was lifted bodily by many hands. She struggled hysterically, trying to escape the hands that held her tight. She kicked and lashed out, once or twice she connected and delivered a solid blow until someone managed to get his arm fully around both ankles and hold them so tight it hurt. Her hands were forced behind her back and held there. She was carried the length of the hall still struggling. As they got her to the door she finally managed to spit the cloth from her mouth.

'I curse you, in the name of Taymar, in the name of *Kisharuk*, you are corrupt and I will be avenged on you!' She screamed with meaningless rage as they carried her through the castle but they did not attempt to gag her again. The volume of her voice grew less as her throat became hoarse. After a while she began to sob, and then they threw her to the floor in her room. The door was slammed and locked.

16

The sun was close to the horizon and no longer shining directly into her room when she came to her senses. She was alone and she was not chained to the bed. She stood carefully. Her joints ached where she had struggled; there were new bruises on her arms and legs, and her ribs stung where the iron belt rubbed. She felt dazed and went to the water jug, poured herself some in a metal goblet, and drank deeply. What did it matter now? They did not care that she was untainted, they did not care that she was pure. They would keep her chained like an animal until she died and then do as they pleased with the heart of Faerholme.

She stood in front of one of the painted glass screens and stared at the intricate bird designs, imaginary birds with long feathers of bright reds and greens. She scraped a gash through the delicate brushwork, then laughed and threw the goblet across the room where it clattered against the wall and floor. Suddenly she threw herself against the screen and pushed; it tilted and hung for moment before crashing to the ground, splintering into a thousand shards.

Elona picked up a piece the size of her hand; pain pierced her and drops of blood spilled from her fingers. She stared at it for a long moment, then held the sliver to her neck pressing hard. The world seemed to pause and she could hear her own rapid breathing.

No one cared, no one loved.

Save one. The one who had never harmed, who never chastised and was always there. The image of her mother swam before her tear-soaked eyes. She fell to her knees, dropped the shard, and cried with blood dripping from her neck. Though her mother lay in nonlife, Elona could not desert her; for her she must keep going.

The door clicked and swung open. Elona looked, but through the haze of tears she could see only that a woman and an armsman had entered, and then the door was pushed closed.

'Little 'Lonie, sweetie. Have you hurt yourself?'

Elona wiped the tears from her eyes with her sleeve and sniffed. Blinking, she saw Nursey hobbling across the floor towards her, wearing a high-collared, long-sleeved dress. A strange terror seemed to chill Elona's hands; she tried to back away from the apparition. It seemed that she had been in her every dream, her every nightmare, always there, always telling her things, always chastising, locking her in the chest. Her knees caught on the edges of the glass shards, cutting through the cloth, and the pain pushed her to her feet. She retreated from the ghost that approached her with open hands.

''Lonie? C'mon dearie. It's Nursey, your lovely Nursey.' The hag giggled to herself and continued to approach. 'C'mon, little 'Lonie, why don't you give your old Nursey a hug and a kiss? I'm so happy to see you.'

Elona backed to the wall and she clutched desperately at reality.

'There now, dearie, that's better isn't it?' A cold cloth wiped across her face and she smiled at Nursey. She felt safe and at home. She had had such a terrible dream. Had she been ill? Elona opened her eyes to the white ceiling painted in details of flying creatures.

'No!' She grabbed the old woman's hand and pulled herself to a sitting position, while the armsman stood by the door. The shattered glass remains lay at the foot of the bed.

'There, there, 'Lonie. You lie back. You've been having a bad time, don't I know it? My mistress, Lady Metrid, is so sorry for you.

But it'll all be over soon.' The old woman smiled the fixed smile she always used for soothing.

'What do you mean?' She demanded desperately, but Nursey suddenly looked sly and did not answer. Anger grew in Elona. 'What do you mean 'all over soon'? Tell me!'

She pulled at the old woman's clothes, dragging her closer and gripping her about the neck. Nursey's face suddenly turned pale and the sweat of fear appeared on her brow. There was a clatter as the armsman rushed over and yanked Elona's hand from the old woman's neck.

'You're upset by the wedding, dearie. I know that. But you'll soon be on your way home again. That's all I meant. I didn't mean no more by it. Honest I didn't. I wanted to see you again. The way they treated you at the wedding, I didn't like it at all. Not the way they treated my little 'Lonie. So I had to come, didn't I? Best I did too. You hurt yourself, I can see that. You shouldn't play with sharp things. Don't you worry, Nursey will look after you.'

The armsman suddenly gave a strangled cry of pain that cut off abruptly. Elona turned to see him slump to the floor. Nursey gave a pathetic yelp. Behind the armsman stood Kienan; his hair was unkempt and there were dark rings around his wild eyes, and his hand gripped a red-stained dagger. Keeping his eyes on them he reached for the door, pushed it closed and turned the key. The click echoed endlessly in the silence of the room. He pulled the key from the door, dropped it to the floor, and kicked it so it slid away out of sight.

'You killed my Savi. Now I'll kill you.' He came closer.

'Killed Savi?' Said Nursey her voice wavering as she stared at the advancing knife.

Kienan paused as if seeing the old woman for the first time. 'Yes! Why did you not strangle her at birth? All these years the demons have been eating their way from her, the demons of her birth, her motherless birth. And you suckled her! Why were you there? If you had not been there she'd be dead and my Savi would still live and our babe would not be motherless!

'This witch fled from the winter's feast and lured my Savi from where she tended our newborn babe. And ... and ... she put her demon hands about my Savi's neck and squeezed the life from her!'

Elona pulled her knees to her breast, turned and slipped from the bed. Kienan stepped forward again, his boots crunching on the shattered glass. Nursey drew back.

'But, Kienan, you played with Elona when you were little 'uns. How can you say this?'

'I'll have my revenge, old woman. Be glad I don't want you too, you who reared her, you who suckled this demon at your very breast. I'll be avenged; I'll have her blood for the blood of my Savi.'

Elona reached the wall by the window, sank to her knees and pulled the curtain to her as if it could protect her. Nursey moved in front of Kienan. Her voice was uncertain but had lost its usual wheedling tone. 'I can't let you kill my little baby.'

'Stand away. I've killed more than one to reach this place; I'll not be stopped now. I will have my revenge on this monster.' He took another step forward and towered above the old woman. Elona shivered and crept on all fours to the window. She breathed heavily. She looked down through the iron grid of the balcony, down to the courtyard so far below, filled with revellers oblivious to her terror; she stared down and the world reeled, and then she shut her eyes and crawled out.

'No.' Nursey's voice was firmer. 'I ... yes, I gave her life. I'm to blame. It's me.'

'Get out of my way, you stupid old woman,' Kienan cried suddenly and Elona heard a crash and a whimper from Nursey. Heavy footsteps on stone, then a clanging and the balcony shook dangerously as Kienan stepped out and stood over her. Elona whimpered with the fear of falling. She rolled over, banging her head against the metal railing, and stared up at Kienan, her eyes drawn to the bloodied knife held in a bloodied hand.

'I will have the life of the one who murdered my Savi. And you'll die the way you killed her.' He dropped the knife and it clanged on the metalwork. He knelt by her and his massive hands went around her neck and squeezed, gently at first, like the lovers she'd dreamed they might be. Elona pleaded with him mutely, don't kill me, don't for the sake of Faerholme, don't for the sake of my mother, please don't kill me. The pressure increased and it hurt; finally, she couldn't breathe. Please don't kill me; please don't kill me, for Faerholme, for Mother, please. Her eyes flowed tears.

'Cry, you witch! Cry as my Savi cried, as my babe has cried for his lost mother.' Then his head jerked up, the intensity in his eyes seemed to fade, and the strength in his hands faltered and pulled away. Elona saw Nursey standing with the knife in her hands. But Kienan stood and turned, blood seeped from a ragged hole in his back. 'You'll not rob me of my revenge,' he hissed; he pulled the blade easily from the woman's hand and plunged it into her stomach. He pulled it free and a gout of blood flowed. Nursey stared at Kienan, then turned her sad eyes to Elona.

'I'm sorry, 'Lonie...' Nursey said and deflated like a pierced *tekra*.

Kienan wavered and turned back to Elona, his eyes unfocused and refocused. He would stab her now, she realised with a sudden clarity as if a curtain had been lifted from her mind. She pulled herself to her feet, her breath rasping painfully in her damaged throat. Kienan lunged at her with the knife; she grabbed at it and missed. Pain shot through her side. The blood-wet handle slipped in his hand as he fell forward, the weight of his body pushing her backwards against the balcony rail. Terror filled her as her body twisted and she stared down at the distant courtyard cobbles. I can't die. I can't die now, for Faerholme, for Mother. She looked into his eyes and saw victory in the seething hatred. His arms came up and embraced her. He pushed her backwards and together they tumbled slowly over the rail.

17

Awareness returned first as cold. Across her body there was a chill breeze that brushed the hairs of her skin; it brought the smell of wild woods, and the scent of burning logs. Beneath her hands, back and legs she could feel raw stone. She was lying on her back, naked on stone. She opened her eyes to the sky and saw blackness pierced with a thousand pinpoints of brilliant white. She turned her head and saw, at the edges of the star-dusted sky, the dark silhouettes of trees, moving gently.

The memory of the fall flooded back and she trembled. Kienan had carried her over the balcony; she could still see the hate and the triumph in his eyes. She felt sick.

But she lived, she lay on stone, and a fire burned nearby.

Carefully she turned and pushed herself up until she rested on her left elbow. She expected to hear the chains drag on the stone. Yet there was nothing, no pull, no rattling, no grating. Just skin brushing stone and the feel of gravel piercing her elbow. She raised her right arm in wonder, realising that the shackles were gone. She sat up and stared at her arms and legs. She felt her wrists, ankles and waist; they were bruised and raw, with hard ridges of skin. It was no dream. They had been there but now they were gone. Her hand went to her throat; Metrid's necklace, too, was missing.

In the distance, she heard a voice exclaim in surprise. Other voices jeered. The first voice seemed to say Look! More voices cried out but she could not understand their words. Elona stared through the darkness in the direction of the sound and saw the dim red glow of fire reflected darkly on lower branches and leaves. Silhouettes of armsmen climbed to their feet and buckled their swords.

Fear overtook her; they had brought her to this place to slay her. Not content to destroy her every hope, they now intended to destroy her body. The men climbed upwards and on to the level plain of stone on which she sat. Slowly she stood and turned to face them, the men stopped and exclaimed again; the swords were dropped and some laughed. Elona backed, slowly moving away. Their voices died away and they moved toward her slowly. The first voice spoke again, gentle, cajoling, but she would not be fooled by this simple trick. Did they take her for a fool? Had she not killed a demon? She heard their boot nails scratching the rock. Her eyes had been adjusting to the light and she saw that she stood near the centre of a circle of smooth stone. Around its edges at regular intervals stood rocks twisted into hideous shapes and beyond, in all directions, dark trees.

She fled.

Tiny stones bit into her feet as she flew across the flat surface. The men shouted at her but she did not heed them, and they pounded after her. Within twenty strides she had reached the edge of the stone circle between two great blocks. Beyond was darkness. She could not see how high she was or what means served for descent; yet she could not pause to find out and if the fall were great. Then the darkness served to protect her from her fears.

She leapt into nothing, her arms flailing, expecting every moment for pain to strike her. For what seemed an endless moment she hung in darkness, with only the feel of the cold wind whipping across her skin. Then something scratched her leg and she crashed into a bush, feeling stings and cuts across her skin. She cried out involuntarily at a sudden pain in her right ankle and collapsed to the moist ground.

Male voices echoed above her, and looking back she could see two of them silhouetted against the star-filled sky. She climbed painfully to her feet, thorns scratching her as she pulled herself up. She took a step, cried in pain, and folded to the earth again as her right ankle crumpled in a spasm of agony. Boots clumped down a series of steps behind her and a gauntleted hand took her by the shoulder. She lashed out with her left fist to where his head should be, gratified by a satisfying impact; it felt like his eye. A hand grabbed her arm and twisted it behind her back, and then a fist pulled her hair, jerking her head into the air.

The man behind lifted Elona to her feet. He shouted something to the others in words that sounded familiar yet did not quite make sense. He turned her round and forced her back towards the ring of stones; she limped on her painful ankle. If they were marching her back for the sacrifice, they had been foolish to remove the manacles. They would have to tie her up again, and she would not lie easy while they sliced her head from her shoulders. They climbed up and crossed the plain of stone, past the centre and towards the other side.

The light from the fire was much brighter now, yellow rather than red. Other armsmen clambered on to the rock carrying lit torches. She could see the salacious thoughts that ran through their minds as they stared at her naked body. The man behind her barked some orders and most of the men looked away, while another came running with a blanket. The hold on her hair was released and the prickly blanket wrapped around her shoulders. She wanted desperately to escape but as they led her off the stone circle, past the now roaring fire and down to a waiting cart, she allowed herself to believe that they did not intend to kill her yet.

The cart started off through the trees. The *kichesa* had to be whipped repeatedly to keep them moving, for lizard beasts did not like to travel by night and this was a cold one. She sat in the back, on a bench, with her captors on each side of her as well as behind. Another man drove the wagon; he did not seem to be an armsman. They journeyed a good while, occasionally passing through tented areas where armsmen moved, until finally they came to a town. Its walls were timber rather than stone, yet they looked thick and strong and she could see the designs of the accursed Patterners marked upon its barricades.

They clattered on to the cobbled main street. She studied the strangely built houses, part stone and part wood, until finally they came to a halt at an inn. On the stone pathway that ran around the building stood two armsmen; small torches burned at either side the main door, throwing wavering shadows into the blackness. The two guards peered at the cart and came to attention as they saw the passengers. One of them stepped forward to assist and gazed at Elona.

Elona was pushed roughly out and down; the armsman quickly averted his eyes as the blanket slipped open, and Elona readjusted it. With her fellow passengers flanking her closely, she was guided through the door of the inn. The interior had few lights and it was darker than the night outside. The main room had scattered tables and chairs, and a dying fire glowed in the huge hearth to the left. People slept on the floor around the fire, and there was the smell of sweat and beer.

She was guided to a table near the fire and pushed firmly into a chair with arms that restricted her movement. One of her guards went off and shouted for attention, raising complaints from the sleepers. Eventually the innkeeper came, grumpy, down the creaking wooden stairs in a nightshirt. He swore vividly and Elona found the words almost recognisable, sounds she felt she should understand but shifted in a strange way; similar to the way the ambassadors spoke when they visited Father.

But she was tired and didn't want to think; no doubt they would use her as they willed. In this state; she could not think well, and though escape seemed more likely now she was unchained she needed to rest, but it seemed they would not give her that chance. The most senior of the men who had accompanied her sat down noisily in the chair opposite and dropped two wooden goblets before her. He poured wine into them, its dark red colour reflecting the fire's embers as it gushed from the mouth of the flagon. He moved one goblet in front of her and took the other for himself, taking a long drink and gulping it down noisily.

She reached out and took hers. The thought crossed her mind to throw it in his face, but she felt it would not please her and she sipped at it instead. It had a heavy, woody flavour at first, then tasted of strawberries, almost syrupy in consistency. She swallowed it and felt it slide down into her empty stomach. Almost immediately warmth spread through her and her fingers and toes tingled. She took another mouthful. Her muscles, that she had not realised were so taut, relaxed and her head drooped towards the table as sleep overtook her.

'No sleep.' The man's voice was gentle but insistent, penetrating the languor of her mind. She lifted her head up again. He nodded and smiled. 'Faerholme.' Then he turned and shouted to the innkeeper who was falling asleep on the bar; Elona understood the word 'food.' Then he said something incomprehensible to the armsman at the door, who saluted and left.

'Find speaker for you, Faerholme,' the man said. 'Eat now.' He turned again and shouted at the innkeeper, who grumbled loudly as he clattered around behind the bar, eventually emerging with a tray. He ambled over and dropped the tray without ceremony on the table before them. There were plates of cheese, dark bread and butter. The man cut a hunk of bread, buttered it generously, and handed it to Elona. She took it and inspected it suspiciously. The man frowned, then buttered himself a piece and bit into it with a great show, and swallowing noisily.

'Good,' he said, cutting some cheese and biting into that too, then washing it down with a gulp of wine. Elona watched him, careful not to stare at the knife that now lay on the table between them. She bit into the bread; it was slightly stale but the butter was creamy and eased the toughness. She chewed it, surprised at the amount of flavour in it; she had not been able to taste anything for so long. She took another sip of the wine and reached out to one of the chunks of cheese, her fingers brushing the cold metal of the knife blade. Her captor did not seem to notice, and she smiled a little sly smile to herself; she would escape from this easily. He had no inkling of what she could do. Clearly she was no longer in Faerholme, so she had to get back. She had to complete her task and rid her beautiful homeland of the corruption that infested it.

18

Elona awoke with a start and opened her eyes. Bright sunshine poured through a small, open window, and a cool breeze blew in laden with the smells of forests and flowers and baking bread. She was lying on, and covered by, white linen. The pillow at her head was soft and the mattress on which she lay was firm but comfortable. Her head felt quite clear and the tiredness was gone from her limbs.

She did not want to move, for the comfort of the bed held her like a mother's embrace. She lay there staring at the low window; through it she could see the roofs of houses and beyond them tall trees. The sky was clear and blue but white clouds moved rapidly across it. She could hear the hissing of wind in trees, shouts of children playing and, nearby, hammering and sawing.

She sighed and pulled back the covers, she had been put into a nightdress that seemed to fit her well. She sat up on the edge of the bed and her feet dangled over, not touching the floor. The room was small, not much larger than the bed, and the ceiling sloped down on the window side. When she stood and stretched, her arms touched the ceiling and the sleeves of the nightdress slipped down, revealing the manacle scars on her wrists, though they were less distinct than before. There was a slight twinge in her right ankle from the fall. Had it only been last night?

She brought her arms down and stared at the brands of her imprisonment, then turned up the palms of her hands, the right one bearing the scars from the blade of Kienan's knife and the glass shard—yet they were healed and seemed like old wounds.

She looked around the room; there was a small table with a wooden jug and bowl. Laid out on a chair on the other side of the bed was a dress of wool and old, soft leather. She washed in the water from the jug and drank a little too, it tasted fresh. The marks of the iron belt were about her belly and on her hips; she had become very thin during her confinement. She slipped into the clothes that had been put out for her and they, too, were a decent, fit if a little loose. There was a rope belt for her waist as well. Under the chair she found a pair of ankle boots, like the clothes they bore the marks of having been worn by another, but she pulled them on. The leather was soft, though they pinched her toes a little. It felt strange to wear shoes after going so long without; the soles clattered on the smooth wooden floor.

She went to the window and looked out. She could see the buildings of the town and the defensive wall not too far off. The houses were all built in the strange wood/stone combination, and had roofs which were much steeper than she was used to. All the windows were small and fitted with shutters, and most were glazed. Beyond the wall were the trees, some whose leaves were still green but and others turning to scarlet and gold. Rising above the trees she could see, far off, white peaks on blue and purple mountain slopes, reaching to the sky.

The sounds from below drew her attention. With only the slightest twinge of vertigo she watched the people go about their business. They were dressed in good quality clothes, though not rich, the women wearing dresses similar in style to the one she wore. Armsmen, she noticed, were everywhere. In the daylight, she could see that most wore the insignia of the tree, while some had another design she did not recognise. She was in Dirdin, but how? Perhaps she had been carried off and brought here? It would be a journey of many days; at least a ten-day of riding hard, three times that of easy travel. It might explain how the cut to her hand was mended. But how had she not died from the fall? And why had she been left naked in the Patterners' ley-circle, which must be the Woodcircle of Dirdin?

Her contemplation was interrupted by a polite knock on the door. Elona turned slowly, tensing for an attack. She looked desperately for somewhere to hide. The door did not open. The knock came again, polite and diffident. Elona waited, hoping they would go away. Then came the very same knock, and a muffled female voice called out in a questioning way. Elona's fear ebbed slightly, for it was probably a maid.

She gathered her courage. 'Come in.' Her voice wavered as she called. The latch clicked up—there were no bolts or locks on the other side—the door swung in. A maid with a laden tray stepped into the room, smiling, and placed the tray on the small table, pushing the jug to one side. She had her back turned. Thoughts of attacking the girl and getting out through the open door flew through Elona's mind, but she held back—there were no locks, so she could escape at any time. And they were bound to have guards below; they would not trust her so easily. The window was too small, they knew that, and with probably a single staircase to the floor they would not need many guards to hold her.

The maid turned and curtsied, said something about the food, then left, closing the door behind her. Elona waited for bolts to be drawn but there were none, and no lock clicked. Elona crept to the door and listened to the sound of footsteps descending wooden stairs. Delicately, she lifted the latch and drew open the door. Outside there was a small landing and stairs, and no other rooms led off. There were also no guards. She crept to the banister and looked down. Her stomach churned as she stared down to the next landing, where several doors led to more stairs down to the main room of the inn. She could hear voices.

She went back into her room and silently closed the door. She brought the tray to the bed and worked her way through the bread. They had even given her a wooden knife with which to spread the butter. There was also cheese, boiled eggs and ham to go with it; even clear water to wash it down. She ate as much as she could.

❧

The sun had moved and was no longer shining in through the window. She lay on her side watching the shadows of birds and other flying creatures flit past. The full meal had made her languid, and even the thought of escape drifted from her mind. Another knock broke the quiet of her room, though this one was firmer than the last. The fears that had faded in the peace of the woodland town reared once more.

She stood and withdrew to the corner furthest from the door. Holding the wooden knife up her sleeve and gathering her courage, she spoke before another knock came. 'Come in.'

The latch flicked up and the door swung back. A man with straight brown hair, over a strangely unsettling face, stood in the doorway. He wore the insignia of Dirdin as part of a black tabard, beneath which hung high quality mail. There was a sword at his waist, the hilt of which was finely worked.

'Good morning,' he said in a clear Faerholme tongue with only the slightest twang of oddness. He made no move to enter, but after a short polite wait he continued. 'I am Jalka of Revor, Captain of Guards.'

Still she did not speak. He spoke a name of Faerholme yet wore the badge of Dirdin? Was he a traitor sent to corrupt Dirdin? She had to know: 'Who are you?'

He looked down for a moment, then raised his eyes to look at her. He smiled. 'Lady, I have given you a name, and that question was my own. Now, we may stand on opposite sides of this garret and exchange such questions. Or we may sit below in comfort, in a room set apart.'

Elona trembled with indecision. He was well-spoken and she could feel none of the poison in him. Perhaps they had perfected their disguise such that she could no longer perceive her enemies

130

for what they really were? 'Tell me how you came to Dirdin first. Why have I been held prisoner?'

'As you wish, my Lady.' The Captain bowed slightly. 'I was born and raised in Faerholme until I felt the need for adventure. Thus I travelled north to Umran, southerly to Raertane and from thence here to Dirdin. I found their need suited my purpose, to fight against the expansion of the empire of Tirnia. I enlisted in the army of the Dirdin King and swore allegiance to him. In the four years since that time I have been a Captain of Guard.

'Last night—early this morning, more precisely—an armsman came to my billet. He told a strange tale of an unclothed woman who had been found at the Woodcircle, and that she seemed to be of Faerholme. I was ordered to come and question you, and to translate for my superiors so that they could enquire of you, whence you came and why?

'As for being kept as a prisoner it is true we have guarded you, but there has been nothing to prevent you from leaving your room. I am glad that the clothes fit you so becomingly.'

Elona raised her hand as if to ward off his compliment. He could be lying. Nonetheless, though his face did disturb her in a way she could not fathom, she felt inclined to believe his tale. She did not truly believe she had lost the power to divine the evil and corruption. She felt no different to the way she had before the fall, save only that here there was nothing that pressed her mind with its devil terrors. 'I will come, Captain.'

He bowed again. 'Allow me to lead the way.' He turned his back to her and moved away from the door. Elona gripped the security of the knife handle in her right hand and crossed the room. He waited for her at the top of the stairs, his hand gripping the round pommel of the banister. As she appeared, he descended.

'It is a pleasant day, though autumn is beginning to turn the trees to brown and yellow. I did not see much of trees and woodlands before I left Revor. I find this time of year to be most beautiful. Do you not think so?'

He seemed almost like the hated Bejeren before he was contaminated by the poison. She answered hesitantly as the words came unexpectedly to her lips. 'It is quite pleasant ... though the woods below Alba are silver in autumn.'

'It is, as I have heard, one of the many wonders of Alba, Lady Elona.' She froze at the sound of her name; he stopped and turned a gentle smile on his face. 'Don't be surprised. Your words, your actions, everything about you proclaims your inheritance. You are a gentle creature; it was first your own voice that betrayed you. For when you spoke I knew you to be of the nobility, and your accent is of the middle lands of Faerholme. There are but two noble houses that could claim such a beauty as yours for their own. Betlain and Corlain, and you are not the daughter of Betlain.

'But, my Lady, I am no enemy of yours, though you may mistrust me. The scars you bear show that you have been sorely used, though I cannot imagine by whom. And, by my honour, should I ever be faced with the ones who dealt you so ill, I swear I will be your right hand and your champion against them.'

Elona let her face smile. The fool, either he was ignorant of the corruption of Faerholme or he thought her witless. He switched from trickery to honesty in a breath. Either way she could not trust him, but he might be useful. 'Let us go down, Captain.'

They continued down to the ground floor. The main room looked airy and light with the sun shining in through the windows, and it was warm enough without it being too hot. A fire had been laid in the grate, ready to be lit as evening came. Two maids were scrubbing the floor and tables but the smell of stale beer hung in the air. The maids both looked up as Elona and her captor entered; one was the girl who had delivered her food. They both smiled in a way that reminded her of Savi's grin. She did not return their favour.

The Captain led her across the room to a slightly open door, he paused. 'Do you wish for refreshment? Some fruit perhaps? A drink?' Elona shook her head. He called out in Dirdin, and they went through into the side room. It was about twice the size of her attic space, though it seemed much bigger since the ceiling did not slope. There were a series of windows along the wall opposite to the door, and two small tables were piled one atop the other in a corner. The centre of the room was occupied by a large rectangular table with six chairs about it. On it were laid out paper, an ink pot, a pouch of fine sand, several quills, a single lit candle, a stick of wax and a small knife. Jalka held a chair near the window for her to sit on, then he took the one opposite. He gathered the writing equipment around him and trimmed one of the quills absently with a knife.

'You must excuse me, my Lady, if my questions appear impertinent.' He paused to eye the nib he had formed and then unstopped the ink pot. 'My seniors are very curious to know how it comes about that a young woman, with the marks of imprisonment on her, appears at the Woodcircle. Did she come there secretly through the forest, with woodcraft defying the finest men of Dirdin? Was she brought there through the skills of the Patterners? If so, where are the weavers of this secret road? Is she a Patterner herself who travelled her own road in secret? Yet if she is a Patterner where has she escaped from that she should carry such wounds? Most important, is she a spy of Tirnia?

'They have many questions, and their curiosity will be further aroused when they discover this young woman is the daughter of a noble house of Faerholme.' She remained silent while he dipped the pen into the ink gently shook it off and inscribed her name at the top of the page.

'Lady Elona, how did you come to be at the Woodcircle?'

19

She sighed. The simplest lies were the best, and the ones that stuck closest to the truth were the best of those. 'I don't know.'

The Captain pursed his lips and rested his writing hand. 'My Lady, that is not sufficient. How came you by the marks on your wrists and ankles?'

His question stirred the memories of a year of confinement, of threat and conspiracy against her, against her mother, against Faerholme. They rose up like a great wave of torture and crashed upon her. Her body shook with sobs and tears streamed down her face. A knock came at the door and she heard a chair scraping on the floor. Jalka walked to the door and spoke briefly to whoever was there. A mug was placed on the table and then an arm placed around her shoulders. She tensed so suddenly and fiercely that he released her immediately. 'Here,' he said, pushing a kerchief into her hands. She mopped at her eyes and sniffed. Through blurry eyes she watched him sit opposite her again and take a short drink, wiping foam from his lip.

'I apologise, my Lady. Let us consider instead the last thing you remember before you were at the Woodcircle.'

Elona sniffed again then blew her nose. She tried to think what she could say that was truth and what she should keep back. 'I ... I fell ... from a balcony.' Then, in a rush, the lie poured out easily and swiftly. 'I am scared of heights, I became dizzy and I fell. Then I woke in your circle.'

'And what day was it that you fell?'

What day? What day? Anger built up in her as she recalled the wedding, the day of that wedding, but she fought it down, she must not reveal her hate. 'I don't know the day—I had been ill for a long time.'

'Where were you?'

'I was—' her words slowed, what could she say? They were certain to check, and when they did they would be told all the lies about her. She had to escape before the Dirdin knew, and it was best to put them off the scent for as long as possible. '—at my home at Corlain ... with my family. I think.'

'You were not at the wedding of Prince Drahail?'

She looked away from him, as a grief she had never felt before rose up and threatened to choke her. She dabbed at unstoppable tears on her cheeks. Jalka looked up, sympathy and sadness in his eyes, and wrote in silence.

'Can you tell me the time of day that you fell?'

'It was late afternoon.' Then she added, 'It was autumn, just beginning.'

'Here in Dirdin autumn comes a little earlier than Faerholme, but even here autumn is not much advanced. It must have been by magic that you were brought. It cannot be that fifteen days have passed since you were last in your right mind in Faerholme. And to carry a person, unknowing, so fast? No, it cannot be. Patterners are involved in this.' He formed words neatly and carefully upon the page and, though she could not see what he had written, he put down far more than she had spoken. Finally, he sprinkled sand across the sheet and poured it off again. Then he rolled up the sheet, placed it into the container and closed the lid. From beneath his tunic he pulled a metal stamp on a chain. He sealed the tube with wax and imprinted it with his stamp. He went to the door and delivered it to an armsman who waited beyond. He turned to her.

'We will not continue for the present. Would you care to take a walk?' The offer amazed her since she expected to be sent back to the attic room. He must have seen her surprise as he smiled. 'You are not a prisoner, my Lady. Leastways, not one to be confined. To tell truth, I am not sure what you are, but at the very least we must keep you safe. Please, accompany me.'

The town was quite large, perhaps three hundred inhabitants, swelled to double that by the resident garrison. Jalka said there were many hundreds more outside and around the ley-circle to avert the threat of invasion from Tirnia. Though as Jalka explained, it had the beneficial side-effect of driving away the outlaws who preyed on the trade through the Great Forest as well. The Captain led her up to the wall and they climbed the wooden steps to the wide walkway that led around the edge. The sun shone down and warmed Elona's skin and she breathed the free, autumn-filled air.

As they walked Elona kept her eyes open for a way to escape from the town. She saw that, apart from the main gate, there were two smaller ones. One of these led to the nearby river and the other in the direction of the mountains, though what lay in between she had no idea—the maps of Dirdin generally showed only trees. The road beyond the main gate led, in one direction, to the Woodcircle while the other headed west towards the plains of Dirdin, and from thence to Raertane and Faerholme.

The walk tired her considerably and she began to limp. She explained to her companion that her long illness had confined her to her bed, and that she had not exercised in that time. He offered her his arm but she refused it.

On their return in the late afternoon, a messenger awaited Jalka. He examined the seal, then broke it and read the enclosed message. Elona watched his eyes as they flicked back and forth across the sheet. She saw as his eyes narrowed, a frown replacing the relaxed smile he had only moments earlier. He reached the bottom and read it through again. He lowered the letter and looked at her as if searching for an answer in her eyes. The fears began in her shoulders and spread, freezing her muscles and weakening her. He knew, knew it all; all their lies had come here to haunt her; and all his sweet lies of the morning were forgotten in the bitter untruths on the paper before him.

'Lady Elona, I have been ordered to confine you. Emissaries of Faerholme are en route, they will be here presently.'

'No. Not so soon, I haven't had time...'

'Time?'

'To live.'

Elona felt the strength go from her legs as she imagined the weight of the chains and manacles pressing once more on her flesh. At the thought of the poisoned foods of Faerholme and the insidious crawling evil, she collapsed and wept. The Captain passed the message back to the armsman, gently took her hand, and led her up the creaking stairs. 'I will send for some food,' he said quietly, and gently shut the door behind him.

Her tears dried. She must escape as soon as possible while there was still a chance. The Dirdin were careless with their charge, so there had to be a way. Perhaps if she could get through the gate unseen and take a horse in the night she could make a good distance before they discovered she was gone. But the woods were full of armsmen.

Jalka returned with the food, a plate of *sikechak* meat and vegetables, and some water. He sat in the chair while she ate.

'The Emissaries have arrived; I have them quartered beyond the walls. They are Patterners, a green and a brown.' Elona almost choked. 'I find it unusual that Patterners should come for you. Can you explain it?'

She shook her head.

'It seems that in your illness you were not aware that you had been moved to the palace.' She gave him no response. 'It seems that Prince Drahail has been married to Hope of Betlain.' Her knuckles went white as she tightened her grip on the utensils. He waited in silence while she finished her meal. 'I have told them you are weak and cannot speak with them today. They are content with that for now.'

As he removed the empty plate and the knife he said, 'I'm sorry about your mother, Elona.' Then he was gone.

Elona came instantly wide-awake from a deep sleep. The sound came again, a scratching at the window then a tapping. She pushed herself up on one arm and stared at the silvery window framed in black. Her stomach jolted as what looked like a huge spider crawled across the pane and tapped again. As the bleariness of sleep cleared she recognised it as a small hand. It rapped persistently on the pane.

She stood and went across to the window. A *Kadralin* boy, perhaps ten or twelve, was standing on the thatched ridge outside the window, the wind blowing his long hair back and forth; his precarious position made her feel queasy. She opened the window carefully. The wind whipped in and tried to grab the frame from her hand but she held on tight. The boy's eyes seemed wide and bright; he grinned, revealing shining white teeth.

'Missy, 'scape,' he said in a loud whisper. She stared at him. With his free hand he gestured to her. 'Come, 'scape.' She hesitated, then shook her head slowly. 'Come now, 'scape lord's men.' Elona looked past him at the roof of the building and the ground.

'Who are you?'

'No time, missy, go now. 'Fore sun.' He pointed to the East.

Elona took a step back and gripped one hand in the other. 'I don't know...'

The grin disappeared from his face and he drew back a little from the window, then suddenly he was back. 'Not go Alba.'

Elona stared at him, then nodded. She turned back to the bed and she threw her dress over the nightgown, tying it loosely, then slipped on her boots and laced them tightly. Finally, she placed the chair under the window and closed her eyes. She gathered her courage and climbed up; it seemed as if the distant ground beyond the roof swam in the silver light. She tried to focus on the window frame as she attempted to see how she could climb through the tiny space.

Holding tightly to the frame above the window, she lifted her left foot and slid it through the window as far as she could. The cold wind blew on her exposed calf. The boy drew back to give her space.

Then, holding tight, she lifted her right leg and poked it through the opening. The frame of the window pressed into her thighs and the strain on her arms stretched her weak muscles. Taking a deep breath, she lifted her weight, turning her hips and forcing her legs further through. Her dress was caught on the inside of the frame, pushed higher and higher up her body.

'Hey! Hey!' The boy suddenly called out. She looked at him through the glass he indicated for her to pull herself up. She heaved; the boy's hand sneaked in under her body and grabbed a handful of her dress. He dragged most of it out and covered up her legs. With the dress out of the way she found she could slide her body sideways out through the window and into the cold. For a terrifying instant she thought she had missed the eaves and would fall from the edge; then her boots came to rest on the roof and, with the wind whipping her hair, she clung to the window frame from the outside.

She finally opened her eyes and saw the grinning face of the boy. 'Good, Missy. Come.' He turned almost nonchalantly and walked along the edge. Elona nervously released her grip on the window and dragged her hands down the outside of the roof as if trying to stick to it. She knelt down and crawled along the edge. It was better than walking but the distance to the ground was very obvious. Moving only one limb at a time, she inched to where the angle of one roof met another. The boy was waiting, sitting with his legs dangling over the edge.

He beckoned to her and she climbed to the roof ridge behind him. He pointed down. Over the ridge the roof sloped away to a second roof sticking out from it. It was the roof of the stable and there was a hole in it where some thatch had been removed. The boy got off the ridge as if he were dismounting, then stretched himself out flat, his feet dangling down and his hands holding tight to the ridge. He released one hand and waved it at her. 'Missy!' She grabbed it instinctively, and he grinned and let go with the other hand. She gasped as his weight pulled her. She let him slide down as far as she could stretch. His feet were an arm's length above the eaves when he let go of her and slid the final distance with his feet pressed into the thatch to slow his descent.

'Come, Missy,' he hissed up to her.

She tried not to think about what she was going to do as she climbed off the ridge. She let herself down, clinging tightly to the thatched ridge. The boy's hand grabbed her foot and pushed up on her heel. She knew it was not far, certainly less distance than the boy had dropped but knowing did not help. She had to let herself fall, she had to let go. The boy released her foot.

'Come,' he said insistently. She let go, terror lurching through her as she slid uncontrollably until her feet struck the guttering. She looked down at his grinning face; she felt sick. He clambered down the short distance to the ridge of the stable roof and walked casually along to the hole. He sat on the ridge with his feet dangling into the dark space. Elona carefully let herself down and sat astride the ridge as before, then slid along. The boy peered down into the blackness of the hole and then jumped off. Almost immediately she heard him hit straw and his voice floated up from the darkness. 'Come, Missy.'

This was worse because this time she couldn't see what she was falling into. She rolled over so that she was face down to the roof and her legs dangled into the open hole. Her mind conjured a bottomless cavern beneath her as she slowly slipped backwards. Her hands gripped tight but this time she was carrying her weight and she could not stay that way for long. She heard the sound of hay being moved about below her, and she slipped little by little. Fear built in again. Her hands lost their grip and for a terrifying moment she fell; even before her head had disappeared below the level of the roof, she came to an abrupt stop.

Then the hay bale she had landed on wavered and slipped away from under her. She gave a cry as she fell into the hayloft. The boy laughed and piled up the bales again, carefully replacing some of the thatch. Elona's eyes became used to the dark but there was not much to see. Through the last of the gaps she saw the sky beginning to lighten with dawn. The boy finally climbed down to her. 'Come.'

He guided her to the ladder down to floor level amid the sounds of snuffling horses, then peeked out through the doors. Slipping out, he pulled her along and they moved quickly and quietly across to a set of covered carts that stood in the inn's courtyard. He climbed up at the back of one and then pulled her up inside, the interior almost completely dark and smelling of bodies and leather. He lifted up a bundle of hides and pointed to a gap underneath, urging her into it. She lay down in the cramped space and he dropped the hides on top. She heard him move away.

So this was how she was to escape, as a bundle of hides. In the stuffy atmosphere beneath the hides, with her mind turning over the possibilities and the unknowns, she fell asleep.

20

___

Light was seeping through the cracks between the hides when she awoke next. The cart jerked and moved as animals were hitched to it. There was plenty of shouting, mostly the voice of the caravan master she had met in the inn. Even the difference in language did not hide the invective mixed in with his speech. Suddenly the light increased, and she drew a sharp breath as the hides covering her face were pulled back. The boy's face was there, grinning ear-to-ear. He gave her a thumbs up, then dropped the hides back and disappeared.

There was another loud shout, a crack of whips and drivers urging their beasts forward. Her cart jerked again and kept moving, shaking its way across the cobbles, the sound of grinding wheels echoing round the courtyard. She heard the sounds change as they went through the inn's arched entrance and out into the street. After a few moments, the sound changed again as they left town through the gate and entered a dirt road. The cart swung to the right abruptly and splashed through a stream.

She knew they must be heading towards the north, to Taltia. The cart rolled on and its swaying motion slowly put her back to sleep.

The cart was still bumping along when she returned to wakefulness, and she was hungry. She shifted the hides a little so that she could breathe and light poured in. The arched canvas ceiling of the wagon waved back and forth as the wheels trundled over the uneven surface. Elona tried to sit up but found the unpredictable movement kept throwing her back. She rolled over and looked forward. Through the open frontage she could see the driver, and occasionally the bobbing heads of the *kichesa* team. On either side she could see trees; the sky was overcast.

She lay back again, wondering if the boy was the sole collaborator in her escape or whether others knew of it. She would have to wait, but she'd had plenty of experience with that. She was free now to turn the tide on the malevolence that possessed her land and her people.

She dozed again and woke to the sound of more orders being given. The wagon had stopped though the sun still shone; the driver was no longer sitting up at the front. She clambered up and peered out from behind the flap. The carts in the caravan were drawn up in an open, grassy space among the trees. The *kichesa* were grazing quietly to one side, and when she lifted the flap a little further she saw the traders eating together. Elona needed to get into the bushes to relieve herself. The back of the wagon faced away from the traders, so she carefully climbed out. The cart moved slightly as she swung down, then she dived into the bushes at the side. There were no sounds of pursuit or anything to suggest that she had been seen.

When she returned she saw that some of them were standing up, as if preparing to return to their wagons. Taking her courage in her hands, she ran the short distance to her cart and climbed in. Again there were no shouts or alarms as she climbed into her hole and covered herself up. The cart jolted as the beasts were yoked again; the boy pulled back the hides and dropped a small packet of leaves into her hands before re-covering her. She heard him clamber forwards.

She unwrapped the packet; it contained a boiled egg and a small piece of bread. She sighed, chewing them slowly, though she had no water to wash them down. The day continued dull and the sun did not get a chance to heat the woods, for which she was grateful. She had had no drink since the night before and her thirst was beginning to nag. It worsened every time the caravan splashed through a stream.

The afternoon passed in a confusion of dozing and waking. At times the traders sang, and other times they called out to each other in what seemed to be a rhyming game that often ended in laughter. But it all blurred into a dream as she breathed the smell of animal skin.

Evening came and the caravan stopped once more, followed by the sound of running water and the animals being unhitched. Elona came to full wakefulness with the strong awareness that her legs were itching badly. There was no one in sight so she pulled off the hides, lifted her dress and looked at her legs. She bit back a cry of disgust as she saw the red lumps covering them from ankle to thigh, and little insects crawling across her skin. Frantically she brushed them, almost sobbing, trying to be silent; then the rear flap was pulled back and a man's face looked in.

Elona froze as his eyes scanned her rapidly from bare ankle and leg to head. Then his eyes narrowed as he failed to recognise her. His frown triggered Elona into action. She turned and stumbled to the open front of the wagon, her feet catching on the hides as she went. To the right were other carts and woodland to the left. She clambered out on to the wooden seat and jumped. Her weakened right ankle failed and she tumbled head first into the long dry grass. A shout went up behind her and a hand grabbed her arm, pulling her into a sitting position. The man's face was pushed so close to hers that she could smell his breath.

He shouted at her but she didn't know what he was saying, and that made him shout more. A crowd of voices gathered around her and they jabbered in a tongue she did not know. Then another voice made itself heard above the rest and they quieted; the hand that held her arm released its grip. Elona looked up to see the caravan master push through the wall of bodies.

He said something to her in a gruff insistent voice; she looked blankly back at him.

'What you do, hey?' Her attention was snapped back to the Master, his accent making the words thick and strange.

What could she say? If she said she had escaped they'd take her back.

'I see you and soldier. Hey?'

'Run away,' she said at last, desperately trying to think of a story that would satisfy him. Someone in the group muttered something to the others and a murmur ran through the group. One of the other men whispered in the Master's ear, and he nodded.

'Long way Faerholme. Hey?'

The boy pushed his way through the crowd and spoke to the caravan master. He paid no attention at first, but at the boy's insistence he suddenly turned on him. The boy pulled a pouch from inside his jerkin and the man took it. He tipped up the pouch and coins tumbled into his hand. The boy took Elona's hand and gently pulled back the sleeve to reveal the manacle scars and showed the old cut on her hand.

The one who had spoken before did so again and a murmur ran through the group once more. More than one craned their heads forward to look at her scars. There were some nods among them, some disapproving frowns. The man who had caught her spoke quickly to the Master, who nodded and spoke.

'You go clean. Stay Yolandra.' He pointed to an older woman who stood to one side of the group. 'You work. We keep you, hey?'

Elona understood enough to realise that she would not be sent back to the town, so she nodded gratefully. The Master turned and walked away, the crowd turned away, the men and children more reluctantly, and then went about their work. Yolandra waited. Elona climbed uncertainly to her feet, her right ankle throbbing as she put her weight on it. Elona hobbled carefully to the woman, who gestured for her to follow as she walked towards a wagon.

As they reached the back of the caravan, a word was shouted from a distance away. Turning to see, she saw it was the man who had found her. Yolandra turned and shouted the same word back in a querying way, and then the man, laughing, confirmed it . Yolandra looked at Elona and indicated for her to pull up her skirts. She tutted at the red blotches and the insects that still crawled through her clothes. She indicated for Elona to stay outside, and then she climbed into the caravan. When she returned she was carrying a rough cloth and a shift yellowed with age but embroidered in detailed patterns.

'Come.' Elona recognised that word and limped after the woman as she led the way through the undergrowth to a stream. They followed it for a short while until it dived over a small shelf and pooled in a basin of rock below. She gestured for Elona to undress, saying the words in her language at the same time. Elona repeated the words carefully and removed her clothes. 'In water.' Elona complied; it was cold but not freezing. The pool deepened towards the middle and the old woman gestured for her to dip her head under the waterfall. She took Elona's clothes and dumped them in the stream as it left the pool. Carefully she went through each fold and cleared out the bugs.

Elona was beginning to get cold but continued to scrub at her hair, watching the insects float away as they struggled against the water. When no creatures had appeared for some time she climbed from the pool. The red blotches stood out on her skin all the way up her legs and on her arms, some on her stomach and shoulders. The scars around her wrists and ankles were clearly defined too. She picked up the rough cloth and dried herself, her hair dripping as she rubbed it without much effect. She slipped the shift over her head; it did not make her feel much warmer but kept the breeze from her skin. The woman eventually returned with her wet clothes over one arm, passing them to Elona as they returned to the camp.

Elona limped up the stairs behind Yolandra. She glanced around before entering and saw several of the men looking at her; she shivered and stepped through the low door. The interior was dimly lit from the two pairs of small windows on either side, glazed in a translucent material. There were cupboards on the walls and a large square bed at the far end. Yolandra indicated that Elona should take a seat while she searched through one of the lower cupboards. She removed some small glass bottles, a bandage and a short black stick. She gestured for Elona to remove the shift.

Yolandra opened a wide-necked blue bottle and the room was filled with a vile smell. The old woman dipped her finger in and spread a green ointment onto the red blotches. The smell intensified but the effect on the bites was almost immediate as the itching decreased. Yolandra tapped Elona's hand and waggled the bottle under her nose. She grinned toothily at Elona's disgust at the smell. Elona took the bottle and spread the soothing unguent on to the blotches. When Yolandra seemed satisfied that Elona could do that properly, she turned her attention to her right ankle. She wound the bandage about it tightly, occasionally dropping a clear liquid from one of the other bottles on to it. She tied off the bandage and, using the black stick, inscribed patterns on to the outside of the bandage.

Elona gasped and pulled her leg back. The old woman was a Patterner. But then she would be the healer for the traders, of course, not part of that devilish hierarchy that sought to imprison and kill her. Yolandra smiled and spoke in a coaxing way, holding out her hand. Gingerly, Elona placed her ankle back into the old woman's grasp and Yolandra continued to draw the patterns, humming quietly as if reminding herself of the shapes needed.

By the time she had finished, the patterns covered the bandage front and back. Then the old woman made her lie back on the bed and began a quiet, repetitive chant. Elona felt herself drifting into sleep as the voice droned in her ears, her ankle tingling with warmth. In the darkness behind her eyelids, Elona could see a great pool of light and a tiny stream that flowed from it, leading to her. It tumbled over a shelf and made a welcoming pool for her foot. Carefully, she dipped her foot up to her ankle and the soothing light flowed over it. She felt its warmth and wanted to feel it throughout her body.

She slipped her other foot over the side of the pool and let it splash in, gently. Then she slid her whole body down, feeling the light rise through her. She relished its warmth, feeling the tensions ease out of her. It covered her belly and then her arms; her wrists tingled excitedly at the touch of the power. Then it reached her neck and she felt she could swim in it forever. Her hair floated out from her head like a halo about a moon as she prepared to dip herself under and feel it flowing through her. The pool shrank and the light drained away, and in a moment she stood naked in darkness and someone was shaking her arm.

Yolandra pinched her hard and Elona squealed, coming fully awake, finding she was sitting up. The old woman released her arm, then jabbered at her for a moment before giving up when confronted by Elona's uncomprehending face. She sighed and lifted Elona's foot. Elona looked down and saw the patterns on the bandage had disappeared completely, and so had the blotches on her legs though a dry green residue remained. The bandage came off and the manacle marks were gone from both ankles. She stared at her wrists, where the ridges of hardened flesh on her stomach had been; they and the scar on her hand were only a memory.

Yolandra watched the amazement pass through her, then handed her the shift. 'Put this on.' The woman pottered around the cupboards and brought Elona a drink in a beaten and engraved silver cup. It seemed to be water. Elona shrugged and drank, and the woman nodded with a smile. Then she sat on the bed next to her, twisting round to face her.

'I am Yolandra.' She said, pointing to herself.

Elona repeated the words. 'I am Elona.'

'You are Elona.' Yolandra said and pointed to her.

'You are Yolandra.'

The woman nodded and smiled, took the cup from Elona's hand and drank down the rest of the water herself.

In the days that followed, the caravan crawled along an easterly trail through the woods. She tried to visualise the maps that the traitor Bejeren had shown her before the coming of the evil. She thought they were heading out of Dirdin and that would take them into Taltia. They were gaining height, though the mountains to the East did not seem to grow any closer. The weather remained cloudy and cold but there was little rain. From time to time they would pass through a village where they traded some of their goods for food.

They hunted, too, and milked the goats that ran tethered to the wagons.

After nearly a ten-day the trees thinned out and they travelled through a hilly land. The road turned north, winding in and out of valleys, maintaining a slow climb. After one turn they emerged on the north-western side of a hill with an unimpeded view to the West. The clouds were high and Elona could see they travelled above a great forest-filled valley. On the horizon, rising from the sea of trees, another mountain. Then she knew that she was looking down on the Gap of Dirdin, the valley that stood between Dirdin and Taltia. The mountain she saw was Mt Liniel, the beginning of the range that split the two kingdoms.

Her work with Yolandra was not difficult, and she learned to drive the wagon—the *kichesa* followed the one in front, and so it was not hard. And as they drove Yolandra would teach her their words, though mostly it did not differ greatly from her own language. Some words, and some ways of putting the words together, were unusual but there was much in common, as all the tongues were given to them and descended from Taymar. When they stopped, Elona learned to handle the *kichesa*, harnessing and releasing them, hobbling them so they could not stray far as they grazed. She fetched water, cleaned the caravan, learned to light and tend the fire as well as skin and prepare animals. At night she slept with the old woman in the big bed.

Yolandra was not impressed with her lack of practical skills and grumbled constantly about her ineptitude. Although, when it came to sewing, Elona found something that her new mistress did find acceptable. It was a shock to become the maidservant, yet the freedom of traders, travelling beneath the sky, always without threat, made her almost happy.

As they passed around the great mountain spur that slashed into the Dirdin forests, guards were set and the children kept within the caravans as dusk fell. The evening air was split apart by the raucous cries of the *sikechesa* as they wheeled through the air on the hunt. Yolandra warned her not to stray far from the fires lest she be taken by one of the huge bat-winged creatures.

During the next few days they descended the other side of the spur. The weather was beginning to turn cold as winter approached. Yolandra left Elona to drive the wagon while she worked inside. Elona asked what she was doing.

'Elona-servant, though you are a good girl, willing if unskilled, you are not one of the People. Our mysteries are not for you. It may be that you become of the People if the signs are fulfilled, but in my wisdom this will not come to pass. Be content for now with the peace you enjoy.'

21

That night they made camp early, in a valley surrounded by high hills and a rapid flowing stream nearby. The men built a large bonfire in the middle of an open space in addition to the caravan fires. The women cooked much more food than usual for the autumn feast. Elona grew excited as she saw the preparations but understood that she would not be permitted to take part. Having prepared Yolandra's fire, she took pleasure in the fact that she had succeeded in lighting it without help. As she worked, several of the young men stood a distance away and watched her. They had done so before but less openly than now. Yolandra had told her to ignore them when she mentioned it, but it was harder now that she was forbidden to enter the caravan to hide.

As darkness fell the big fire was lit, blazing into the sky and lighting the thin drizzle that fell. The people of the caravan drew around the fire and meals were handed out, though without the careful precision of a proper banquet she was accustomed to. Here, anyone took food as a plate came past. Elona's stomach grumbled. Yolandra had not prepared any food and Elona did not know how. Besides, the supplies were in the locked caravan anyway. All she could drink was some of the wines from the skins that hung on the outside of the wagon. These were for trading but Yolandra did use it for herself too. So Elona sat at the front of the caravan, leaning against a wheel, with the skin in her lap, sipping at the coarse heavy liquid and watching the celebrations. The Kadralin sang songs, some bawdy, told jokes which she could not catch, and ate while her stomach grumbled and her head grew light with the wine. And still Yolandra did not appear.

Elona's head was beginning to nod when the crowd hushed suddenly, and those still standing sat down. Yolandra stepped from the caravan and walked past wearing a white dress embroidered with patternings. As she passed, Elona saw that her face, hands, arms and feet were covered with intricate designs as well. Elona raised her head but felt dizzy; she took another drink to steady herself, though she couldn't taste it. Yolandra threw up her arms and screamed, then she stamped around the fire while chanting in a low voice. Her form seemed to blur to Elona's eyes. She rubbed them to clear her vision but it had no effect. Yolandra had become a fuzzy white flame that moved round and round the fire, but the people who sat silently watching were still perfectly clear.

The flame that was Yolandra seemed to merge with the bonfire, turning white and forming shapes. The first had the aspect of a flying *sikechak*; it leapt from the fire and swooped over the people before flying away. Elona closed her eyes and found the fire still burned white behind her lids. Once more she saw the stream of light flowing, but this time it was a flood. It was not directed at her but to the fire. Another shape formed, a creature like a *kichek* only bigger, and instead of flat teeth its mouth was filled with knives. It reared its head and roared into the night. She knew this to be the *nachak*, the demon hunter that prowled the southern lands.

Elona rolled forward onto her hands and knees, desiring the light, wanting to feel it flowing through her. At her desire, the river that flooded to the fire spread and split; a stream of dazzling light bubbled towards her, like the molten metal fresh from the furnace, yet she could feel no heat. As the diverted stream swirled towards her, the fire it fed dimmed and she reached out to the steaming strand of light that flowed to her. She touched it, her body jerked and the light ran through her.

The glowing form that was Yolandra stood above her angrily and lashed out; Elona struck back seeing her arm shining from within. Yolandra drew back, and a shape of power formed between her hands and she caught Elona about the neck with it, twisting it until she gasped. Then she struck her about the face and the dream vanished. Another hand slapped her face hard, and another forced her head back. She threw up her hands to protect her face, and opened her eyes. Yolandra stood above her, her white dress blackened and singed with fire. Behind her stood the People, scared and angry.

Yolandra forced her to sleep outside that night. In the morning Elona's head throbbed and ached as if to burst, but Yolandra drove her mercilessly to her chores. She only gave her a crust of bread and water but Elona did not care, as the smell of food that drifted around the grey encampment made her feel sick.

The caravan moved on. Yolandra no longer spoke to her save to issue instructions. Elona was permitted in the caravan to sleep at night but its floor was now her bed and she had to spend the rest of the time in the open. Elona tried to talk to Yolandra to explain that she had meant no harm but the woman would not listen. The young men of the caravan no longer watched her.

Two days after the ruined feast the procession of wagons re-entered the forests. Winter had withdrawn slightly, and autumn made the avenues they travelled glorious with colour. The Master came to consult with Yolandra. As Elona drove the caravan she could hear the voices rising and falling from within. At one time there came a shout from Yolandra, a vehement "No!" followed by loud words she could not decipher from the Master. Not long after he emerged from the rear and trotted past up to his wagon, climbing up beside one of his sons.

That night Yolandra seemed to have mellowed towards her, and instructed her to enter the caravan earlier than the usual time for sleep. Elona entered timidly and sat on the floor near the door in a suitable position of humility. Yolandra picked up a skein of wool to untangle it.

'Elona-servant, we have never spoken of your past. There has been no need; I have known your path to be through shadowed valleys and seldom upon the sunny ridges. Thus it has been and thus it will be.

'Though we have walked the same path for the now, the time comes when we shall walk apart.' She stopped and hummed a little as she concentrated on a tangle in the wool.

'There is power within you, and if you were of the People I would make you my daughter, to follow on. To be the thread that never ends from the dawn of the beginning, to the time when the great *Nachak*-master consumes the world as he does the moons in each of their turnings.' She sighed and pulled a thread; the whole tangle fell to pieces in her hands. 'But it will not be. Sleep now, Elona-child. I release you from your bondage, for this night sleep free.'

Elona suddenly felt very tired and curled up where she lay. She heard the old woman sigh and move about. Moments later a quilt came down over her body and frail, dry lips kissed her cheek.

The caravans did not set off in the morning. Elona stood confused at the front of Yolandra's wagon, staring at the inactivity of the camp, as no one had risen. Save for the boy, he came and stood before her, his face was no longer grinning.

'What is it, hey?' She asked.

'The *sikechasa* come to feed from our carcasses,' he replied with a sing-song tone to his voice.

Elona frowned. 'Then the men will fetch arrows to bring them down.'

'These *sikechasa* have two legs, and they wield swords and fire. They are many, we are few. They will eat us and let us pass, until we come again.'

'You mean bandits?' Elona used the word from her own tongue; she did not know the trader word. But the boy shrugged.

'When will they come, hey?' Elona concentrated to get her words right.

The boy answered. 'When they are here.'

Elona left him standing and rushed to the back of Yolandra's caravan, knocking urgently. 'Yolandra-mistress, please!' It seemed an age before the woman opened the door.

'Elona-child, I have released you,' she said quietly.

'You must pattern a magic to protect us from the bandits.'

Yolandra cast her gaze to the ground and smiled sadly. 'Elona-child, you are not of the People, you do not understand. The *sikechesa*-who-walk have fed upon us for as long as memory can tell. In the days of the beginning the People wandered the land freely and where we wished and we were many and we were strong. Then came the Taymalin from beyond the furthest mountains, and they spoke sweet words to some and showed the sword to others, and we were lost.

'In the days that came after, the People became weak and we lost our tongue and our hope. And the Taymalin preyed upon us as *sikechasa* from the sky. We endured though we were not strong. It is the way of the People to endure. We will not fight and bring the wrath of the Taymalin upon us such that it crushes us. We will pay the price of defeat until the day the sins of the Taymalin cast them down and we are free once more.' She jerked her head up and put it to one side as if she were listening, then shut her door and left Elona in the cold.

Moments later Elona heard the thundering of paws. Suddenly the camp was full of armed men on *kichek*-back, waving their swords and whooping. Finally she saw a man on horseback enter camp and the bandits drew in a circle about him. She walked to the front of Yolandra's caravan and watched him shouting orders in another tongue of the Taymalin; she only recognised the word "search".

The Caravan Master appeared and walked to the mounted bandit. He spoke with him for a long time, though she could not make out the words. All around her the bandits were searching through the laden carts, throwing out selections of their contents, especially dried foods and wine, though they stayed away from Yolandra's wagon. The bandit leader seemed to listen carefully to what the Master said but under his helm Elona could see no expression. Then he shook his head. The Master grabbed the man's leg, and the bandit raised his sword above his head as if to strike him dead.

"Take me!" Elona shouted.

The bandit leader jerked his head in her direction. His arm relaxed and he brought his sword to his side. He urged his horse across to her; she drew away until stopped by the wagon. He loomed above her and pushed up the front of his helmet, showing a face that was white with scars, eyes peering from twisted flesh. Elona's eye was caught by movement at her side. Yolandra stood a short distance away, impassively.

Elona looked back at her. It was the Taymalin who had crushed the Kadralin. Yet they had helped her, there was a debt to pay. She looked back at the twisted face beneath the metal helm, and walked forward from the safety of the wagon.

"I have value," she said clearly. "In Faerholme."

She came to a halt beside the horse and raised one arm. His inexpressive eyes stared down at her; he reached for her, grabbed her arm and lifted her on to the horse behind him.

22

———

For several days they traced back along the track the traders had taken, travelling faster than the trader caravan. They headed south into the mountains, twenty bandits with two carts laden with the spoils from a summer's raiding. There were fewer of them than the first impression of their ride into the camp had given. Elona rode in the back of the second cart, bouncing along with the kegs of beer and barrels of fruit.

Each day they would set traps for smaller animals and a few of the bandits would ride ahead or behind to hunt. She soon learned which of them were the better hunters. They would return with animals that she would have to clean in the freezing water of a stream each night till her hands were numb with cold. They did not fear to give her a knife. They did not treat her well, but she was surprised to find they did not treat her badly either. She had expected to be used that first night by the bandit leader, Styvan.

After she had given herself to him at the trader camp, he had carried her about on his horse supervising the rape of the caravan. Yet she knew he had not taken as much as he would had she not been part of the trade. The Caravan Master had looked her in the eye only once and there had been no expression in his face. Yolandra she did not see.

As they left he had dumped her in the cart with the rest of the booty, and that's where she had remained. He took no further interest in her. The ancient cart driver, Pitra, talked to her the whole day, though at first his accent and the strangeness of some words garbled his speech into nonsense. When he was not talking he was coughing, a long painful cough that tore his throat and lungs. The bandits slept in the open, in large skin bags with the fur on the inside and oiled on the outside to keep out the rain. Elona was not given a bag but Pitra slept under the cart, so she did too, wrapping up in a coarse, smelly blanket he gave her.

The meat from the animals she skinned was salted down and the skins left behind. When she tried to salt the pelts as well Pitra hit her on the ear, knocking her to the ground and complaining about her wasting salt. She did not respond, as she did not want him to know that she understood every word, or how wasteful she considered them to be.

As they travelled she listened to their talk. Most of it was repetitive boasting as they told each other how many they had killed, the women they had taken, and the treasures they had contributed to the store. But as the days passed she managed to glean information about how they had spent their summer raiding the towns and villages of eastern Dirdin, southern Taltia and even into western Tirnia. They respected no authority but the strength of Styvan's sword and fist. Their journey into the mountains was to their wintering valley, with fresh water and wood to burn. The only route to it would fill with snow in the winter storms. Thus it had been for many years, for Styvan was a successful bandit.

On the second night she woke in the cold needing to relieve herself, so she scrabbled out from beneath the cart. The second moon, Colimar, hung just above the tree-tops casting its wan light; Lostimal had yet to rise. There was a convenient bush not far away and she trudged out and squatted, then cried out as a hand landed on her right arm, pulling her off balance. She fell back into the bush. She swung her left hand and struck the leathered jacket of one of the bandits. The man batted her hand away and dragged her from the bush. He laid her out on the stony ground and grunted like an animal as he pulled up her skirt.

Elona held her skirt down with her free hand and wrestled her other arm free. She grabbed at his neck and squeezed hard on his wind-pipe; he choked and grabbed her wrist again. Bringing up her other arm, she twisted round and jammed her elbow into his neck, then pulled up a knee under his body. Shoving as hard as she could, she pushed him off and he crashed to the side. She rolled the other way and came up to her knees.

'Leave her.' Styvan's voice seemed unnaturally loud though he had not shouted. He loomed out of the dark and her attacker pulled back. 'She has more value whole. Get back to your bed.' The man took a wide circle around Styvan before heading back to the camp. 'And you.'

Elona climbed to her feet, brushing the stones and dirt from her dress. Hugging her bruised arm, she walked back to the cart. She lay down and pulled the blanket round herself, seeing the bright points of Pitra's eyes staring at her. She shivered and turned her back to him.

On the seventh day, they left the path the traders had used that descended to the right into the forest-filled plain. They turned south-east and upwards. The mountains ahead were clear and bleak, their snow-capped tips shining bright in the sunshine of late autumn when their heads were not thrust into the clouds. In the evening, *sikechesa* wheeled about their sides and along the mountain spur. Pitra grumbled about how they were late and would not make the bridge before the snow.

On an overcast evening a five-day later, the threatening grey clouds hung almost to the ground, making an oppressive roof, and the dew had frosted the ground with white before dark fell. The day's hunters caught up with them, carrying only a few animals and without the usual cheers and whooping that accompanied their return. The group's leader rode directly to Styvan and dismounted with only the slightest courtesy of a bow.

'We are pursued, Styvan.'

'How many?'

'More than five.'

'How far?'

'Half a day, they are a-horseback.'

'Armsmen.'

Styvan looked round at the *kichesa* huddled together near the fire, with hides thrown over their backs to keep the worst of the cold from them. Then he brought his eyes to rest on Elona as she stood by Pitra's cart. In the trader dialect he said:

'So, you do have value, almost I did not believe it.' His ravaged face smiled grimly. 'But the timing of this is not good.' He turned back to his men and switched dialects. 'There is nothing to be done this night. We will light the fires as usual in case their scouts spy on us also. Let them think we have not seen them. On the morrow you will spy them out, find their numbers and their armament. We will move quickly to the bridge and lay an ambush. Do not hunt, we will have their horses and their stores as recompense.'

Elona approached the hunters' *kichesa* and untied the dead animals from them, then returned to the small fire by Pitra's wagon. She sat cross-legged on a pile of hides to protect herself from the cold ground and skinned the already freezing bodies. At the back of her mind the itch of fear rose; armsmen were coming to return her to her living death.

Elona hardly noticed when the high-pitched keening began. But when she became aware of it three of the *kichesa* were already calling in a strange whine she had never heard before. Pitra looked up from where he huddled in his sleeping bag by the fire and coughed in the cold air.

'Too late, they are too cold.' He muttered. 'Never supposed to be this cold, won't last the night.' He tailed off into more muttering interspersed with fits of hacking. The piercing keening from the *kichesa* went on for a long time before Elona slipped into sleep.

~

Their mounts had not died in the night, but they were difficult to get moving in the morning. They could barely manage the pace Styvan demanded, yet as they travelled the animals seemed to move more easily. Pitra complained incessantly as the cart crashed along the rocky path in a long climb towards the high ridge of the mountain spur. Elona was tossed from side to side and had to kneel up. She gripped the rail of the cart tightly as she willed the *kichesa*-team to pull harder and faster; she almost felt they responded to her command. The morning passed through to midday and the temperature dropped. Elona's hands were blue and she could scarcely feel her feet. The clouds threatened snow.

The carts passed over the highest point of a ridge. After a short pull down the other side they came out onto a wide stone road running along the contour of the bleak land. Each of the great stones that flagged the way measured three paces in each direction and was ridged with the passage of countless wheels. The grass and bushes that grew between the cracks showed it had been a long time since it had been in regular use, yet it afforded easier travel and they picked up speed.

Styvan shouted orders and the mounted bandits moved off at a faster rate, leaving the carts with two escorts. It was mid-afternoon when the scouts who had been left behind overtook them, their *kichesa* flying along the road. One of them shouted as he passed, 'Armsmen of Dirdin!'

A horror spread through Elona. They were coming for her. They would take her back to Faerholme, a prisoner – they must escape.

The afternoon was dying and the road they travelled turned sharply to the right. Elona gasped as the land fell away before them. Ahead, at a distance she could not judge, rose a sheer wall of rock, but between the wall and her there was nothing. The road dived downwards and vanished into an abyss. Elona cried out in fear as the cart rumbled towards the precipice, Pitra suddenly pulling on the left rein and turning the cart right again. Elona's head swam as she looked down into a green river valley far below, and the cart clattered along barely an arms-length from the edge.

Elona slammed her eyes shut and ducked down in the cart. She buried herself among the barrels, but the image of the precipitous drop hung before her minds-eye and she felt she was falling.

There was a shout from behind and she heard Pitra call out. 'They come.'

Elona did not understand, and she opened her eyes Pitra was staring behind; Elona felt a wild impulse to shout at him to watch where they were going. Gripping tightly to the cart, she twisted her head around. Behind and to the side was one of their escorts keeping pace, but past him she could see moving spots on the road. They were here.

Elona turned to look ahead, peeping over the driving board to hide the sight of the cliff edge. Beyond the leading cart the road lay like a winding ribbon, sloping down slightly. Pitra coughed and said, 'Won't make the bridge.'

Staring into the distance, Elona could make out where the ribbon ahead twisted to the right and crossed the void in a massive grey span. Pitra lashed the *kichesa* and they pushed forward.

The barrels and frozen meat thumped back and forth as the speed of the cart increased. The mute thundering of *kichesa* claws and the clatter of iron-shod wheels on the stone took another tone. Ahead of them the other cart was slowly moving away from them. Elona looked behind and was shocked to see how much closer the pursuing horses were already. The dull light glinted on armour and she thought she could hear the riders shouting.

She looked ahead again. The road bent sharply to the left and she watched as the two right wheels of the leading cart ahead of them slowly rose into the air. The cart lurched suddenly and spun into the air, her stomach turned to lead as she watched in horror as the driver flew off into empty space, the cart careening over the edge and pulling the screaming team into the abyss. The terrified cry of the driver came to their ears. Elona closed her eyes and felt her cart swing round, but it did not follow the other into oblivion. Their pursuers disappeared from sight. Pitra had stopped complaining; she looked up to see him fixated on the road ahead and his hands tightly gripping the reins. Periodically he shook them, urging the team on, but they were *kichesa* and could not run long at full stride. Horses had more speed but less endurance; they were less affected by the cold yet their thin legs could not gallop on the stone flags of the road. There were too many risks.

The road ran straight for a distance and, sooner than she expected, the armsmen came in sight. The thundering of hooves floated down the wind to her, mingling with the crashing of the cart. A humming whistle broke the air and an arrow pierced the wood to her left. Already they tried to carry out the execution; they would not rest until she was dead.

She loosened one hand from the edge of the cart and grabbed the skinning knife that hung in its sheath. She looped its thong over her head and hung it at her breast beneath the remains of the dress she wore. A jolt of the cart pulled her other hand free and sent her flying backwards. Her cheek scraped painfully against the side of the cart. She grabbed hold again and pulled herself hand over hand along the racing cart, and as she did another arrow whistled by though she did not see where it went.

There was a cry from behind; she spun her head around to see an arrow sprouting from the back of their escort. Yet he hung on, urging his mount forward as blood soaked his shirt. The cart swung again, hiding them from the hunters for a short time. Elona looked ahead, see that the bridge was closer; perhaps they would make it. The thunder of iron horseshoes filled the air and Elona turned to watch the armsmen pour like a wave around the curve in the road. She could hear their shouts clearly now.

They needed to go faster but Pitra was holding the *kichesa* back, not giving them full rein. She looked up at him. He still stared fixedly ahead, grim hands holding the reins, then she saw the thin stream of red that leaked from the corner of his mouth. There was an arrow in his back. The *kichesa*-team was slowing.

23

Elona jumped up, nearly losing her footing in the bouncing cart; she stumbled to the front, climbed on to the driving bench and screamed at the *kichesa*. The sudden noise scared them into a burst of speed and she was pushed back on to the seat. She grabbed at the reins and pulled them from Pitra's dead hands. He held on for a moment and then yielded, his body falling towards her. In sudden revulsion, she heaved and pushed him from the cart.

She shouted and lashed with the reins and the *kichesa* leapt forwards. Elona tucked her legs under the seat and gave the team its head, screaming and shouting at them to make them go faster. She reached under the seat, found Pitra's drinking horn, and threw it as hard as she could at the left *kichek*.

From behind she could hear the armsmen shouting for her to stop but she lashed the reins harder. The cart streamed round a right-hand bend almost out of control, and the rocky ground seemed to slide towards her as the two frantic *kichesa* pulled her round.

She could see the bridge ahead, its huge stones making a massive arch across the gulf; on the far side she could see figures.

Almost in slow motion they took a left-hand bend, and she felt the wheels lifting from the ground and suspending her above the cliff. A wave of terror slammed through her as the moment passed and the cart's wheels crashed down again. Twin terrors fought within her, too slow to be caught or too fast and be cast into the abyss. The road went straight for a way so she let the *kichesa* run. Then a corner loomed, nearly the last before the bridge; she felt exultant, she would make it.

An arrow whizzed past on her left, close to the *kichek*—they were trying to bring down the team. She reined in slightly and the cart took the corner comfortably on all four wheels. She saw her escort riding past a second arrow protruding from his leg, his face confused as she urged the team faster again.

He jerked his head back and Elona threw a glance over her shoulder. The armsmen had not gained anymore; their horses had to be tiring, Elona laughed out loud as they took a left-hand bend; she could see the bridge clearly, and it seemed to grow out of the cliff-face on each side to meet high in the middle. Now closer she could see the road widened on the approach and two lanes split off on either side. The bridge had two levels: the road flowed straight onto the upper arch while the two outside lanes curved round and down to the lower span.

The curvature of another bend hid the bridge for a moment, then she whipped up the *kichesa* again and they picked up speed. Another curve grew from nowhere, and in shock Elona heaved on the right rein, sharply pulling the team round. The right wheels lifted and the cart hung precariously before spinning over. She catapulted from the seat and crashed into the rock face, knocking the wind from her lungs. Her ears were filled with the splintering of wood and the screaming of the *kichesa*. She heaved her lungs trying to draw breath while pains shot through her arms and legs.

Suddenly a hand grabbed her arm, and she fought to pull away. 'Come,' said a voice in the trader tongue. She saw the remaining escort trying to pull her up. She took his hand as an arrow pierced his chest, then watched as his eyes unfocused and his body slumping. Reaching up, she dragged him from the saddle and climbed in.

The clattering of hooves filled the rocky valley and her pursuers came in sight.

Elona grabbed the reins and jammed her heels into the panting beast as it jumped into a run, almost unseating Elona as it leapt the remains of the cart. The poor creatures scrabbled to free themselves from the wreckage. She kicked and kicked the tired mount, shouting into its ear. It ran on to the bridge and Elona closed her eyes to hide the appalling view of no parapets guarding the fall on either side. The animal pounded away underneath her, and she could feel its muscles working at each stride, carrying her closer to safety. She heard the bandit leader's shout and a flight of arrows flew above her head; cries of pain came from behind.

She knew from the shouts in front that she had reached the other side. She opened her eyes and Styvan stood before her as she reined in her mount. He stared up at her, his twisted face almost hiding the suspicion and confusion that she knew must be there. He gave her an arm to let herself down. An arrow hummed over and he pushed her behind a boulder.

'Stay there,' he ordered, before stalking back to the bridge.

A light touch fell on her arm and she snapped her head to look—snow was falling. Despite the cold the excitement kept her warm. She cautiously peered out from behind the rock and watched as the armsmen carefully made their way across the upper bridge, using the pillars for cover. The opponents exchanged volleys of arrows without success. The snow continued to fall, increasing in intensity, the far side of the bridge becoming invisible in the greyness. Elona saw the figure of Styvan, moving from man to man, encouraging them.

He came back up to the boulder. 'Go to my horse, yonder, wait for me.' He nodded further up the road. Elona stared out towards the bridge; the nearside was disappearing in the swirl of snow, covering the ground with its crisp whiteness. She stood and made her way carefully uphill, unsure of the exact location of the horse and *kichesa*. Moments later she heard the keening of the cold creatures and headed for them, even so she almost bumped into the bandit holding the mounts.

'How goes it?' he grunted above the high-pitched whine of the animals. She chose not answer and instead went to Styvan's piebald mount and held herself against its body. She could feel its warmth flow into her when a cold dagger pressed hard against her breast. The guard shifted to the trader tongue. 'It goes well, hey?'

'I am but a woman, I cannot tell. I live, I am content.'

'Cold, hey?' he asked, his gaze running from head to toe. She remained silent. 'Share my cloak, hey?' Elona moved round to the other side of the horse's neck, away from the man's lecherous glances. The snow fell in great white clumps that covered everything that stayed motionless while the *kichesa* trilled their pain.

'Share my cloak,' he grunted, his request becoming an order as he stepped up and looked down at her from the other side of the horse's neck.

'Styvan comes. I'm worth more whole.' She held her ground, held the horse's neck. The dark-faced guard looked like Krazak. She saw his face again, leering over her, tearing at her clothes.

He turned away. 'Aye. Styvan,' he muttered. The keening of one of the *kichesa* suddenly changed into a gurgling and it fell silent. Elona and the guard turned to look at the creatures through the dim light. The animal's back legs crumpled and it fell heavily forward. Its breath gusted as it hit the ground and the gurgling was replaced by uneven breathing. The guard stepped over to the dying creature and drew his dagger. Kneeling by its head he hacked at its throat. Blood spurted and the breathing changed to a bubbling, then ceased altogether. The man pulled his drinking horn from his belt and placed it under the neck of the animal to catch the blood that flowed from it. She watched him sit back on his haunches and drink, spilling the thickening red liquid down his cheek. He refilled the horn and stood, offering it to her. 'Good, make you strong like a *kichek*. Drink, hey?

Elona looked down at the dead beast and at the man offering the cup; she was hungry. She took the horn from his hands. It was sticky with blood. The guard licked his fingers, grinning at her. 'Drink.' Dropping the horse's bridle she held the horn in both hands. She pressed the horn to her lips; the blood smelled foul. Abruptly she tipped it back and allowed the liquid to flow down her throat, trying not to taste or smell it as it slipped down into her empty stomach; there it lay slowly, spreading through her body in a lethargy of warmth and cold.

'Taste good, hey?' He said, grinning all the more. He stepped closer put his arms around her, pinning her arms between their bodies, the horn fell spilling *kichek* blood over them both. He shoved his hand between her legs. 'Feel good, hey?'

She struggled, pushing against his chest, and felt the dagger she had hidden. They overbalanced and fell beneath the horse, and in an effort to save himself he released her and she rolled away. Facing away from him, she pulled out the knife; the handle was slick in her blood-covered hands. She heard him cursing behind and getting to his feet. She listened to his feet crunching through the brittle snow. Suddenly she turned and stabbed wildly with the knife. It struck him in the thigh and he threw himself back, clutching at his leg.

'Bitch. You bitch. You bitch.' He repeated the words over and over as wet blood mingled with the congealing *kichesa* blood on his trousers. 'I'll kill you.'

'You won't.' Styvan's voice was there and his bulk loomed over her, but faced the guard. 'Get down to the bridge. They're crossing over, you're needed.'

The guard stood defiant for a moment, then seemed to deflate. He turned and hobbled downhill, swallowed up in the snow. Turning on Elona he plucked the blade from her hands and tucked it inside his jacket.

'Come. We're leaving.' He gathered up the horse's reins and mounted, reaching down and grabbing Elona by the forearm to pull her up behind him. 'Hold on to me. You may try to kill me but if you succeed, you'll die in the snow. Do not become any more problem than your value, you have already cost me much.'

With that he turned the horse up the road. The sounds of battle began behind them, mingled with the dying gurgles of the *kichesa*. They rode into the snow and the darkness.

24

———

The darkness of the night enclosed them. Elona wondered how Styvan dared let the horse walk through the black and freezing night with the threat of the abyss so near. Abruptly he reined in their mount.

'Off,' he ordered. She slipped to the floor, her feet skidding on the snow-covered stones. Styvan dismounted and searched through his saddle bags, finally pulling out a lantern. He set it on the ground and clicked his tinderbox under the protection of his hood.

Elona wrapped her arms about her shoulders and shivered; freezing rivulets of melted water soaked through her clothing and ran down her back; her hair hung in drenched locks around her face.

'I'm cold,' she said as the warm lantern light silhouetted him against the white ground. Styvan stood and hung the lantern from the saddle; it showed the way ahead for barely an arms-length. He turned to face her, his face hidden in the shadows of his hood. Then he shook his head and went to the saddle-bags again. This time he took out a blanket and threw it at her; it struck her in her middle and fell to the floor before she had a chance to grab it. She picked it up and pulled it around her shoulders and head, grateful for the slight respite it gave her against the weather. They remounted and the warmth of the horse penetrated the damp cold of her thighs.

'There is a cave not far,' he said as he urged the horse into a slow walk. The horse's hooves plodded silently on the carpet of snow. The snowfall lightened and the huge flakes gave way to tiny specks. The lantern's light stretching further, Elona looked to her left and saw the distorted shadow of the horse leading to the edge of the road and an impenetrable void. She shuddered at the thought. She turned to the right and stared at the snow-softened edges of boulders and stones reaching to the cliff that rose a short distance away. It was craggy and deeply gouged as if a giant had ripped away the surface of the land, leaving the cliff behind.

The rhythmic plodding of the horse and the whiteness of the terrain was hypnotic; Elona's head slowly moved forward until it rested against the rough jerkin of her captor, and she stared at the passing rocks.

'Get down,' he said roughly, jerking backwards and nearly toppling her from the horse. She clutched at him as she felt herself fall, waking from her dreamlike state. The night was still dark and the snow had stopped.

'Get down,' he said again, prying her fingers from his arm. Stiffly she dismounted, collapsing to the ground; she couldn't feel her legs. She sat and rubbed them, trying to restore their circulation. Styvan lightly dropped from the saddle and his boots crunched into the frosted snow. He reached under the horse to unbuckle the girth strap and pulled the saddle to the ground.

'Give me the blanket,' he ordered. Elona looked up at him in incomprehension . He tutted, stepping forward and ripping the blanket from around her shoulders, tumbling her headfirst into the snow. As she recovered, she saw him adjusting the blanket on the horse's back. Her legs were beginning to tingle.

'Get the lantern, follow me.'

He led the way off the road and toward the cliff-face along a barely visible track. Elona climbed awkwardly to her feet, her legs and feet filled with pricking that increased with every passing moment. She whimpered slightly with the pain, and was rewarded with a snarl from Styvan. She stumbled across to the lantern, burning her hand on the glass. As they passed behind some bushes they came to a small stream bubbling from a cave entrance. He took the lamp from her and examined the ground outside the entrance.

'No wolves, good. Too cold for *tikak* up here now.' He straightened and turned. 'You go in first. I'll wait here.' His face twisted into a distorted grin in the lantern's light. 'If you see anything, scream.'

Elona stared at him in disbelief. She shook her head slowly. His hand moved and held a long dagger. 'You go in, stand near the door.'

She swallowed and cast her gaze to the ground, then shuffled across to the cave mouth. 'Give me the lantern,' he ordered as she passed him. She handed it over and walked awkwardly to the dark entrance, splashing in the freezing water. The blackness engulfed her; she knew he couldn't see her anymore and the feeling of freedom washed through her. She breathed deeply and the air smelled clean. She could hear the water splashing behind her, and before her was a deeper pounding of water pouring without end. She took another step forward and her foot struck a loose stone, hearing it skitter across the ground and give a deep-throated splash.

'Nothing's here,' she said, her voice thin in the darkness, echoing through the unknown space. Styvan did not reply but Elona heard the splashing of hooves in the brook and the light from the lantern threw jittering shadows across the walls. She looked about. The cave was high with a domed ceiling, and the almost circular walls were scored with deep horizontal cuts. By her feet, covering most of the cave, was a pool of dark water. Far off on the other side she could see the tunnel from which a stream of water poured.

'When the snows melt in spring this place is filled with water. But it is safe for now.' Styvan led the horse into the damp cave. 'Go outside and find some wood.'

'None'll be dry.'

'Don't talk back to me,' he barked, turning on her. She stared defiantly into his eyes for a moment, then looked away. She gathered up the horse blanket, pulled it around her shoulders, and stepped out through the narrow opening.

The fire blazed fitfully, cracking and spitting loudly as the damp wood hissed and steamed, but its warmth was welcome. They sat on opposite sides, the flickering light making the shadows on Styvan's face even deeper. He did not prepare any food.

'You didn't escape,' Styvan said into the flames. 'At the bridge.'

Elona placed a damp branch next to the fire to dry and did not look at him.

'You took the reins of the cart; you rode the *kichek*. You were running from them, same as us.'

Elona huddled beneath her blanket. The weather beyond the cave mouth had turned to drizzle, and the snow had become patchy before she had returned with the wood.

'You are of noble birth. I hear it in your words. But you flee your rescuers. Why?'

Elona sighed. 'They would tie me in a loveless marriage with an old man.'

Styvan reached across the flames and slapped her across the face, knocking her to the floor.

'Don't lie to me,' he growled. 'That may do for simple traders. To be in that life would be a blessing compared to this.'

Elona pushed herself up, and held her hand against her stinging cheek. 'They sold me to you.'

'You gave yourself willingly!' She ducked to avoid another blow but his hands snaked out across the fire and grabbed the blanket. He pulled her towards him, suspending her above the flames. 'You will tell me the truth.'

Elona could smell the dangling strands of her hair burning. The blanket steamed in the heat and she closed her eyes, feeling the heat against her eyelids. She shook her head.

'You will or I will burn you.' She hung helpless from his hands, her hair crackling and her face burning in the heat; she could not breathe. She nodded her head violently. He pushed her back. She pulled in a breath of cold air and coughed.

'Tell me.'

'I ... killed people.' Though she said it, it seemed unreal, as if it had been another person. Styvan laughed and his voice echoed around the chamber. For a long time he laughed. Then he stood and went to the entrance, staring out for a long time.

'I will take a price out of those traders if ever I should find them again,' he mused. 'I should be more careful.' He gave another short laugh and turned toward her. 'So, you have a price on your head. I wonder if it is as much as mine. I doubt it. Is it worth redeeming your value? I doubt that too. How many did you kill?'

'Three—by my hand or because of me.' Tears welled in her eyes as she thought of Savi; not a demon, it had been Savi.

'Noble, guild or commoner?'

'Commoners. I stabbed a guildsman, but I didn't kill him.' She thought of Bejeren, her emotion a mix of hate and remorse.

'I am unimpressed.'

'There was treachery, I had to do it.'

'It matters not to me. You have no value, only your body. I will keep you for now, but cause me further trouble and I will kill you.' He gathered up his sleeping sack and spread it out. 'Prepare the fire for the night.'

Elona shivered as she gathered large stones from the floor of the cave. She squatted before the fire and built up the rocks one at a time around it, feeling the heat on her breasts and face. She heard his boots scrape on the stone directly behind her and clutched the blanket closer around her neck. His hands fell on her shoulders, pulling the blanket from them. He gripped her upper arms; she felt a warm, damp breath at her ear; and she stiffened involuntarily as his lips touched her neck. She lifted her head sharply as teeth nipped her skin.

She dropped to her knees, the heat from the fire's embers scorching her dress. Awkwardly she turned to her left and his mouth moved round her neck, his left hand sliding from her shoulder and cupping her breast. The sharp bristles of his face scratched along her cheek and she could not suppress a whimper as he bit her neck again. She heard him grunt in reply as if he imagined she welcomed him.

She turned further, his left hand slithering across the top of her dress as she felt its cold hardness on the skin of her right breast. His right hand held her left shoulder, and she choked again. Her left arm snaked up under his arm and came to rest at his neck. She felt him pull away a little, pulling her up with him, feeling his breath on her face. She hefted a rock in her right hand, feeling its weight, then smashed it with all the force she could muster into his left temple.

The weight of his body slumped forward. It pushed her towards the fire, then slipped sideways to the floor. His trapped left hand dragged her down as he went, and in a panic she scrambled backwards and stood up, still holding the rock and ready to strike again. But he did not move. He did not breathe. She smelled burning flesh and saw his right hand resting in the embers, blackening.

She let the rock drop to the floor and pulled his hand from the heat.

'Four,' she muttered. 'Perhaps I could claim the bounty on your head.'

She rolled him awkwardly away from the fire and his dead eyes stared accusingly at the wall. She closed them. A wave of exhaustion flooded through her; she was free at last. Alone and free. She dragged herself to his sleeping sack, climbed inside, and slept.

25

The vaulted ceiling of the cave glittered with reflected sunlight, and the crisp air was filled with the unceasing echo of cascading water. The horse stood by expectantly and Styvan's body lay rigid by the fire's remains. She investigated the saddle bags and found plenty of strips of dry, salted meat. She chewed on a piece as she tried to make some plans.

There were two possibilities: Jalka had won or the bandits had. Either way she needed to get away as soon as possible. Perhaps her pursuers would not be able to track the route that Styvan had taken last night, but it was not a chance she could take. She knew Styvan had stayed on the stone road, which made the chance of being followed more likely. She made her way to the exit and peered out.

The snow had melted away to rivulets that ran through mud and grass to join the stream that flowed from the cave. The sky was clear except for a few clouds scudding across it. She couldn't see any betraying foot or hoof marks in the ground beyond the cave entrance. About twenty paces away she could see the stone slabs of the Slissac road. Keeping to the splashing brook, she crept further out. Beyond the road was the drop-off and she could see the sheer cliff on the other side of the chasm climbing upwards.

Then she heard it, the clopping of horse hooves on stone. Jalka had won. He would try to take her back, return her to the poison of Faerholme. She shivered in sudden fear, turning and creeping away as fast she dared along the stream, back into the cave. She stood in the centre, panic filling her mind. What could she do? What should she do? There was no time to escape on the horse; no way to escape on foot, as she could not climb up the cliff or down into the ravine. Her eyes came to rest on the tunnel from which the water poured into the pool.

It was large enough for her to crawl into and low enough that she could get into it from the pool. Even if they came into the cave they could not know which way she had gone. If the tunnel did not lead far, she would wait until they had gone and come out. Otherwise she could follow it as far as it would go.

She grabbed a saddle bag and stuffed it with what it would take: the food, Styvan's knife, and his tinderbox. Buckling it up, she threw it into the tunnel mouth. It disappeared into the blackness and she heard it splash. She followed. The pool was deeper than it looked and her foot did not touch bottom; she fell forward into the freezing water. Her clothes tried to pull her down but she thrust hard towards the other side. She grabbed the rock with the numbingly cold water pouring on her. She pulled again and managed to get both arms on to the rounded lip of the tunnel.

Glancing back she saw shadows moving at the cave entrance. Desperately, she pushed up with her elbows and landed with her upper body in the tunnel. She rested for a moment with her legs dangling in the rush of water, managing to get her left leg over the edge and putting her weight down on it. She pulled up her other leg and crawled forward into the darkness.

Moments later, above the constant roar that echoed through the passage, she heard a man's shout behind. She clambered further in, bumped into the bag and lifted it from the water, praying to Taymar the contents weren't completely soaked. She crawled deeper and the tunnel twisted to the right, blocking the view of its mouth. She turned and sat down in the rushing water. Reflections of sunlight played on the wall and water at the turn but nothing more could be seen or heard.

She turned round again and looked into the dark upstream. She had to go on. She slung the bag across her back and crawled forward on the slippery stone into the darkness—her ears numbed by the constant thunder, her legs and hands like ice.

~

She had been travelling for a long time, and the skin of her hands had become soft from the cold water when the pounding roar suddenly seemed to fade. Abruptly her hand went into deep water; she overbalanced and plunged forwards. She broke the surface, gasping for breath with the tips of her toes pressed against the stone floor of the bottom, her coarse breathing echoing round a chamber. Cautiously, she explored with one toe and found a place where the water became shallower; carefully she tiptoed that way, paddling with her arms. Her fingers grazed a rock wall and she grabbed at the rough surface, pulling herself against it. As she made progress she brushed against twigs and small branches drifting back the way she had come in the current.

She judged that she was halfway round the chamber wall when it curved away, and she found herself standing on a perfectly flat stone. She took another pace and found her foot resting on a higher surface. A step. She tried for another and found it, and again. She climbed from the water and stood unsteadily on a platform of smooth rock in pitch blackness; water dripped from her sodden clothes and hair.

Reaching out with her arms, she took cautious steps forwards until her fingers grazed a stone wall. She traced intersecting straight lines carved into its surface and brushed over patches of thick moss. Where her fingers ran across the moss they left a faint trail of bluish-white light. She found a larger patch of moss, and when she pulled her hand back there was the shining imprint of her hand. Its light illuminated the surface around it. She was able to see the faint outline of her hands in the darkness, as well as the mist of her breath.

A shiver of cold ran through her. She unslung the bag and

dropped it to the ground. Feeling for the ties, she opened it and pulled out the sodden blanket. She wrung it out as best she could, the water splashing on to the stones beneath her feet, and wrapped it around her shoulders. It was not much of an improvement.

She looked back at the wall; the finger streaks and her palm print still glowed gently, though perhaps a little more dimly. She sat on the stone floor and felt across the wall, feeling were more patches of moss. She pressed both hands onto the moss, releasing again and again, steadily increasing the illumination until she could see the bag and the floor for some distance around. She turned and sat with her back pressed against the mossy wall, and she waited while the light behind her grew and she could see to each side. Finally, she moved aside and the whole cavern lit up.

She was on a smooth-cut ledge with steps that led down into the water. The ledge came to a dead end against the cavern wall to her left and, in the other direction, curved around the pool to disappear into the wall as a dark passage. Along the edge stood low arches supporting a higher, parapeted gallery still shrouded in darkness. The walls and arches were decorated with geometric patterns covered with the moss clinging the edges of the shapes and dangling in damp, disorganised clumps.

Elona pulled the tinderbox from the bag; the tinder itself was soaked. She pulled it from the box and spread it out near the wall. She ripped some moss from the wall and placed a pinch of it into the tinderbox, then snapped the flint. After a few attempts she gave up, the sparks fizzling on the damp plants. Elona sighed; she would have preferred the warmth of a fire but the light would do for now. At least the food was edible, the water clean and fresh.

When she had eaten she sat with her back against the wall and stared into the water, shivering in the cold, waiting to dry.

~

She did not know how long she had dozed but the light of the walls where she had placed her palms had dimmed to nothing. She rolled stiffly onto her hands and knees, her cold muscles complaining, and the cavern was lit even more brightly from the moss she had being lying against.

The far side of the pool was twenty paces distant and around the walls were metal loops at intervals just above the surface of the water. The wall opposite the tunnel where she had entered was rough and natural, save for a tall door-like section in the middle that descended into the water. One of the loops near the door had a rope tied to it, which descended into the water. There, distorted by the angle, was the skeletal shape of a sunken boat.

She stood and moved to let the light flood up the passage. Within ten paces there were more stairs heading up into the gloom. The gallery followed the passageway into the rock, and along both sides of the passage was a stone shelf from which hung the moss.

The blanket and her clothes were now reduced to a simple dampness which clung to her awkwardly as she crouched down to examine the rest of her equipment. The tinder was still damp to the touch; she doubted anything would be able to dry down here. She took another two mouthfuls of food then looked around at the moss on the wall, still glowing brightly, and at the surface of the water where the occasional twig and branch floated past.

She ripped a glowing section of moss from the wall and wrapped it around the biggest branch she could find, then used the knife to cut the bottom of her dress into strips and bound the moss to the branch. She pulled large wads of dark moss from the walls and pushed them inside her dress close to her skin. She packed up her gear and hung the bag over her shoulder and walked briskly to the bottom of the steps.

She climbed a short flight of worn steps that turned to the right and opened through an arch into a long narrow cavern, a dark wide channel chiselling from the rock to her left. The walls were smooth save for the detailed lines of patterns that ran around it in strips and the ledge of dangling moss. She stepped into the room; her feet slapped on the stone and echoed above the sound of splashing water. She approached the channel and got down on her hands and knees to peer over the edge. Below was another river of water, the echoing sound of water coming from more stone doors set in the channel further ahead where water cascaded through. From where she looked over the edge, a ladder reached down into the water below.

She crawled back from the edge and stood. Above her the second gallery level continued, and at the far end of the chamber a set of stairs joined the two floors. She walked to it and climbed quickly, not looking back into the deep channel. This level was also carved in patterns, and hung with damp clumps of moss. The floor was covered with some dark material. She went down on one knee and brought the light closer. The damp remains of rugs covered the floor, laid end to end along the gallery. Though everything seemed to have taken on an almost uniform brown colour, she could make out the same geometric patterns as covered the walls.

She sat down at the top of the stairs, leaned against the pillar for comfort, and chewed on a dry strip of dried meat. The light from the moss was dimming, so she replaced it and put the darkening material by her skin. She started up the wide steps.

The new tunnel was decorated like the rest and the floor covered with mouldering rugs. She kept to the sides and brushed her hand along the wall. The steps were broad and she took them two paces at a time . The climbing tunnel curved slowly to the right; she had gone through almost a complete turn. A yawning void opened up in front, for the ceiling had collapsed and taken the floor away into the lower tunnel. Beyond the gap the passageway split, and the left tunnel went straight and flat while the one to the right continued to climb.

She crawled to the edge and looked over. A short distance below lay the remains of the passage roof, lying in the lower tunnel that also split as hers did. She crawled to the right side of the passage, the remains of the stone floor providing a narrow ledge. She threw her torch to the far side, gripped the edge of the moss furrow with both hands, and, with her face to the cold, patterned stones, edged slowly round the hole. She tried not to imagine the black fall behind her as waves of vertigo made her stomach churn.

She sat heavily on the other side and cradled the torch in her arms for a long time.

Finally, she pulled herself together and continued along the climbing tunnel. She tripped on a chunk of rock lying on the steps; there were small ones at first then, larger ones, not to mention more of them than the former. The footing became difficult until she had to clamber over them, occasionally dislodging a large rock that went tumbling and crashing down the way she had come until, at last, she looked up in dismay, her way completely blocked by collapsed stone. Here and there she could see green moss and stunted blades of grass, and the droppings of some small animal.

Elona sat down and stared around in tired disappointment. She had hoped to come out somewhere far away from her pursuers; now it looked as if she would have to return the way she had come and hope that they had searched and gone on. But they would have taken the horse, and the prospect of those heights and cliffs was not attractive. If it must be she would do it, but she would rest here a while longer to give them more time to go on. Twisting herself among the rocks to get comfortable, with the bag under her head and the horse blanket over her, she slept.

A glow of white light shone on her eyelids as she returned to wakefulness. Her whole body was stiff from being held motionless by the enclosing rocks. She opened her eyes, then squeezed them shut against the brilliant light that poured through a gap in the boulders piled above her.

There was an opening. Carefully she stretched her arms and legs and climbed up a little way, looking at the gap. It seemed very small. She gathered the now darkened moss from the branch into the bag and climbed. The rocks here were jammed solidly together, cemented by countless seasons of wind-blown soil and rain. She pushed the bag before her, then pulled with her hands and pushed with her toes, her body barely able to bend in the tiny gap. She could smell the open air and wet grass; a small animal leapt away from her, up and out. The walls of the tunnel pressed in on her as she pushed harder. Above her the bag suddenly fell away from her fingers as it escaped into the outside. She pushed again, squeezing through, the rocks scraping at her flesh.

Finally, her hands were free and she could flap them in the

breeze, a crazy image of herself as a flower rushing through her mind. She could only push with her feet now. The rock beneath her left foot gave way, giving her a sudden wave of vertigo as she lost her footing. It lodged beneath both feet and she was able to use it to force herself another hands-breadth upwards and out. At last her arms were free enough to add leverage, and she pressed them down and out, not caring how the sharp-edged stones cut into them.

The top of her head came free; she pressed down with her elbows and moved up again. A plain of stones and boulders came into view in the white light. She twisted one shoulder up and pressed with her toes once more. The rocks below shifted again and she felt them tighten against her waist as she got one arm completely free. She pushed again and cried out as her dress tore and the rocks bit viciously into her hips. But her other shoulder was free, and with a final thrust the rest of her body followed. She sat on the edge of the hole, rubbing at the cuts and scrapes on her arms and legs.

26

A white mist hung in the air, making it cold and damp, but she knew from the brightness that the sun must be high. She was sitting at one side of a heap of rubble, fallen pillars and walls; in the mist the more distant objects were shadows. To her right and behind two walls still stood, in some places reaching into the mist and in others broken on the floor.

Between the fallen stones she could see a flagged floor, covered in the same intricate designs that adorned the walls below. She pulled her legs from the hole and rested them on the edge opposite, examining the damage. Her dress was torn at the hip and beneath it the skin was lacerated and bleeding. Using the remnants of the hem she dabbed at the cuts, when suddenly the back of her head tingled and the wounds seemed to burn. As she watched, the bleeding cuts closed and sealed as if they had never been.

Elona stared at the place that had healed, the heat dissipated and the tingling vanished. She ran her fingers across it, pressing gently and then harder. Not even a bruise. A wave of panic ran through her as she saw light pouring from the cracks in her bag. She felt warmth inside her dress, pulled it open, and was almost blinded by the brilliant glow of the moss within. She pulled it out, and shining like gems in sunlight was a cold, blue-white light. She had somehow thought the moss responded to the warmth of her skin, but that wasn't it at all: it glowed from magic.

Healer's magic.

She sat and thought as a thousand tiny incidents suddenly made sense: a thousand bruises and cuts that had lasted less than a day. She was a healer, as Mother had been. She smiled at the thought, as it gave her a closeness she had not felt for a long time with the woman who lay in Faerholme. Yet with the thought of her home, the horror of it flooded back—but it did not linger.

The malevolent presence that haunted those memories faded away even as it came to mind. She knew how she had felt then, yet could no longer feel it. Ever since her escape she had found it harder and harder to feel the horror and the hate; and now it was all gone.

The sting of her other injuries called her back from her reverie. If she were truly a healer she should be able to do something about it, but what pattern should she make? She was not trained; all magic had to be done with the proper preparations, patterns and conjurations. If she did not know them how could she do it? Yet she had already, and she had used something before, with Yolandra; could she recapture it?

She had been drunk then; it should be safer when she was sober. Looking around, she saw an opening among some fallen rocks, not deep enough to be darkened but sufficient to hide from casual observation. She gathered up her bag and stumbled across the stone-strewn floor. Carefully, she lay down in the space with the bag under her head and closed her eyes. She recalled the flow of light she had felt with Yolandra, once more conjuring it in her mind's eye and sensing it at a great distance, like a tiny light.

Yet around her a similar light burned strong. This fallen building enclosed a ley-circle, not one of the earth-wrenching great circles yet it was there and she could use it, unlike before when the light had flowed to her in a stream. Now it was as if she bathed in it. She let it pour over and through her, a deluge of light; she was aware of her body, every part of skin coming into sharp relief; she could sense all of it in every instant. Her whole being tingled and she could feel the healing power surge through her.

With the energy of the circle she looked outwards. The rock and stone buildings were grey shadows, but plants and little animals glowed with their own patterned light. She could look for her enemies, her pursuers. She thought of Jalka and instantly she knew where he was—not far, not far enough. A bright group of living lights unaware of her, and yet ... she drew back as the light that was Jalka brightened as if it recognised her.

Mother, she must find Mother. She cried out in the blackness, how could she? She did not know her, the body an empty shell. She looked back deep into her memory, trying to touch the woman that bore her. Mother! Yet all she could see was herself—and, nearby, a group of bright shapes, not men but somehow familiar. She reached out to them and then she knew—they were wolves.

The shock drove her back and she jerked upright. The light of the mist was dimmed, and she opened her bag seeking her magic lights to see they were gone. The dark moss crumbled to black dust at her touch. Too much power, they could not survive.

She stood shakily, every scratch and bruise gone but replaced by a hunger that seemed to call from every muscle and bone inside her. At the back of her mind she could still feel the wolves, at a distance but aware of her location. She had to find safety from them, but once they began a pursuit they never gave up.

She needed meat and pulled a strip of dried meat from her bag. The wolves were to the right, Jalka and his men to the left and behind, and far below her. Once she had picked her way out of the ruined building she found herself on moist grass cropped short by some grazing animal.

She was climbing a gentle gradient and the ground became more solid but the mist was denser and darker. She could sense the wolves searching for her but they had not yet reached the building. Though tired, she pushed on through the white featureless world, and it seemed almost as if she were unmoving while the ground flowed beneath her. Her confidence from the healing seeped away and nothing changed about her, save the ground, which had now flattened out and she no longer marched uphill.

A large, shadowy shape loomed out of the mist towards her and she stopped with a wave of paralysing fear. She could not sense what it was; even her contact with the wolves was slipping as her courage faded away. The shape stopped too, its tall rounded bulk towering above her. She stepped forwards, realizing it was only a huge boulder; she touched it with a sigh. Just rock.

She sped up to a steady trot but her fear persisted; the wolves were coming. she knew that, though she could no longer feel them, they were there behind her and closing in. The daylight was almost gone and she wanted to run, but the fear of the unknown ahead held her back. Another boulder took shape through the mist; as she passed it the ground dipped.

She returned to a fast walk, breathing heavily from the exertion. She was weak and she cursed herself for the foolishness of trying magic, as everyone knew that magic was tiring. The large rocks and boulders appeared with greater frequency. As she descended, the mist thinned out a little and the remaining light brightened.

Despite the protests of her body she trotted again, through the boulders and rocks that now lay strewn about as if some giant had smashed an enormous pot on the mountain side. Silence filled her world save for her own hoarse breaths and her footfalls in the grass.

She knew the wolves were near and terror seeped up her spine. She felt that any moment she would feel the weight of a wolf crashing down on her back; or one would appear before her, leaping at her, tearing at her throat.

Then she did hear it, not her own breathing but the sound of a wolf panting, the sound of paws padding rapidly through the grass. First one, then another and another, then she couldn't count them.

Perhaps they could not see her; perhaps they thought she was one of them. She knew there was one pacing her to the left; it seemed to be moving faster, going ahead of her, trying to cut her off. She pushed her legs into a run, the downward slope carrying her forward.

The wolf to her left and front couldn't be heard any more but the ones behind were still running with her. Why didn't they attack? Why didn't they get it over with? Her breath came in short gasps and rasped in her dry throat.

The slope steepened and she moved faster still, legs moving on their own; she felt powerless to control them. Another rock appeared, barring her way. She had a moment to see that this one was different: tall, thin, regular in shape with patterned faces. She desperately forced her legs to steer to the left and almost succeeded.

She struck the obelisk. Her right arm scraped hard against it and the pattern of razor-sharp stone sliced the length of her forearm. She choked at the sudden pain. Her legs continued to carry her forward in automatic movement on her new course. The ground was smoother now but still sloped too much for her to slow down. Twin pillars appeared on each side every few steps as she pounded forward, gripping her arm tight and gasping hoarsely.

A small boulder loomed up in the dark directly ahead and took the shape a wolf; it was waiting for her. She tried to veer round it, but her legs would not respond and she ploughed straight at it. At the last moment, she screamed at it and it dodged to the side. She had the idea it looked surprised.

The ground flattened and she was slowing. Behind her she could hear the panting of many mouths. They had run her down; run her to exhaustion. She wanted desperately to stop, to give up, to let them have their prey; but she could not, could not fail. Within the misty, muffled world there was only her breath and their breath, her padding feet and theirs—so many of theirs.

The paired stones on each side grew smaller as she passed by them, and they became more frequent despite her slowing. She had dropped to a tired and aching walk. The wolves matched her pace, following her carefully, spreading out around her, flanking her left and right. She could hear them, almost sense them. She glanced left and right but it seemed they were beyond the small circle.

The surface of the ground changed abruptly, and she was no longer walking on low moss and grass; now it was smooth, cold stone. She quickened her pace with renewed energy. Perhaps there was shelter ahead, perhaps even a door that she could close on these stalking monsters. Whatever the difference was, she could no longer hear the wolves, no padding feet, no panting breaths. The path split in two, the main route climbing the beginning of an arch, the other descending and curled round to a lower level. She took a few more paces forward and stopped abruptly; the greyness of the stones at her feet had turned to black. She took another two steps forward and froze. The stones ended and there was a drop into the ravine. It was quiet but not silent. Below, she could hear water tumbling and gushing.

A claw scraped on stone.

She stood up straight with her eyes closed. She did not need to see them to know the pack stood behind her. They had crept closer in silence and now she stood between two deaths. But she could not meet death with her eyes shut, so she opened them once more and stared ahead; the blackness of the void did not go to infinity, and she could see the other side of the bridge ahead, the upper level of it beyond her reach but the lower path beneath not so far.

The wolves were waiting, but for what? She slowly unslung the saddlebags and reached in, pulling out a strip of dried meat. Very slowly she turned around. The wolves were further back into the mist than she had thought, but she could see their shadowy shapes, shoulder to shoulder, nudging, pushing and shuffling silently. Their dark eyes glinted, and they did not take their gaze from her.

To reach the lower level she would need space to run at it, and to distract them with the meat she needed to be closer. She took a deep breath, and at this they froze. She took a step forward and a ripple seemed to pass through them, but they did not move forward or back. She took three more paces, until she could make out differences in their markings. A part of her screamed in terror commanding her to run, but she held it back.

These are beasts that chase; if I am to run it must be when they are not ready. But they are wolves, they are always ready.

If I do not flee they will not chase. I have food; I am going to give them food. I am not food, I am a wolf, I have chased down my prey; I will share my food with the pack; here!

She flung the strip of meat close over the head of the wolf in the centre; faster than she could have imagined, it raised its head and snapped the meat from the air. The ones around it snapped too, and there was confusion and conflict as they grabbed at it.

Elona paused long enough to see the meat torn from the air, then she spun round and ran full tilt at the void. She covered the distance in three strides and sprang from the edge, leaping high.

27

Her fear demanded she close her eyes, but she kept them open as the edge of the lower pathway came at her. It struck her midriff, knocking her breathless, but her arms and chest were fully over the top.

Moments later a crushing weight struck her back, driving her ribs into the stonework; paws dug into her shoulders, and the creature tried to climb up her body, scratching her legs with its back claws. She felt herself slipping with the combined weight, the wolf's hot breath in her ear. She pushed herself upright and twisted her body. The wolf's paws lost their grip and tore their way across her shoulders and down her back; it slipped into oblivion and into silence.

With desperate energy, Elona managed to pull her leg over the edge and roll on to the path, facing across the chasm. The wolves stood there on the upper level, silhouetted against the misty sky. She grabbed at the saddlebag to get the knife to defend against them if they jumped. Then a shudder ran through them and their intensity faded; they turned and disappeared.

Breathing heavily, Elona rolled to her knees and climbed to her feet. Holding the heavy dagger in one hand she staggered across the paved bridge as it rose to its apex and then down to the opposite bank. The twinned pillars of the Slissac road continued, and she followed them until the light was fully gone, then turned off to one side. She gathered the blanket around her tattered clothes and bloodied body and slept.

The morning brought a clear winter's day with a strong wind blowing from the north. The long gash on her right arm, from the collision with the boulder last night, oozed blood. Chewing on a strip of meat she looked back across the ravine, the Slissac ruins from which she had come were lost behind a ridge. She could see the wide field of grass strewn with boulders across which the wolves had chased her. The roadway came down from another ridge to the right and crossed the wide ravine in an elegant two-level span broken near the opposite side.

The road continued from the bridge past her and alongside the ravine as it curved away to the east. She considered where to go next; down did not seem an option, so she would have to re-cross the ravine with all the terrors that could bring. It seemed likely that this road was the same one that Jalka had been travelling when they nearly caught her. They may have come this far up but would not have crossed the ravine, and more likely they had turned back; perhaps they would think she had fallen.

Then there was Styvan and his bandits. Where had they been travelling to? They would not have tried to cross the ravine with the horses or *kichesa*, let alone the carts. This could not have been the way he intended to come. So, if she continued this way she would not meet her pursuers or encounter more bandits. She started up the abandoned Slissac road.

At first she counted the markers, but as the numbers piled up she lost track and watched as the unchanging scenery passed her by; the grass gave way to heather while rocks and boulders showed through more often as she climbed. The wind was bitter. Occasionally the road approached the ravine and Elona could see part way into its depths, see the tops of trees growing from its base and hear the crashing waters tumbling through it.

As the evening drew in she built a cocoon of earth, stones and heather around the base of a pillar to keep the wind out. Then, using Styvan's tinderbox, she managed to make a small fire, but it needed too much heather to keep it going and there were no trees or bushes. She promptly gave up.

She slept better and walked on. She rationed out the food, and the frequent streams of water chattering down across or under the road kept her thirst at bay. The cold was intensifying, the wind blowing steadily from the north and the amount of cloud flying in tatters across the sky increasing. She judged it to be about midday when the road reached its destination and plunged off to the right and down into the ravine.

She followed it, thinking that the ravine might provide better shelter from the wind, when she saw the smoke. At first she took it to be a late mist, but it did not blow away and kept renewing itself from below. Elona ducked behind one of the markers and peered round it; she could see nothing. Carefully, keeping low and taking one marker at a time, she closed in on the cliff edge until she could see well down into it.

The smoke was rising from one of dozens of windows cut from the sheer face of the ravine on the opposite side. There were balconies, stairs, rooms and columns in the Slissac style. For a moment she thought she had found the creatures themselves, until a human child ran from one door to another. The bandit Pitra had been wrong; they would have made it before the snow closed in.

She crept away; she did not know whether they could cross the ravine, but if they did not know of her so much the better. Besides, what story would she be able to tell them? That Styvan was dead because she had smashed his head with a rock? And if this was his wintering place she would not be safe from the men.

A little way back along the road, as it turned down into the ravine, there seemed to be a vague track that led further up into the mountains. She took it.

～

On the sixth day from the fight at the bridge, she reached the snow-line and continued trudging upwards. Her thoughts seemed to have frozen; all she could see was the whiteness and all she could feel was the need to keep on walking.

She trudged slowly upwards for another two days. The sky remained clear and the wind had diminished. She became numb to the cold and at night curled up in whatever hollow she could find.

On the ninth day the wind picked up again and clouds filled the sky. It was almost by surprise that she found herself standing in crumbling snow on a ridge between two peaks, as the sun sent fading beams through holes in the clouds. Ahead stood mountains and snow while behind the hills stretched out to the dark forests far below. The lowlands called to her with comfort and warmth, but also suffering and death. The bleak whiteness had the pain of cold, and its simple purity was to be preferred. She started the descent into the next valley.

She came to a ledge that afforded a little shelter and tripped on something under the snow. She fell into a circle of stones and old heather. Carefully, she dug down into the snow and pulled out a rubbery shell bigger than her hand, torn across half its length. A giant *kichek* egg—no, a *sikechak*, the great flying beasts. This was a nest, abandoned during the cold of winter. She cleared the snow as best she could and found a huge mass of heather that smelled of dung surrounded by a ring of stones. She quickly buried herself in the heather and slept.

When the dim light of day pushed itself through the heavy clouds, it accompanied a huge downfall of thick snow. She did not move that day, sleeping and chewing cold dry meat. The rest restored her to the point where her wounds in her arm and shoulders ached; her feet ached with the cold and she could not feel her toes. She did not dare to use her power to heal herself in case it brought down wolves on her, or something worse.

The next day the snow stopped and she dug her way up through the new layer, almost her body height in thickness above her. The mountains looked unchanged. The sun reflected dazzling bright from the snow and there was no wind. Using threads prised from the blanket she tied two of the flexible *sikechak* shells over her feet. She stared for a moment at her bare and aching feet before covering them; her toes were black. She used two smaller shells for her hands.

She set off walking downhill, making slow and awkward progress in the deep snow. After a short time, she looked back and could see she had travelled very little distance. She stopped as a crazy thought came to her. Though she herself had never been permitted, she had seen the children of Corlain playing when the snows fell. They slid down the low slopes on pieces of wood and bark. Before her was the greatest hill of snow she had ever seen stretching smooth for what could be leagues below her.

She put the saddlebag down with the worn and shiny back to the snow. She sat on it with her feet sticking out to the sides. With one hand holding tight to the front of the bag she pushed off with the other. She rapidly picked up speed and felt elation as she rushed down the hill.

The increasing pace unnerved her and she dug her feet into the snow; she slowed a little but the effort was tiring. The slope was not as smooth as it looked and she was bumped and shaken every moment, but it was a small price to pay for the progress she made.

After a long time the slope flattened out and her speed became less reckless. She did not know how she could stop. The valley into which she was descending curved to the left and she struggled to keep herself on course. A stream came flashing into view at her side and the ride became rougher; there were trees ahead. She dug in her feet, in trying to slow herself. Her left leg caught on something under the snow and was wrenched backwards; she screamed in pain and spun round, coming to a sudden stop against a snow-rimed tree trunk.

Elona opened her eyes and stared at the white virgin expanse above her, corrupted by the single line stretching from infinity to where she lay. She blinked twice and something inside her snapped. She laughed. Her throat was dry and she could not remember the

last time she laughed but now she could not stop herself. She
coughed and spluttered with the laugh, aching in every part of body.
she could not feel her toes, her thigh was twisted from the abrupt
stop, her right arm and shoulders burned with old pain; but still she
laughed.

28

After a while she ran out of laugh. The branches of a tree hung a few feet above her. Around the arc of the tree's edge she could see the blue sky and the beginnings of other trees; every moment threatened another giggle. The air smelled of pine and she could hear water splashing nearby. She was very cold.

Pushing with her elbows she tried to rise, but pain shot through her stomach and back. She tried to roll to the right but another spasm forced her back. Finally she succeeded in rolling the other way and came to rest, face down in the cold, damp pine needles.

She forced herself up to her knees. When the distress of her muscles subsided, one leg at a time, she climbed to her feet and leaned against the tree. The saddlebag lay a short distance away and her head spun with dizziness as she lifted it painfully from the ground.

Stumbling from the support of one trunk to the next, she worked towards the sound of running water and finally broke through the line of trees. A few yards away a river bubbled and rushed; she staggered over and collapsed beside it.

She drank some and ducked her head below the surface. Her body was almost bare of clothes and her skin was ablaze with red cuts and purple bruising. She had to find some shelter and warmth or this coming night she would die. The humour of it made her giggle.

Mud from the river caked her legs as she took another stumbling step, her frozen, blackened foot sinking deep into the bank. She looked up from the endless mud and saw it was growing dark again. The gash in her right arm ran from her elbow to her wrist and blood still oozed from around the clots. She stared at it, not daring to even think of the magic that could bring it back to health. The effort would drain her of what little strength she had left and bring who knew what to eat her. She had stopped walking again; with concentrated effort she forced her legs into motion.

It was when the darkness was almost complete that the acrid smell of burning pine brought her to a halt. She could hear nothing but the constant murmuring and splashing of the river at her side. She peered hard into the gloom but no light betrayed itself.

She forced herself into calmness and suppressed the desire to shout for help. She breathed deeply, forcing the cold air into her lungs—wincing at the stabs of pain—in an attempt to clear her mind. The pain succeeded better than the coldness of the air.

There was a chance the fire she smelled was a farm, or perhaps a hunter who would give her shelter. Or it might be danger. She felt inside the bag and pulled out the knife, then moved forward hoping the noises of the river would hide the sounds of her approach.

The shape of a large boulder loomed ahead of her, outlined in flickering orange light. She heard the crackling of the fire above the splashing of the water. She went down on all fours and crawled forward, trying to make out the fire's owner through the gloom.

She was close enough to feel the heat of the small fire on her face, arms and shoulders while her lower body and legs froze in the night. The fire's owner was sitting with his back to the very boulder that had shielded her approach. There was no way to see him without circling the fire at a distance.

The tempting warmth of the fire kept distracting her. She saw a gauntleted hand reach out with a stick and prod something large and round from the heart of the fire. The hand was joined by another and she watched in fascination as together they cracked the large shell at one end and broke away the pieces.

The delicious smell of cooked meat flooded her senses and forced an uncontrollable sob from her throat that emerged as a cough. She froze in terror of having betrayed her presence to the hands. The gauntlets did not react; they simply withdrew, taking the food with them.

She did not know how long she held her breath, but as her body cried out for air she silently exhaled, then carefully drew in a breath of cold air. Then a hand came down on her shoulder. She jerked to the side and jabbed up with the dagger at the shadow that loomed above her. It was knocked from her hand as a wave of unconsciousness overcame her.

Elona was roused by the pain in her chest. On the other side of her closed eyes the light of a fire flickered, yet she dared not open them. She was lying on her right side and could feel the heat of the fire on her face. The coarse blanket that covered her prickled those parts of her skin that could feel.

Her face had been cleaned and she could smell the cooked meat, but as she remembered the shadow she jerked open her eyes in fear. The blazing fire blinded her and she saw nothing but dancing reds and yellows. As her eyes adjusted she saw across from her, a third of the way around the fire, a hooded figure, his face hidden in shadow. He seemed slight of build, perhaps just a boy. An involuntary shiver ran through her as the hooded face looked round and stared at her with hidden eyes.

He said something gentle; his voice was light and young. The words made no sense but she felt no threat. The boy put the clutch of small bones he'd been gnawing into a wooden bowl near the fire and moved round to her. He spoke again, and there was familiarity in the flow of words yet they were spoken in a strange, clipped way. The boy gently raised her up; a young boy perhaps, but there was strength in those arms.

Satisfied that she was able to sit by herself, the boy went to the fire and used a short stick to lift a black metal pot from the embers gathered up on one side. He pulled a pewter mug from within his cloak and a small pouch. Setting the mug down he poured in the broth, which sent up a pungent and mouth-watering aroma. From the pouch, he took a pinch of salt and sprinkled it into the cup. He held it up for her to take but her strength failed her. Understanding, he raised the cup to her lips and gently tipped it up.

The broth flowed across her tongue and the taste almost overwhelmed her. He withdrew the cup while she tried to swallow the tiny amount of liquid. She turned her head to look at her kind benefactor; his eyes reflected the light of the fire but the depth of the hood hid his features. The eyes looked back and she tried to smile, but her face would not respond.

Instead he raised the cup again and she drank more deeply, feeling the liquid slide into the emptiness of her stomach. Soon the cup was empty and she lay down again, and the boy withdrew to his seat. She listened uncomprehendingly as he spoke again but his voice seemed very far away.

It was daylight and raining—but a canopy had been erected over her, which kept most of it from away. Her head ached and hunger was eating at her. The boy was not in view but a large brown mare stood nearby, dripping forlornly in the rain. The boy must belong to some wealthy family if they had a horse for him.

Moving her feet she discovered they were encased in boots, and from there upwards she was completely outfitted in a man's stitched leather and woollen travelling clothes. The trousers pressed tightly against the skin of her legs and a wave of embarrassment flooded her at the thought of being dressed by the boy.

An increase in the intensity of the rain interrupted her. The cloak about her shoulders had a hood and she pulled it over her head. Looking around her small shelter she found a large pouch placed under the blanket that served for a pillow. Opening it she found small pieces of cooked meat, a piece of old cheese, some bread and a small bottle.

She ate the cheese immediately and, while she chewed it, unstoppered the bottle. The liquid inside was water, which she drank gratefully. The dark bread took some time to chew but she wanted to leave the pleasure of the meat to last.

Though the meal was barely enough to feed a *chakik*, she felt bloated. There was a pile of kindling under the canopy as well but she decided not to try to make a fire, for the rain was too heavy.

The sky was filled with tatters of cloud that streamed past and the rain had stopped. The valley floor was in shadow but the sun's light glowed on the opposite cliff. The horse seemed happier now but the grass and bushes around it had been stripped of greenery.

She stood carefully; her muscles ached and her joints cracked. She shuffled over to the horse. She held out her arm and murmured quietly, and it snuffled her hand then her clothes.

She tried to say, 'I have nothing for you' but she had no voice.

Undoing its rein, she led the horse from the shelter of the rocks, away from the sound of the river. She came out into the open. With the river to her right she looked down the valley stretching into the far distance, disappearing only as it curved to the left. The land-scape was filled with broken rocks among areas of open grass, and large copses grouped near the water's edge.

Letting the horse feed, she sat down and watched it as the shadow of a mountain moved up the far valley wall. It had almost reached the top when she saw movement in the distance, near the river. Quickly she gathered up the reins of the horse and drew it back within the shelter of the rocks.

The boy walked into the circle of stones. He was tall and very slim, and still kept the hood pulled over his head. He carried the carcasses of two long, lithe animals she did not recognise. He said something, waited for a moment as if for a response, and then, with the slightest of shrugs, turned to the soaked fire. Very shortly after-wards a small fire blazed.

The boy quickly set several small iron pots in the hot embers, their contents bubbling and steaming, giving off mouth-watering aromas. Carrying a wooden bowl, a sharp-looking knife and the two animals, he disappeared in the direction of the river. He returned a short time later with the skins in a bundle and the bowl brimming with fresh meat. He deposited all the meat into the largest of the pots and stowed the skins in a bag.

They sat in silence around the fire and breathed in the delicious smells. Elona wondered about the boy hiding his face. She had seen deformed people sometimes and those disfigured by disease, usually on the road heading towards the Guildhouse of Healers in Heaton. Perhaps out here in the wild there were no healers for the boy.

It was dark by the time they finished eating. She felt satisfied at last. The night was silent save for the occasional crackle from the glowing heart of the fire. The sky was clear and the air very cold. She spoke not knowing if he would understand:

'I am Elona.' She pointed to herself. 'Elona.' There was a long pause.

The boy sighed then raised his hand to his hood. 'Elona,' he repeated and the hand pulled back the hood. 'I a' Tek.'

At first Elona did not understand what she saw, for the colours did not belong to the shapes that should be there. Then her senses adjusted: A reptilian face, shaped like her little Ichen; scaly skin patterned in grey and green; simple ear holes with tiny flaps cupping them; a hard ridge beginning from what would be the fore-head and travelling over the head; large pale eyes, shining like milk in moonlight; a hard, lipless mouth that was slashed from the muzzle and filled with razor teeth.

A Slissac. A female.

Tek studied Elona's face then went back to watch the flames. Elona pulled herself to her feet and tried to think how she could escape; she felt as if she was falling and her vertigo swallowed her. After all she had done to escape, to become a slave now...

Tek glanced up at her and spoke quietly. 'Ssit down. 'Efore you vall down.'

Elona collapsed to her knees and cried in long deep sobs with her arms over her head.

~

The sky was greying towards dawn when Elona woke again. For the briefest moment she couldn't recall where she was. Then the cold wind, stony ground, and the dark figure, no longer hooded, moving to and fro, reminded her. She shivered; her head felt stuffy and her eyes were tired.

Tek looked over to her and spoke; something about the river perhaps. The Slissac's voice was stern as she repeated her words and she clicked her mouth. 'Wash.' She pointed towards the river and obediently Elona went.

The ground was cloaked in dark shadow, the sun still hidden behind the far ridge. Elona stumbled down to the riverside, the frost crunching beneath her feet. Without a thought, as if she were still a child, she went through the motions. The freezing water brought her fully awake, though she still seemed to be thinking through wool. Loosening the unfamiliar clothing she examined the bruises and cuts covering her body. The gash on her forearm had been treated and was healing—faster or slower than normal? She did not know. She felt she had the strength to heal herself now but did not have the desire. Besides, it might not be wise to reveal herself to her captor.

When she returned to the camp all the blankets and pots had been stowed and the horse stood waiting. Tek was obliterating the traces of their camp, then turned to face her.

She pointed to the horse and gestured that Elona should mount, saying the words with it. Elona recognised the "you", and the second word should have been "mount" but it was said wrong. Tek's hard lips could not pronounce the sounds correctly.

Elona moved alongside the horse, and without another word Tek grasped Elona's left leg and pushed her into the saddle. Elona felt insecure; the horse had a wide girth and her straining body ached.

Once she was satisfied that Elona was firmly seated, Tek took the reins and led the horse down-river. Elona tried to adjust to the unfamiliar riding position and gait but her exhaustion left her like a sack on the horse's back.

29

The horse had stopped. They were between two steep cliffs that ran with streams, cascading down to the river rushing headlong on their right. The previous day they had forded the river where it ran slow and wide, but now it raged tight and fast. The clouds hung so low that it was as if she could reach out and touch them. The air was cold and thick with moisture. Her head ached worse than ever; her nose ran and she sniffed repeatedly.

'Down.' When Tek spoke, the word came from the back of her throat. She gestured for Elona to dismount but her legs would not obey. When Tek tried to force her right leg over the back of the horse, Elona whimpered in pain. Her legs were stiff, muscles frozen from the unaccustomed position. Finally, they managed to push her leg forward and bend it over the horse's neck. Elona fell to the ground weeping, unable to feel anything but pain below her waist.

When she could finally stand Tek forced her to walk, clinging to the saddlebags for support. The horse's hooves clattered and slipped on the stones while the river frantically rushed by.

Elona felt ill and the dampness of the air clogged her throat. They plodded on, the pounding noise of the river slowly fading as it fell into a gorge beside the road. Presently they came to an arching double bridge across the river. It was certain that Tek was taking her to her masters. She closed her eyes and clung to the horse saddle as they crossed the arch by the higher span.

The road beyond mounted the cliff in sharp switch-backs. By turns, she was safe between horse and cliff face, then terrified as the next stretch had her back to the cliff edge and gorge. Tek let her rest when they reached the top, and there they ate. Elona glanced repeatedly at her captor, yet she seemed disinterested.

The rest was barely enough for Elona but they pushed on along the paved road across an expanse of cropped grass. Elona's head was throbbing; she felt hot and then shivered with cold. Did this creature not care that she was ill?

Low mists protected her from her terrors as the road descended, cutting back and forth down a second cliff. The sound of another, bigger river roared up from the depths below, beating their ears.

When they reached the bottom of the descent another double bridge awaited them. Tek led them across. On the other side she helped Elona mount the horse again, and they followed the road alongside the new river with cliffs on either side once more. The road slowly sloped downwards, winding left and right in a channel cut through the rocks. Elona felt a little better as they came out of the mists and the air cleared.

The crashing of the second river was gradually overtaken by a deep-throated roar that seemed to shake the air. The cliffs at each side fell away and they came into a wide, open space. On their left the river was in turmoil; the first river they had crossed emerged from the cliffs beyond and the two joined in a mad confluence. Looking ahead, Elona felt her stomach churn and fear gripped her as she looked forward and down; there was no sloping landscape. The ground disappeared in a fall so great that she could see nothing below. The two torrents cascaded over the edge and vanished, roaring as they went. Elona gripped the saddle in terror, doubled over, hiding her face and weeping with fear and illness.

The young Slissac woman spoke, the tone of her voice gentle and coaxing though the individual words were lost in the roar. Tek placed one of her hands on to Elona's—that clung desperately to the saddle—and at her touch Elona went rigid.

'No. Please. I will fall. Please. I can't. I can't.'

Tek spoke slowly. 'You will get down or you will die.'

Fear of the Slissac concentrated her unfocused mind, and Elona carefully lifted her leg and slid from the horse's back. The Slissac caught her and bound her wrists loosely to the saddle pommel. It rained again. Tek went to the horse's head, gathered up the reins and stood for a moment staring down. Then she started forward, clicking to the horse, dragging Elona step by step.

~

Elona returned to awareness lying on a damp stone floor. Her head pounded if she dared to move it, her throat was dry, and she could not breathe through her nose. Every joint in her body ached and her thighs and hips threatened torture if she dared to move them. She was lying on her side with her head pillowed by a saddlebag. Directly in front of her she could see a dim cold light filtering through a misty opening.

She shivered uncontrollably and a rasping cough tore at her lungs; she tried to sniff and failed, coughing again. Her eyes watered and blurred the image of the light through the stone. She wanted to wipe her eyes and tried to move, but her limbs ached painfully and felt too heavy.

She lay there in mournful self-pity until she felt a heat on her back and legs. With a great effort she rolled over to face the fire and sobbed as pains shot through her. Tek was sitting on the opposite side, dropping something into a pot that hung steaming over the heat. The horse stood behind her at the back of the cave.

Tek looked up at her and said something. It wasn't a question but Elona felt too heavy to respond anyway. Tek rolled some small leaves between her black, scaly fingers before dropping them into the pot.

The memory of her terror at the cliff-edge returned, only slightly blunted by the pain in her head. Tek went to a large pile of branches that lay near the fire. As Elona watched, she laid out six parallel to each other before taking another and weaving them together, humming as she did. Elona recognised the tune, a song she had learned to sing when embroidering; a working song for the elite about soldiers and knights. Elona's attention flagged and she dropped her gaze to stare at the flickering fire, but the light hurt and her head pounded all the more.

The next day passed in a dream. She was lying on a pallet, her body bound tightly to it, being dragged along by the horse. All she could hear in the brief times when she was lucid was the crunch of horse hooves on stone. She watched the grim mountains and cliff faces receding as she was dragged backwards into the future.

She was hot; her head was muffled with fur above and below. A cloth was drawn up over her mouth and nose so that only her eyes were open to the air. She sweated profusely and the furs were clammy against her bare skin. Every once in a while Tek would come and give her flat-tasting water.

When she dozed she dreamt terrors: a corpse with a battered face bit the index finger of her right hand, then pressed itself on her trying to kiss her with its lipless mouth. She was naked, fleeing through a forest of pine with wolves howling at her, and she fell with the hot breath of the wolves against her skin, bound in a dungeon while Lady Metrid forced pieces of orange between Elona's lips. But the juice burned her tongue and she saw her home in flames, with a great dark tide washing over it while she stood by helplessly, all the while Tek beside her, pointing and laughing.

It was drizzling when they stopped for the night. She was still on the pallet, though it now lay flat. The horse munched noisily a little way from the small fire, and further off she could hear the constant roar of the river.

Seeing Elona awake, Tek picked up a water-skin and brought it to her. Carefully she lifted Elona into a sitting position and helped her drink. Elona felt so weary; every part of her body ached and she barely had the strength to move her arms.

Tek's voice was gentle: 'I an taking you to ny hone; nother will hel' you.' She let her down again, and for a long while Elona lay. She stared into the fire; her head did not hurt as it had, though her scalp prickled.

'You shouldn't help me, I don't deserve it.' She gave a half-coughing laugh—becoming a slave would be a fitting reward for her crimes.

In the morning Elona was stronger and Tek unwrapped her from the litter. With the reptilian woman's help Elona pulled herself to her feet and stood, swaying. Tek brought her a blanket and wrapped it around her. The air was cold but the sky was clear at last, and the sun warmed her skin. Tek watched her for a short while, then went to her bags to search for a moment, pulling out a grey stone that fitted neatly into her fist.

'Take thiss to the river, rud it on your sskin.' Tek gestured towards the river, but Elona didn't move. Tek pretended to rub her arm vigorously with the stone, pointed to the river again and offered the stone. Hesitantly Elona took the stone and stumbled across the broad flat rocks until she came to the river bank. Tek had chosen a spot where the river was wide, shallow and slower moving. Elona dipped her toe into the water and found it was freezing. She didn't dare go in and instead she wrapped the blanket around her shoulders, kneeling at the river's edge.

She cupped her hands and splashed water onto her arm, then took the round stone and began rubbing it against her skin. The stone was covered with little indentations, a gentle roughness that scoured her skin. It was refreshing.

She was gentler over her bruises, which were many, yet all seemed to be healing well. She ran her fingers along the rough surface of the stitched cut on her arm; the outer skin was completely dead and the ridges of thread pulled at her skin.

Finally she was done and used the blanket to dry herself as best she could. When she returned to the camp Tek indicated a pile of clothing, which Elona pulled on awkwardly. Then she took the bowl of steaming porridge and spoon Tek offered. Elona had never liked porridge, but it had been sweetened with honey and she felt a new strength beginning to stir in her muscles. After Elona had eaten Tek took the bowl, refilled it, and ate from it herself.

When Tek had finished she handed the bowl, pan and spoon to Elona, pointing to the river once more. 'Clean then.' Elona looked down at the implements and walked slowly off to the river again. She knelt down and carefully washed the items, watching as the bits of porridge separated and floated downstream. She kept at it until she was sure that they were spotless.

Tek had broken camp and the litter had been cast aside. She took the items from Elona and stowed them in a pack, then gestured for Elona to mount the horse again. Elona approached reluctantly and took hold of the saddle. She held up her left foot and Tek boosted her up. It did not feel as awkward or as uncomfortable as before.

They set off again, Tek walking beside the horse's head. They continued to follow the course of the river valley; here the river had cut a wider path, though for the present it meandered in a much smaller bed.

The sun rose slowly and when it was high Tek stopped. She helped Elona dismount, then unpacked some crusts of dry bread and cheese, let the horse graze as she did so. Tek broke the food into equal portions and gave half to Elona. Tek watched her while they chewed.

After a short break they went on again. Tek seemed to be hurrying, as she picked up the pace and kept looking at the sun as it moved across to the western ridge. The river turned to the left abruptly and then descended in rapids.

From this height Elona could see, in the distance, smoke rising from a cluster of tiny buildings. The valley was very green and large, shaggy goats grazed across it. They descended the main slope by a well-worn path that threaded through the rocks, while the river roared beside them. Elona could not remember when they had left the Slissac road.

Then suddenly they were out of the rocks, the valley lay before them, then the river widened out and turned to the right cutting across their path. They stopped. Without a word Tek pulled the reins back across the horse's head, gesturing for Elona to move backwards along the horse. Tek mounted in front of her and then urged their mount into the water.

The water level rose until it covered their feet; they pushed on and out the other side, water dripping from the horse's legs and belly. Tek didn't dismount but urged the horse into a trot across the grassy meadow. The horse seemed to enjoy the change of pace despite the extra weight. But Elona, taken unawares, grabbed onto Tek, who suddenly laughed. Elona jolted along unhappily.

As they moved towards the village they passed a goat-herder sitting on a rock; his face was frowning as they passed by. He was human.

30

———

They passed small cottages. Here and there more people who watched them pass, though none were Slissac and none smiled. Perhaps they were all slaves, yet they did not give any sign of deference. Tek steered the horse through the centre of the village and left it behind. Elona turned her head to look back and saw the faces of men and women staring after them.

Tek slowed the horse to a walk and they crossed a small brook. They turned up the side of the valley and she saw ahead of them another cottage, not large but in good repair. A brown and white *zatek*, with a muzzle grey with age, lay at the door. It lifted its head at their approach and sniffed, then blew a deep nasal note and lay its head down again.

Tek brought the horse to a stop a few yards from the door and dismounted. She tied the reins to a post and walked to the *zatek*, who stood at her approach. She rubbed its head and scratched behind its ear; it gave her a single lick and settled again.

'Nother!' called Tek, then the latch snapped and the door creaked open. An old human woman with grey hair shuffled out. Her hands were white with flour and she had smudges of it on her cheek. Tek embraced her.

'Look what I vound,' Tek pointed to Elona. 'She wass in the

nountains, she wass sick.' The old woman looked up and stared at Elona still seated on the horse.

'So,' she said. 'You're here after all these years. Better bring her in, Tek my love.'

Tek walked back to Elona, helped her dismount, then supported her as she walked stiffly to the house and followed the old woman in.

The room they entered occupied the whole ground floor of the cottage with a stone staircase on the right. Light from the small windows revealed wooden chairs surrounding a table in front of a large fireplace, embers glowing hotly at its base; various pots were hung about it. The bare rafters were hung with dried plants and tools.

Tek guided Elona to a chair and sat her down. The old woman shuffled across to the fireplace and ladled a liquid into a bowl, gathered up a spoon, and brought it to the table. Placing them down in front of Elona she sat down opposite. 'Eat.'

The smell from the bowl was delicious and hunger rose within her. She picked up the wooden spoon and ate the thin soup. The warmth of the cottage seeped through her clothes and took away the chill that had inhabited her body for days. By the time she had finished the soup she was very tired.

'And what's your name then?'

Elona tried to answer but somehow could not force her mouth to form the words.

'Tek, my love, she'll sleep in with you, make up the second cot.'

When Elona woke next, light was peeping through the closed shutters and she could hear rain splashing on the roof and walls. Her muscles were very stiff but she pulled herself into a sitting position under the low rafters and thatch. The sleeping pallet was straw but the linen and blankets were of reasonable quality. Her clothes had been changed again and she was wearing a cotton nightgown. The air was cold but the smooth wooden floor felt warm.

The second bed on the other side of the room stood empty and neatly made up. A plain dresser was placed at its foot nearest the window with a water jug and bowl on it. The wind gusted suddenly, and for a few moments rain drummed against the low window.

Carefully, slowly, she climbed to her feet and went to the stair-well. From below there was no sound, but appetising smells wafted up in waves of warm air. She peered through the window; outside it was bordered with ivy and all she could see was the muddy ground running with water.

Using the bannister rail for support she descended the stairs, peering at the room as more and more of it came into view. The *zatek* was lying on the hearth. It looked up at her as she came down but did not consider her worth more than a short, breathy note before going back to sleep.

The old woman was seated at the table peeling apples.

'Feeling better today?'

Elona's voice came out in a rasping whisper. 'Yes, thank you.'

'Good. Have an apple. It'll be better for your throat.'

Elona took a bite and delicious juices flowed into her mouth.

'Sit down, dear. What's your name?'

'Elona,' she replied between mouthfuls.

The old woman waited expectantly but Elona said nothing more. 'So Tek said, but that's not all, is it? You're noble-born; you've got a bigger name than that.'

'Elona Corlain, daughter and only child of Veona Corlain, wife to Lord Taniel Corlain of Faerholme.'

'You can call me Usala, or mother. Never had a daughter, but Tek calls me that and I like it. I love stewed apples, don't you?' She finished peeling the apple and cut it into sections. She placed it with others in a pie dish which she covered and placed in an alcove by the fire.

There were no more prying questions. Usala spoke of the weather and the village. After a while Tek came in, dripping from the rain. She stripped off her outer garments and hung them by the door, then went upstairs. When she returned she wore a simple shift with a belt—the first feminine clothing Elona had seen her wear. It looked very odd with her dark scaly skin, though now Elona could see that it was not a flat colour, each scale sparkled with iridescent blue and greens.

'I have mucked out the sstable, mother.'

~

Elona woke early refreshed, as if her past no longer threatened to drown her with horrors at every moment. Elona sat up and looked through the window. It had snowed heavily in the night and through the window the world was covered with a blanket of crisp white.

There was movement in the room; Tek was still asleep in her bed. For the first time Elona looked properly at her face: elongated, reptilian face with a small, bony ridge running from between the eyes over the head and down the neck and back. According to the records Bejeren had shown her the males had more of a crest. Then there were Tek's claw-like hands, possessing the same number of fingers as her own. Most alien of all, no breasts. Elona wondered how they suckled their young, and then felt embarrassed. Tek's eyes flicked open.

'Good morning.' Tek rose swiftly and sat on the edge of her bed, looking at Elona. 'You sslept well?' The 'w' sound was breathy as Tek spoke it.

'Thank you, yes—and you?'

'I did, thank you.' She paused, then continued. 'It'ss so cold. I'd like to stay in bed.' She widened her eyes and clicked her tongue rapidly. Elona jumped at the unexpected sound, then Tek stopped. 'Sso sssorry, I forgot. That's what my people do—at leasst, I think— to laugh. Your vaces change eassily, mine is not so ... verssatile.' She clicked again and Elona wasn't sure if she was demonstrating or laughing.

'Do you mind if I ask...' said Elona.

'How I'm here?' Tek looked out the window. 'I try to remember sometimess. I don't know. Mother found me when she was looking for a losst goat.' Her voice trailed off.

'Perhaps we could stay in bed,' said Elona.

'Mother wouldn't like it.' She clicked again then stood smoothly, pulling her thick woollen nightgown over her head and picking up her clothes.

'Oh,' Elona said. 'You haven't got a tail.'

Tek froze for a moment and then turned her head slowly. It turned further than a human neck would have allowed. Elona felt hot, she wanted to crawl into a hole and disappear.

Tek took a deep breath, then replied, 'Neither have you.' She pulled on her leather clothes and went downstairs, clicking loudly.

When Elona finally summoned sufficient courage to go downstairs, Tek had already left; Usala was preparing scrambled eggs and there was bread and butter on the table.

'No, they don't have tails,' Usala said as she turned the eggs over in the pot. Elona cringed. 'Tek thinks the men don't either but she's not sure.'

'I'm so sorry—'

'Not to worry, she laughed all through breakfast. She said your face was a picture.' Usala came over with the pot and turned out a large pile of scrambled eggs onto Elona's plate. 'Eat up, there's work to do.' She inspected the stitched gash on Elona's arm.

'That's nasty. Tek sewed it neat, hope it doesn't turn bad.'

Elona lay in the dark, listening to Tek's quiet breathing and trying not to scratch her itching wound. She knew she could mend it if she dared. And why not? She was safe now. Nobody knew where she was, or even if she was alive—except Jalka, but the mountains and snow stood between them now. She just needed to be careful.

She closed her eyes and relaxed, picturing her arm, picturing the wound; and saw it. A damaged pattern as if someone had scribbled across her arm. She imagined what the pattern should look like and overlaid it on the scribble, though nothing happened. The pattern she had made was like a gossamer spider web. The scribble was hard and harsh. Somehow, she had to strengthen her pattern, though she could find no source of light nearby.

She imagined the smaller ley-circle at the abandoned Slissac ruins. She felt for it and pulled a tiny trickle of light from it, slowly strengthening the pattern she had made. As she took each step her confidence grew. The new pattern for her arm was strong enough and dissolved the injury; she could feel the skin of her forearm tingling as the new pattern took hold. She wondered in passing what it would be like to watch it happening.

Finally, no trace of the injury remained and the pattern of her arm looked whole; she released the light that streamed to her, expecting it to disappear. But it did not. It no longer flowed into her but into another channel, a thin almost invisible line that led from her into the distance. Curious, she encouraged the light to fill the channel; it widened, thickened and exploded with power that blinded her. She sat up with a cry.

Tek was at her side in a moment. 'What's wrong?'

Elona began to cry.

'It's alright, Elona,' said Tek, putting her arm around her. 'You're ssafe here.'

'No, I'm not,' she sobbed. 'I saw her, she tried to kill me, and she's going to kill them. I have to stop her. I'm the only one who knows what she's doing.'

'I don't know what you mean but you can't go anywhere 'til Sspring.'

31

Trying to hide her arm was pointless. The dead flesh fell off in clumps, revealing pink, unscarred skin below. Usala frowned at her.

'Your mother was a healer, Elona of Corlain. You have the gift, it seems.'

'I'm sorry.'

'Sorry? It is a wondrous power, a mighty strength. My sisters built an empire on it.'

'Did you know my mother?'

Usala paused in her kneading of fresh dough, looking into the past.

'I did not meet her, I knew of her. I heard with sadness what became of her. It was shortly after I followed my own destiny and came to this place.' She went back to the dough and pounded it. 'But why sorry, child?'

'I must go, Usala. I cannot stay; I put you and Tek in danger.'

'Danger fills the world, child.'

'If you know of my mother then you know of Lady Metrid of Betlain?'

Usala pounded the dough harder.

'I met her when she was a novice. I know her.'

Elona spooned her porridge in silence. Usala stopped pounding, took a clay pipe from the mantel and a taper from the fire, puffed it alight. 'Perhaps I will tell you. The Lady Metrid bore a daughter shortly before your birth. To her you are a threat on her designs on the throne. Her family once occupied it and she believes is hers by right.'

'She tried to kill my mother! She tried to kill me! With Hope now married to Drahail she will kill the King and the Prince himself and she will rule. What pattern can a healer use to kill instead of heal? But worse we are linked, somehow, something she did to me; even now she knows where I am. She will send soldiers to finish the job she started, that's why I have to go.'

'You are a good girl, Elona. But she cannot reach you. The passes are closed; nothing will reach us here until Spring returns.' She breathed in the smoke of her pipe and exhaled it slowly. 'For now you are safe.'

Winter came to the mountains. Thick falls of snow blanketed the slopes and houses, the passes into and out of the valley were choked off and Elona fretted. Usala put her to work as soon as she was able, building up her strength. Life became a repetitive round of daily tasks, clearing snow from around the house, taking care of the animals, bringing in wood to dry by the fire, and cleaning.

With the spring melt the valley came alive with water; the frozen river transformed into a rushing torrent and overflowed its banks. The days became longer and Tek would disappear for days at a time, returning with fresh meat and skins. There was more work to do and Elona chafed as Usala insisted the higher passes would still be blocked.

'When can I leave?' Elona asked one evening when Tek had been away for three days. She and Usala sat facing the flickering fire sipping at warm goat's milk flavoured with sweet-tasting roots. 'When will the passes be free of snow? I have to warn them what she is doing.'

'Why not stay? Your hands make life easier here.'

'I can't, they will come for me anyway, she will send people to kill me and if I am here they will kill you and Tek. I have to do this; she will kill the King and even the Prince. Somehow she brought the madness to me so that Hope would marry the Prince. It was because of her that I killed my best friend and brought more grief to my father. I have no choice. I can't change what she has done, but I can stop her from doing more.'

There were sounds of a horse outside and Elona went to the door. Tek came trotting up through the mud. She leapt down and, without unsaddling the horse, rushed past Elona and into the house. Elona turned to listen. 'Soldierss of Tirnia are coming from the north.'

'How long?'

'They may not arrive until tomorrow night. I rode hard.'

Elona followed her in. 'You see? I've delayed too long already. I have to leave now.'

'In the morning,' said Usala. 'They have to sleep too, and the horse is tired. Stable her, rub her down well.' Tek went back outside; Usala came to the door and spoke to Elona. 'Seems you're right. Tek will go with you.'

'Why should I endanger someone else? I can look after myself.'

'Because she can guide you, and if they come here they'll not be kind to her. The villagers are not bad people but even they don't take kindly to her, even though they've known her from a babe.' Usala ran her hands across her eyes. 'She can take you to where you need to go; then she'll come back.'

'I am sorry.'

It was before dawn when Tek shook her awake. 'We must go now.' Elona dressed hastily in Tek's clinging clothes and stumbled downstairs in a tired daze. Tek and Usala were outside by the horse that was already saddled and loaded. The sky was the insipid blue of pre-dawn and frost crunched beneath their feet. Elona pulled the hood over her head.

Usala clasped Elona to her and kissed her. 'My blessings go with you. Be brave, child, do what you must do.'

And to her own surprise Elona cried as well. 'I will.'

Then Tek helped her mount the horse before turning to Usala.

They stood apart for a long moment then rushed into a tight embrace. Tek kept repeating 'Mother. Mother.'

Tears flooded from Usala's eyes. 'I love you, my daughter. My love will go with you wherever you are. Be strong, be strong for her and come back when it's safe.'

'Mother, I don't want to go. I don't want to leave you.'

Usala tried to pull herself away but Tek still clung. 'My dearest daughter, you must show her the way. Please.' Then the passion seeped from them and Tek pulled back.

'I do as you will.'

'You are a good girl.'

'I love you.'

'I love you. I will be with you.'

Tek turned and mounted in front of Elona, took the reins and turned the horse. Tek guided it down to the frothing river and, where it was widest, they forded. When Elona looked back she could see Usala still standing, watching until they could see her no more.

A strong southerly wind had blown up in the night and tattered clouds streamed across the dark sky, underlit by the rising sun. They travelled southeast, heading deeper into the mountains. A frost highlighted the rocks and as the light of dawn grew each rock and boulder was outlined with a white glow. The horse walked slowly along a track. Elona sat behind, her arms around Tek's waist.

'Where are we going? Shouldn't we follow the river northwards?' Elona asked.

'We will run into their arms if we do. There is a higher pass this way, it should be clear.'

The light grew but Elona found herself slipping into a dream halfway from waking. She felt the pull of the earth beneath her. The trees sighed and moaned as their branches crackled in the cold and horse's footfalls crunched the stones and frosty grass.

The visual and aural images of the world faded until she perceived only the patterns. The magic that filled the land, the patterns that made the world as it is. From the complex patterns of the horse and the greater complexity of Tek to the simplicity of the grass and the trees. Beyond sight she reached out and touched the small animals that hibernated among the roots, and the ones that flew or prowled.

Then she drew a sharp breath as she reached out and touched minds that she knew, patterns that she feared: Wolves. A pack not far, yet she knew they did not as yet hunt but lay quiet in a cave.

Elona opened her eyes, the sun had yet to rise above the mountains ahead but already the mountain tops shone in raging whiteness, and the line of morning sunlight sank down their slopes. 'Wolves,' she said.

'Yess. Do they hunt uss now?'

'How do you expect me to know?'

Tek paused. 'You know. You know there are wolvess here though I see no recent signss. How many are they?'

'Twenty or so including the pups, maybe eleven adults and adolescents.'

'Which way are they?'

'Ahead and to the right, in a cave. They seem content for now.'

Once again Tek was quiet and the horse plodded on, needing no guidance, following the path.

'You see them with your mind's eye. I knew they were there; the cave is only a short time away at a good trot. They have hunted and killed and eaten, yet there will be but a day, if that, before they hunt again. The young get hungry quickly and the pack will seek food. This afternoon their scoutss will be afield. They will find the trail of a single horse; we will not be far ahead, not far enough for wolves on the hunt. They smell us and they will come for us, like the soldierss.' Tek sighed.

They did not stop to breakfast, but Tek rummaged in her bags and handed Elona cheese and dry bread that she ate as they walked. Presently they dismounted and walked, letting the horse rest from their weight. The scenery barely changed as they moved, but the walls of the valley slowly, almost unnoticeably, closed in and the path approached the river to their left. They reached a bridge, not a double-arched *Slissac* bridge but a rickety human construction of stone and wood.

They crossed carefully and continued with the river tumbling on their right. The valley became filled with fir trees and the sound of the river was muffled.

Destiny. She had been attacked by a mad wolf and a fall into the river had saved her. She had been attacked by a mad man, and the fall from a tower had saved her. She had been chased by a pack of wolves and leapt a gap over a river. Now it was wolves again. Less destiny, more a pattern. The pattern of her life seemed set and unchanging; she fled and she jumped or fell. Wolves and men, men and wolves. Someone, somewhere, making a pattern and imposing it on her, imposing destiny.

'Well, I do not like the pattern others have chosen for me. I don't want it.'

Tek swung her head around unnervingly far and stared at her with her impassive face. 'To defy the pattern of life is not easy.'

Elona blushed and laughed inwardly at her own presumption, then bristled against her own reaction. 'It is foolish to obey it if it is not of your own making. I have spent my life in a cage made by others for me and I am tired of it.'

'Are you not free of it now?'

'Being locked in a tower and imprisoned for insanity is not the cage, just one of the bars. Every day I have been in the cage, even with you and Usala, all I did was exchange one cage for another. Destiny. I have had enough of what others have destined for me.'

Tek waited for her to continue, their feet stepping noiselessly across grass and mud, while the river splashed its infinite song. Elona considered her possibilities of choice.

'For now I choose to continue.'

Tek's face remained impassive, as ever.

～

Elona opened her eyes in the dark, or she thought they were open, yet the dark was as dense as black velvet. They had camped in a clearing in the woods. She lay on her back but there was no sign of sky, not a hint of moonlight or of stars. She could not feel the cold on her skin, and instead there was a warmth across her entire body. She was dreaming.

She peered into the darkness and shapes emerged. The horse; Tek sleeping beside her; as Elona concentrated on each she grew aware of the life force, the patterning, within them. The horse was simple in structure though hot with power; Tek was a mass of complex, moving patterns. As she watched, Tek turned in her sleep and there were bright twists to her patterns.

Elona looked beyond and the solid patterns of trees now stood out against the blank rocks, which themselves held no pattern. Roots seemed to hang in thin air. Small animals, like bright sparks, flitted through the dim undergrowth or lay in quiescent sleep at the roots and branches.

She looked further back along the path and her consciousness moved like floating gossamer. The water of the river sparkled with motes of life that defined its depth and edges. She could not judge distances but it was not long before she came upon a dozen sharp forms glowing with the complexity of man.

They were closing in. They came to take her or to kill. For Tek they would show no mercy; they would kill her, and perhaps worse before they killed.

32

She knew what to do and scouted quickly about until she found her quarry, the wolves that lay peacefully asleep or rested on guard. They were far enough away; she hoped she could bring them in time. From what she had been taught, and what she had experienced, she knew the wolves could sense strong patterning, so she floated before the ones on guard and attempted to alert them. But they did not respond. Perhaps she was not really there, perhaps it was a dream.

What would happen if she collided directly with it? She directed her attention and drove into the wolf. Her selfness sundered in an explosion of sensations: Hunger, passion, focused intensity, love of the pack, feelings of the pack, then fear, fear of strangeness. Every wolf leapt to its feet, she could sense them all as if she were one of them. She could feel the stone beneath her feet, smell all the scents of the wind, all reinforced and complemented by the individual sensations of the pack.

They were in confusion, woken by strange feelings, by fear in the one on guard. They drew together sniffing the air for danger, ears listening for any sound beyond the movements of the pack.

Elona's individuality coalesced but still she found herself connected. In her mind she composed an image of the location of the men. The pack's attention caught it and their attention turned to food and attack; from the pack she felt the drive for direction and she supplied it. One by one the mature animals drifted away from the young ones and drove down the hill. They broke into a run, covering the ground between their cave and their prey in a fast, easy gait.

It did not take long and the wolves' instincts took over. They spread out, smelling the different scents of each of the men as they moved slowly and carefully through the woods, stealthily approaching the sleeping forms of Tek and Elona. The men did not notice the silent death approaching.

One man, then two, was identified at the rear of the group. Elona felt the elation and power that sped through them as they leapt silently and brought them down. The two men screamed but their screams turned to gurgles and were cut short as Elona tore their throats out. Their patterns disintegrated and swirled away.

She was being shaken awoke roughly by Tek, the bedclothes pulled from under her and thrown onto the horse.

'Quick! Wolvess!'

Elona pulled herself together; the remnant of her connection to the wolves told her that they were in chaotic combat with the men. Tek was already retreating, moving fast in the dimness of a spring dawn. The sky was cloudless and the air bitingly cold, the ground covered in frost. Elona shivered and pulled the hood tighter over her head, then forced her legs into pursuit of Tek.

'They are attacking the soldiers.' She panted as she caught up. Tek swung her head round with a snap.

'How do you know?'

Elona said nothing.

'And you were sscared of me?' Slow clicks.

They hurried on in silence; the sun crawled up from behind the mountains ahead and warmed them. The air lost its chill and Elona broke into a sweat as they toiled up a slope. Tek did not seem to sweat at all. Below them and to the right they could see the river hissing and leaping down the steep slope; looking back, they caught a glimpse of movement.

'We have no time to take the pass,' said Tek. 'You did not delay them long. We will climb to the ridge and, on the other side, I do not know.'

Elona was short of breath and did not answer.

They reached the top of the ridge. Spread out before them, in a ring of cliffs as if scooped from the mountains, lay a great hollow filled with water. She searched in vain to see a way out.

'You know this place? How do we get out, or hide?'

'We should have turned before, but they would have caught us. I have not come this way before, I feared it. This is where Mother found me; I thought there would be sssomething.'

'Did she live here?'

'I don't think ssso, no one lives here. The village says it is cursed.'

They started down the slope towards the water. There was a slight wind which kept the water lapping the gravelly beach, the sun reflecting dazzlingly off the water. Where the river flowed from the lake a bridge spanned it in a Slissac two-level arch. They reached the lake's edge and turned to the right crossing the bridge by the upper arch.

'We can't fight soldiers,' said Elona.

'Then they will kill us both.'

The horse's hooves clipped loudly on the stones as they moved along the edge of the water. The wind was cold and the sunlight gave no warmth. The water of the lake was perfectly clear and the slight ripples barely disturbed the view of its bed, sandy and rocky by turns with lines of green plants trailing through it.

The false peace was broken by a distant yell of triumph. They looked back and saw eight soldiers topping the ridge. Six descended towards them, two remained on the height. It was eerie to see fate so clearly and yet at such a distance.

Elona stopped and turned to face the water.

'I am tired of being a victim!' She shouted across its surface and the echoing words mocked her. A pattern in the water caught her eye, a regular triangular shape, with a line below it. Another beside it, patterns in the water carved into a rock.

Elona became excited, but suppressed it and glanced up at the soldiers, who were halfway down the slope; it would not be long. She looked back into the water. 'Why would this place be cursed? Why would people not live here? If this were a place where Slissac dwelt, perhaps they caught and killed my kind. Perhaps they're still here?'

'Mother never said there were Slissac here.'

'There was you! You came from here! There must be a way in; why else would they have made a bridge? You came out; somewhere here. Come on!' She moved faster along the water's edge towards the cliff face, staring into the deep water.

Every now and then, through water weed, she glimpsed more markings and writings. Finally, they reached the cliff, and it too was carved with Slissac symbols; but there was nowhere else to go. Elona climbed on to the wall of stone and clung to it. Using the carved shapes as handholds and she started along the water's edge.

'Are you crazy!' shouted Tek.

'There has to be a way in.'

Tek looked back, the men were coming along the water's edge at a fast pace. They weren't running but their strides were purposeful, they were confident they would have no difficulty with two women, and they had yet to recognise the nature of their second quarry. Tek breathed deep, took the saddlebags from the horse, and climbed out onto the wall.

Elona followed the carved patterns of the Slissac; once her foot slipped into the water, it was numbingly cold. Tek was stronger and soon caught up to her. They had gone for less than half an arrow-shot when the writing ran out and they were stranded without a guide.

'Where is the entrance?' Elona yelled in desperation, banging her fist against the smooth rock. 'There must be a way in.'

Voices of the soldiers could now be heard, jeering and taunting for them to return. They still had not seen Tek's face. Elona looked back and down; the water did not seem deep but she knew that could be an illusion. The weed lay flat in a kind of arc, each strand pointing towards them. Pointing below them, driven by a current.

'The entrance is below us. The current makes the weed lie flat, it points the way.'

'But how do we get in?' asked Tek.

'The same way. Down there.'

'But if you're wrong?'

Elona hesitated. Her heart beat hard in her chest; without another word, she took a deep breath and threw herself back from the cliff.

The cold water gripped her and numbed every part of her skin. She opened her eyes to see a black hole in the grey stone. She turned towards it, the current grabbing her and shooting her like an arrow, feet first, into the void.

Pressure built in her ears; her eyes were open but she could see nothing, and her ears were beaten by a rushing, bubbling sound. There were twists and turns; more than once her knees struck smooth rock, once her head was struck a glancing blow. Everything was happening so fast that it seemed an age before she needed to breathe, yet the pounding journey continued.

Feelings of languor seeped through her, tiredness coursed through her veins as her blood became ice, and her lungs throbbed and cried out to be released.

33

———

Just as she felt she couldn't hold out any longer, the water pressure lessened and she found herself falling through air. She breathed in deep and crashed into another pool of water. Her numbed skin transmitted little pain and she floundered to the surface in utter darkness. As she surfaced she heard a second body gasping for air and plunging down with a vicious splash beside her. Moments later she heard another intake of breath above the continuous crashing of water around her.

'Tek!' She tried to shout, but her voice was thin and cold, her teeth chattering. All she heard in return was a grunt. 'Can you swim?' There was a second grunt. 'Follow me.'

Elona swam slowly away from the continuous downpour of water. Every other stroke she repeated the words 'follow me.' Behind her she could hear the movement of Tek in the water.

She reached the edge of the pool. Like a huge bath, the side was smooth stone that rose above the waterline to a sharp edge; Tek reached it behind her. She could find no handhold nor foothold in the wall. Elona desperately tried to pull herself out but her numbed arms and legs would not obey her. Tek put a hand beneath her, and with the extra push Elona managed to heave herself out. Immediately she reached down and helped Tek out. Both lay panting and shivering on the rock.

'H-h-h-hold me c-c-c-close,' Tek said. They crawled together and wrapped their arms and legs around one another. There seemed no heat that they could give one another, yet Elona was comforted and relaxed.

She awoke cold; her muscles ached ferociously and she was stiff. She tried to raise her head and it pounded with pain before letting it back down to the floor. Her ears were filled with the constant splashing from the waterfall. She placed her palms flat on the stone and pushed herself up. Her joints creaked painfully and some muscles in her neck felt like they were tearing apart, but finally she reached a kneeling position.

There was nothing to see but blackness all round. Only the occasional splash of water reached her and sprinkled her skin. Tek was nowhere in reach. She hoped there would be the glowing moss somewhere here; she just needed to find it.

Elona tried to clear her mind, tried to concentrate, to generate the energy to activate the moss. She shivered. The darkness remained without form. The last time she had burnt out the moss she had been healing herself. She conjured an image of her own body, kneeling in the deep underground. She reached out for the energy that would heal her. The cave lit up.

'By the...!' cried a voice from a good distance away. Elona stared around the brightly lit cavern; every patch of moss was glowing.

From a hole in the roof, at the centre of the cavern, poured a continuous flood, the water rippling out from where it fell in all directions. The cavern was thirty paces wide and around it was a walkway at water level and an upper gallery set slightly back into the walls. Intricate, almost familiar, patterns were inscribed all around. Ahead of her the path led up a short flight to a tunnel from which more light streamed.

Tek's shape appeared silhouetted in the tunnel mouth.

'What happened?' she said. 'Wass that you?'

Elona climbed to her feet and walked stiffly to the stairs; movement came easier with each step, though her head still throbbed.

'I think so ... but it wasn't like this before. The moss shines when it's fed with magic. It happened by accident before, and I had to touch it. This time...'

She climbed the wet steps; Tek turned away and went through into a second chamber. The noise of the water faded as Elona followed her through. This bare room was smaller than the one below, but on the right was a set of stairs leading to the gallery level. There was a second opening almost directly opposite. Apart from mossy patches on the walls the room was featureless.

'How far does it go?' Elona asked.

'I'n not sure, without the light I couldn't explore far. You'll need to do your magic again.' She pointed at the moss on the far side, which was barely glowing. Elona turned to the wall behind and gently pulled off a strip of brightly shining moss.

'I can make the light, but they don't get hot.'

'Will it burn?'

'Too wet,' she said, staring around at the room. 'There's nothing here, let's go on.'

Tek looked at her for a long moment. 'I want to go up the stairs.'

'Why?'

Tek shrugged. 'I don't know; I feel odd, down here.'

'We can go up.'

'No, I th-think I'll stay down, it scares me too.'

Tek pulled her own strip of moss from the wall and led the way from the room through the second opening. There was a long stone passage which led through another opening. From there, wide steps led down to a quay at the side of a wide expanse of water; the glowing moss did not show the other side. Tied up at the side was a small boat which gently bumped against the stone quay. Above, along the edge of quay, ran the gallery with stairs at intervals.

On their right were more doors, some normal-sized but others double in width and height. Slissac inscriptions were written neatly across each, large and small. Elona and Tek looked in through one entrance to a hugely wide space, completely empty.

'Warehouses,' Elona said, and her voice echoed uncomfortably across the water.

'Warehouses?'

'Big storage places for trade.'

'What trade?'

'I have no idea, can't you read this?'

'I feel like I should but I can't.' she stared around again. 'But I do know this place, someone holding my hand, pulling me. Others running, screaming and fire and death—' her voice had grown louder, now it trailed off. Elona watched her sink to the floor, the moss making strange shadows as she hugged it to her breast.

'They had come, they attacked, we ran, mummy took me and we ran. We came through here. Soldiers fighting and killing, screaming and crying. We came down from up there, I didn't understand why we came down from the gallery, we never had before. But she kept going. We ran through one of these warehouses, it was full of chests. There was a door—' Tek paused. '—then stairss up. She pushed me out into the daylight. I turned to ask her, but there was only stone. I couldn't see the door, there was no door and she was gone.' Her voice broke into sobs and tears formed in her eyes reflecting the moss-light. She whispered 'Mummy.' And howled in grief.

Elona came forward, crouched and put her arm around her shoulders. Tek turned and sobbed on her shoulder.

'She saved you. She was what a mother should be.' Elona replied.

Tek straightened up and roughly brushed the tears from her eyes. 'There is nothing here, we must go. We don't have much to eat. Trade and travel were on the water. We have to take the boat.' She turned to stare down at Elona. 'You think my mother saved me? She abandoned me. How could she know I'd be saved? You should know what it's like!'

Elona opened her mouth but changed her mind. 'We'll need to find oars or something; I don't think there will be a wind down here.'

'No wind. Current like a river. The water flows in, it must flow out. But we will need something to paddle and steer with.'

They went back to the boat and found it had a rudder with a small tiller, but there were no oars nor anywhere to put them.

Searching through a burnt out warehouse yielded two rough pieces of wood, which would have to serve.

Elona climbed nervously aboard the boat; it rocked violently until she sat down. Tek untied the rope and kept the boat pulled into the quay while she climbed down into it. It rocked threateningly again but remained upright.

With both paddling, they made erratic progress out into the pool. As they reached the middle the current took hold and carried it along parallel to the quayside.

The light from the far end of the cavern barely lit the end wall of the cavern that loomed ahead of them. The current pulled them smoothly towards a darker patch and into a tunnel. The water carrying them along at a slow but comfortable pace, there was no need to paddle and steering was a simple affair.

'They will think we have drowned,' said Tek.

'Until they are told otherwise.'

Unchanging stone came and went around them, never varying in width or texture. The light travelled with them and it seemed as if they were still as the tunnel moved past them. Every now and then the usually featureless blocks of wall would have a Slissac inscription cut into it. If there were any kind meaning or pattern to the marks they could not tell, and they soon stopped noticing.

Quiet reigned, save for the gentle lapping of water or the occasional creak of wood as Tek or Elona shifted their position. They did not talk because the words made huge echoes in the blackness.

After a long time Tek whispered. 'Let me steer. You sleep.'

The boat rocked dangerously as she clambered to where Elona sat. Tek took a position on the other side of the tiller while Elona carefully climbed forward clinging to the sides of the boat. They both relaxed once the positions were changed.

Elona closed her eyes. She did not feel tired, but as she relaxed her body's aches overwhelmed her and she fell deeply to sleep.

She awoke once more to darkness, accompanied by the creaking of wood and the gentle lapping of water. She remembered where she was.

'Tek?' She spoke quietly.

'I am here.' The voice floated through darkness to her.

'What happened to the light?'

'It went out.'

'How long ago?'

'A long time.'

'How long have I slept?'

'A long time.'

'You should have woken me.'

'It wass no matter.'

'I could have restored the light.'

'We don't need it. The boat does not approach the sides very often.'

Elona stopped arguing, as there seemed little point. Tek could be obstinate. Elona was stiff and hungry but felt less tired. At least she could exercise her power and generate light. The boat rocked as she sat up on one of the cross benches facing the rear towards Tek. She closed her eyes, then smiled at the lack of necessity and opened them again.

Each time she did this it seemed to get easier. To reach down inside and stretch out that magic sense, to reach out and touch— suddenly the bench on which she sat was ripped from beneath her. something crashed into her shins, spinning her forwards.

34

———

She heard Tek cry out at the same moment. The tunnel filled with light and Elona saw Tek tumbling backwards from the boat as it shot beneath her. Elona barely had time to raise her hands to stop her head striking the rear of the boat. Her outstretched hands pushed the tiller aside; the boat turned abruptly and crashed with an echoing thud, then the ground along the wall.

The boat coasted forward. Elona could see Tek splashing in the water behind, swimming in strong strokes to catch up. Elona reached down and helped her back into the boat. Elona turned to look at her companion. The Slissac's eyes were wide staring back at her.

'What did you do?'

Elona looked at the boat. No oars. No mast. Just a tiller. The glow-moss was shining again in the boat, as they drifted they left the bright patches on the walls behind.

'I was trying to light the moss.'

'Try again—but more gently. And let's sit in the bottom of the boat.' They secured themselves firmly.

'At least it only happens when I concentrate.' She closed her eyes against the light.

Elona reached out very gently with the lightest possible touch she could muster. The light became brighter through her eyelids and she felt herself being pushed backwards as the boat tried to pull away from them again. Tek breathed in sharply and her beak clicked again.

'It's working. We are going faster.' Her voice trembled. Elona lost her concentration and opened her eyes; the boat slowed. The moss did not seem to be suffering and the tunnel was clearly passing them much faster. She turned her head and saw a whole stretch of dimly lit tunnel behind, clumps of moss glowing. She could see the tunnel was now dead straight and seemed to pass away into the infinite.

Keeping her eyes open Elona once more concentrated and the boat picked up speed. It was thrilling and a broad smile expanded on Elona's face.

'You like this?' Tek's voice held a tremor.

'Oh yes. This is power. If my destiny was to be chased forever at least I can set the pace.'

They sat in silence a while longer. Elona found that she could add an intensity to her concentration that made the boat respond with more speed. Tek moved uncomfortably as the boat moved faster. After a while she let it go and they drifted with the current. 'You must be tired. Let me take it while you sleep.'

Tek looked reluctant.

'I will not drive it too fast.'

Tek sighed and let her have the tiller, looking as if there were something she wanted to say. She climbed forward and lay down. For a moment she lay still, then raised her head.

'You promise?'

It was not long before Tek's breathing slowed and became deeper. Elona once more concentrated, the moss brightened a little and the boat moved forward in the water. Both effects simultaneously, light and power. It did not really make sense; she must be doing it wrong, there should be a way to tune in on one or other. She knew it was the moss that glowed, but what drove the boat? What was there on the bottom of it that made it drive forward? Something that had been there the whole time while the boat had been waiting for them by the quay. Something that did not die in twenty years?

She ceased to concentrate and the boat returned to its snail's pace. Once she was sure that it was no longer powered she reached out one hand and dipped it into the water. Cautiously she touched the underside of the boat. It was furry with short, straight strands covering as much of the bottom as she could feel.

Hardly daring to breathe, she applied a little concentration. The strands vibrated and moved in fast, tiny waves; she felt her touching fingers being pushed backwards. It felt alien and she pulled her hand out of the water quickly with a shiver. Little hairs, little living things on the bottom of the boat that responded just-so to her command. The moss was easy to understand, in a way, she gave them power and they gave it back in a different way. But this was not the same, and under her command the creatures on the bottom of the boat cooperated to drive it forward. Was it thousands of single creatures or one big one? Her skin crawled at the thought; better to think of them as lots of little things, as one creature alone would give her nightmares. Perhaps if she understood more they could go backwards, or turn. She remembered what had happened when she had put too much power into the moss. She decided she would not try just yet.

Hours passed and they had made a good deal of progress when Tek finally woke. Elona had been rehearsing what she wanted to say over and again.

'How far do we go?'

Tek looked at her with a slightly confused look in her eye. Elona felt an anger churning inside.

'Where are we going? How far is it? This tunnel goes on straight as a poker. Nothing has changed in all the time I have been driving us forward. I am tired and I am hungry and we don't seem to be getting anywhere.'

Tek shifted her weight in the boat as she sat up straight, facing the rear, making it rock back and forth. She looked back down the tunnel, its patchy mosses glowing away into the far distance. She looked to the sides at the speed with which the tunnel sped past them. She turned her head back to Elona's taut, strained face.

'You should rest.'

'You haven't answered my questions.'

Tek sighed and looked down, then up again squarely at Elona's face.

'I don't know. I was young. I know some things but I don't know where we are going. I don't even speak my own language.' She paused, rubbing her beak with one finger. 'But I'm sure we'll get somewhere in two or three days.'

'How do you know?' Elona insisted.

'The traders on the boats would say.' She leant forward and put her hand on Elona's knee. 'Won't you please rest?'

'And when we get there? You'll be alright, but I'm human.'

'I don't know. Maybe they're all gone.'

Elona pulled back, straightening herself. She closed her eyes and sighed. The boat lost speed. They exchanged places and Elona curled up in the bottom of the boat. Elona lifted herself on her elbow and pursed her lips.

'I'm sorry, I—Thank you.'

Tek said nothing.

'And I am very hungry.'

'We may eat tomorrow.'

'Or the next day.'

Once more there was darkness and silence. Elona came slowly to consciousness. Cold air filled her lungs. Her clothes hung heavily on her and clung with a dampness that refused to dry. She wished she were anywhere but here. Her mind slipped back to chains in a freezing tower. Almost anywhere.

There was the sound of water lapping between hull and quay, distant dripping. She was not on the boat, she lay upon stone. It was damp like everything else, covered in patchy moss that pressed against her cheek. Her stomach yearned for food in that familiar way that insisted it would be easy to feed.

Elona rolled on to her back and stared blindly at the ceiling. Perhaps she should stay here forever. The cloak of dark supported her, hid her and clothed her. None could touch her here; there was no one here at all. The realisation struck with its second blow that made her sit up so fast her head swam. Where was Tek?

With an instantaneous reaction of terror she flooded the darkness with her awareness and wall to wall moss exploded into light, flaming briefly; then going black. She heard water sloshing violently and the boat grating against the stones of the quay. Her eyes were dazzled with after-images and she cursed her own stupidity. Yet she could see the water tunnel now or at least where it entered the cavern; there was no exit. Moss further away from her that hadn't burnt out glowed brightly. In front of her was a doorway and that too was backlit by mosses further away.

Footsteps came running and a shadow moved swiftly through the doorway, followed by a figure that stood silhouetted against the light.

'What's wrong?' Tek's clipped words echoed through the cavern.

'I thought I'd lost you.' Elona sobbed, she held her knees and cried. Tek put her head on one side then walked slowly across the floor. She knelt by Elona and, once again, tentatively put her arms about her.

'Shhhhhhh...' Tek made the soothing sounds of her mother as she held Elona. 'I am here.'

'Sorry, it was just—sorry.' Tek held her for a long time and stroked her hair, long after her sobs had subsided. It felt comfortable and warm.

'You know,' said Tek. 'I wish I had hair.'

Finally they let each other go and Tek went to examine the boat.

'You should be more careful.' She examined the hull of the boat. 'You could break something.'

'It wouldn't be the first time,' Elona replied and smiled gently. She shook herself and broke the spell. 'What did you find?'

'Animal bones. Old ones. I did not recognise it. And fresh *sikechak* droppings, down the overflow.'

'Is there a way out?'

'If they are getting in then we may be able to get out.'

Elona stared around the dimly lit cavern.

'I really am very hungry.'

35

The smell was terrible, and it became worse when they had to plunge their fingers into thick layers of *sikechasa* droppings as they scrambled down the incline, freezing water rushing past their feet. Small *sikechasa* hung and clambered above their heads letting out the occasional cry.

'It is night outside,' said Tek when they paused to catch their breath on a level section.

Elona was standing ankle deep in water with her arms clasped round her body, trying to retain some warmth. 'How do you know?'

'The adults are not here. This may be a good thing, otherwise they'd be putting down another layer of droppings.' She clicked her jaw but Elona didn't know if she was laughing or cold.

The quality of the sound changed, and the echo gave way to open splashing and fresh air wafted in to replace the atrocious stink. They squeezed through a low opening and emerged on a steep hillside covered in long grass; the sky was filled with stars that silhouetted ridges and peaks that edged them around. But dawn was edging up behind the mountains.

Ahead a valley spread out the occasional light illuminated the dark landscape, but directly below them dozens of large, shadowy buildings clinging to the mountainside made a blacker night. Strange smells rose from it.

Elona stared at it. Fear ate at her stomach and she flexed her fingers that seemed to have gone numb. A Slissac town, full of the creatures that had enslaved her people all those years ago—but what did that mean now? She knew Tek; she was not different, she was just a person, she was good and kind and had not killed her or enslaved her. She had to get back to the human world and stop Metrid.

She glanced at Tek, who was also staring down. 'Do you remember it?'

'I think ssso.'

A cry went up from behind them and figures rose from the ground. A stream of noises and clicks poured from behind. Tek breathed in sharply, and haltingly spoke with the same clicks and noises.

'Don't move, they are thinking of killing us where we stand. Please pull your hood over your head a bit tighter, they don't know you're human yet.'

There were more clicks. Tek put her hands on her head and stumbled down the slope. Elona copied her and followed. The armed party fell in behind them. The sun's light brightened the sky. The slope flattened out and they came to a high stone wall surrounding the town with rounded towers at intervals. Its stones were covered in moss and lichen. The voice issued further instructions and Tek went towards the right.

As the light increased a wide road became visible. It was divided into three sections: a central raised path flanked by two smaller ones. As dawn came, carts moved along the outer lanes. Elona pulled the hood closer round her face and followed Tek.

They approached the road, and where it intersected the wall an arch with twin towers stood; the three parts of the road split and three sets of gates barred the way. Slissac armsmen stood at the nearest gate waiting for them and opened a door as they approached. Suddenly Tek stopped.

A furious exchange took place as she refused to go any further. Elona could hear her voice wavering with fear, but she stood firm. Elona was desperate to know what was happening but the guards were too close, so she hid behind Tek's back and kept her face covered.

There was confusion and they argued among themselves in long streams of incomprehensible hisses and clicks, when finally Tek turned around and leant down to Elona.

'I am ssso ssscared.'

'What's happened?' Elona asked as quietly as she could.

'They want us to go through the ssshthrakasa door. I won't, it's inssulting.'

'Why?'

'I don't know! I jussst reacted, I wasssn't thinking.'

Further explanation was interrupted by a guard, who addressed Tek directly and guided them to a set of steps leading up to the central lane. A door in the central gate opened, and there they climbed to the higher level and went through. A new set of guards escorted them through the wide, covered gatehouse and a second door into the town proper.

Elona expected to see a town similar to her own, or even the city at Canvor with the same streets and buildings, the same shops and signs. In the half light of dawn she did not understand what she could see. Streets in two levels crisscrossed and tunnelled into the mountainside; high walkways, always with two levels, crossed from one building another. But each building looked like a fortress, with no windows on the lower floors, arrow slits higher up; they had crenelated tops and everything was in grey and black.

Her hood was ripped from her head and noise erupted all around them, with clickings and hissings, and a dozen spears pointed at her from a dozen scaly hands. Her nerve broke and she grabbed the only person she trusted. 'Tek!' she cried and hid her face under her arm.

The noise was chopped off at her word, as if by an axe.

∾

Elona jumped at the sound of the bolts on the door being slid back, and she backed into the corner behind the door. The stone room was filled with sunlight that lit up the bed and chair. A shadow walked across them as a *Slissac* wearing a light grey woollen tunic over trousers stepped through.

'Elona?'

'Tek!' she cried. There was a glint of metal in Tek's hand. 'W– What's happening?'

Tek sat on the chair. The door was closed behind her and the room was plunged back into semi-darkness, the bolts drawn again.

'What's happening? Are we safe?'

'No, I don't really think so. But they don't want to kill us yet.'

'You can understand them?'

Tek clicked. 'I could talk before I was losst. I thought I had forgotten how.' Tek turned the metal object over in her hands.

Elona came and crouched beside Tek, putting her arms about her waist. 'I thought I would lose you.' She felt Tek's hand caress her hair.

'I don't think I an sso eassy to lose.' Tek sighed quietly.

'What's wrong?'

'I have to do something I don't want to do.'

Elona's fear increased as a dozen possibilities shot through her mind. She let go of Tek's waist and stood, backing away to find the comfort of the corner. 'What is it you have to do?'

'I have to cut your hair off.'

'Is that all?' Elona laughed nervously. 'Please don't do that again, I have lived through much worse than having my hair cut off.' She sighed. 'It's because I'm supposed to be your slave, isn't it?'

'How did you know? We have to talk to a ... a grandmother. And nobody else is willing to touch you—I wouldn't want them to anyway.'

Tek still looked reluctant. Elona came to her and gently took the shears from her hands. She gripped them firmly in one hand and bunched her hair with the other. She squeezed the shears and they sliced effortlessly through, strands of hair drifting to the floor. She repeated the action again and again, until she could not find any more. Tek took over and trimmed it as close to her scalp as she could.

Elona ran her hand across her head, feeling the uneven bristles scratch her palm. She wondered what the Sisters of Taymalin used to keep their heads so smooth.

Tek went out briefly and returned with a change of clothes and a bowl to wash in. It had felt good peeling the leather from her skin and she wished desperately for a bath. She still had to wear trousers but at least they weren't so tight. Tek left again, telling her she had to prepare and that Elona must wait.

Later, guards had come, and they stared at her with their snake-like eyes; it was worse than when she had been mad. It was as if she was a monster. As if they'd never seen a human before. There had been many flights of stairs until they emerged into late afternoon sunlight. She glimpsed Tek on the upper lane, while she was pushed along the low path. There was no one else on the street, but there were many eyes peering from high windows and the occasional shout in an otherwise silent walk.

The lower path slowly rose as they approached one huge building set partly into the cliff, side roads curving off into caves in the rock face. She was only a little below Tek's level when they came to the three sets of doors in the tower and were admitted.

Elona was taken by a circuitous route through the building, eventually emerging in a large hall cut into the rock of the mountain at the back, but the front faced out to the sun. She caught a glimpse of a group of Slissac seated at the far end before she was forced to walk behind a screen that ran the length of the hall. She could hear Tek and her guards walking up the centre of the hall.

They came to a halt where the screen ended, Elona was prodded forward. She understood this much of protocol. The grandmother was so exalted that she should not look at her, so she kept her eyes fixed on the smooth dark stone at her feet and moved forward in small steps until she stood behind Tek. The air felt unnaturally cold against her scalp. There was a long pause and she prostrated herself. There was an audible reduction in tension as many Slissac breathed out.

36

A wooden block was struck three times. One of the Slissac at the front stepped forward and spoke briefly. There was a pause and Tek gave a long, rhythmical, almost chant-like reply. At her words a murmur started round the hall; clicks and hisses of arguments, and then the noise grew.

Elona couldn't contain herself and whispered, 'What is it?'

Three strikes of the wood block brought silence back to the hall. The interrogation continued with short questions from the old Slissac, followed by long, detailed answers from Tek. And then it was at an end. Tek whispered, 'We have to go. Don't turn your back on them.'

Elona suppressed the "I know" that was on the tip of her tongue. She managed to get to her feet and backed behind the screens then kept her head down as she made her way out of the hall.

The streets were still clear but things changed when they got back to the original building. She could hear Tek arguing vehemently with someone. And instead of being brought to her cell she was taken to another room with windows. Tek was waiting and her guards left them alone.

'I didn't want to leave you there, I inssissted they bring you.'

'I am your slave.'

Tek clicked. 'At least we're alive. Come to the window, I like the view. The moons are up.'

'Are we high up?'

'Yes.'

'I'd rather stay in here. Can I sit down?'

Tek clicked again. 'Of course. You don't have to ask. The bed is comfortable.'

Elona sat on it, and put her head in her hands. Trying to calm herself, everything felt so wrong and so different.

'What did she ask? The old woman.'

'My name. She asked me my name and I told her—my real name —I didn't know I knew it.'

'What is it?'

'Chara ko-Tek Tegina ar-Tek Guala ar-Gey Aytrueth Aka Hanna ar-Ku Jyrna ko-Ku Jyrna Aka Kalenaye. That's not all of it but all I can remember.'

'So, what should I call you?'

'Chara. Not Tek.'

'What does the rest of it mean?'

'Chara of the Aytrueth family, third daughter of Tegina, firsst daughter of Guala the Matriarch, of the Hanna area, the first ssplit of the family in Jyrku, which was the third ssplit of the family in Kalenaye.'

'So the Tek means daughter?'

'No, it means mother, or mistress. That's why they didn't kill you. You called me your mother.' Tek sighed. 'But I suppose my name is different now. They are all dead, sso I am the Matriarch. Chara ar-Gey Aytrueth. The Mother of the Aytrueth family. Jusst me, the mother and nothing else.'

Elona stood and went to her. She slipped her hand into Tek's, which closed about hers and clung to her arm. Tek looked out on to the dimming landscape, while Elona stared at the floor.

'I was always alone too. It was different for me, I know, but I was alone surrounded by people. I lost my mother before I knew her. She's there but not there. My Father never seemed to really care for me—'

'I'm sure he did.'

'Perhaps. Anyway, I have felt alone. You had Usala, who always loved you. I didn't seem to have anyone.' Elona then realised how pathetic it sounded. 'I have had few friends, and the two I did have ... they ... died. Then I seemed to have nothing but enemies.'

'I think it's the same in this place. At least with Mother I was safe, but there are some who don't like the fact I'm here, they don't want to believe it. It's like we're playing a game, and I don't know the rules.'

'We're the sisters of adversity,' Elona said suddenly, running her hand across the bristles of her hair.

'Yes, we are sisters.' said Tek. 'Elona tu-Gey Aytrueth.'

'Chara,' whispered Elona. 'Chara Corlain.'

Elona had prostrated herself once more before the Matriarchs in the great hall. Chara stood beside her and answered questions again. Elona heard Chara growing angry in her responses; at first she restrained herself, but as time wore on her temper frayed and finally tore.

Elona's heart beat faster. She didn't know what she should do, lying there on the cold stones waiting for judgment to be passed; her anger welled up. To be helpless in the face of these women—Slissac — who dared to judge. She had a task to fulfil; there was a murderess who would kill her King and his son, and take command of her land.

'I will not listen to this!' She suddenly shouted. She leapt to her feet. A ripple ran through the Matriarchs.

'Ask them why they found us on the hillside.'

'What?'

'When we came from the tunnels, they were waiting for us— why? Ask them that!'

Chara hesitantly formed the words. When there was no response she asked again, louder, stronger. Elona stared at them, and whenever she made eye contact with one she looked away. Finally the oldest responded.

'Magic. Someone released a wild magic.'

'That was me, I did it.'

Chara translated and listened to the response. 'They don't believe you.'

'Yes they do. They don't want to admit it because I am a slave and they're scared.' Elona wiped her hand across her cheek, trying desperately to think. But the old one spoke again.

'You are one of the slave race. You are the ones who destroyed the empire. You are accursed, you will be executed.'

'I am not a slave. I am Elona di-Gey Aytrueth, I am her sister! And if you dare to harm me or my sister, I will destroy you.' Elona took Chara's hand and looked the oldest Matriarch directly in the eye. The guards stepped forward as if to protect the Matriarchs, who pulled back and began arguing.

Chara turned to her. 'Now we've said something. Could you really do it?'

'I don't think so. Can you make out what they're saying?'

'No, but I keep hearing the word for sister, that's what's really got them bothered. They didn't want to believe I'm who I say I am.'

The discussion continued as the sun rose and warmed the hall. Elona and Chara stood and waited. As the sun reached them the Matriarchs came forward again.

'It has been decided. The families of Chara tu-Tek Aytrueth and the human shall be joined in sisterhood.'

'It's a trick,' Elona said vehemently. 'Why won't you listen to what I'm saying?'

It was late afternoon and they had been returned to Chara's rooms. Food, wine and water had been brought and now they stood once again by the window. Elona had her back to it so she could not see the drop.

'But they've given in.'

'It's politics; I lived with it long enough to know how it works. They've said it to appease us, well, probably to appease me. They're scared. They're scared of me because of what I might be able to do and they're scared of you because of what they've done. Don't you see?'

'No, I don't. They've accepted me because they said I could join my family to yours.'

'But I'm not Slissac! And they hate me.' She dropped her arms and sighed. 'Listen, why were you put outside by your mother?'

'Because of the attack.'

'And who is left of your family?'

'Me. Do sisters normally upset each other deliberately?'

'I don't know but that's not the point. Who killed your family?'

Chara turned away and walked into the room. 'I don't know.'

'Look at this place.' Elona threw a glance out the window. 'Every building is a castle. They are scared of each other; they don't know who's going to attack them next. This isn't a town, not really, it's a ... a battleground. Someone here killed your family, one of these Matri-archs, maybe more than one, sent her armsmen to kill your mother and your sisters and you.

'You're trouble to them. They think you're like them, that you'll do what they would do. They think you're going to try to find out which one it was and get them back. To take back what's yours and to take what's theirs too.'

Chara picked at a bowl of fruit. 'What will I do?'

'I remember what it's like to think that everyone is trying to kill you.'

37

Elona longed for human faces. She did not hate the Slissac, but she wanted to see something that wasn't iridescent green or blue. Once more she was isolated from those around her. It wasn't only physical form but language, though Elona managed to understand some of what was said. The constant jabber of hissings and clickings could be very hard to follow and she found it hard to make herself understood, as her mouth could not form the sounds properly.

The council of matriarchs insisted that she do something about her hair. That they hated her was patent; they wanted her to be a slave but she was willing to completely remove the hair on her head and her eyebrows for Chara's sake. The knife they delivered made her heart beat faster, as the patterning on its surface looked the same as those on the knife Metrid had given her. And it was as sharp. With Tek's help she shaved her head.

Chara had depended on her at first. She was a matriarch without resources of any kind and she needed allies. The family Kakrueth had offered their support; they were one of the smaller houses, and in the privacy of the matriarch's sanctum Chara had been told how the larger houses had wiped hers out. Elona wasn't sure about trusting them, but apparently they were related—not that that made much difference—and they were keen for power. They saw that aligning themselves to a reborn house of Aytrueth was one way to get it. There had been days of negotiation with Chara asking Elona for her advice on every matter. She didn't mind, but every day was one more day that the Lady Metrid tightened her hold on the Faerholme throne.

'I cannot stay, Chara.'

'I need you. How I can play this game by myself? You know the rules, I don't. I know how to catch and skin animals and here they have people who do that for me.'

'They're not doing it for you, they're doing it for the Kakrueth matriarch. You get to eat what she doesn't want.'

Chara took her hand. 'You understand these things. Please don't go yet.'

'I don't even know where we are.' Elona turned away and stared out the window into the north. The valley and the river must go somewhere, perhaps Tirnia.

It was like standing on the edge of a cliff. The hall was filled with Slissac; it was if the whole town was there, hundreds of them. It was the wedding all over again, but now, without her insane confidence, Elona trembled. Her hands were cold and her breathing ragged. She tried to control herself but it was hard. She glanced to her right. Across the room was Chara, though she couldn't see her at all beneath the volumes of black robes. She was wearing the same, and it was the one saving grace. At least the Slissac did not stare at her as a freak, for now she was another matriarch, of the House of Corlain.

She pursed her lips at the thought. Could she really call herself that? Was this all a sham and a lie? They had asked her if she was the elder female of her house, and she had explained that her mother still breathed but did not truly live, and that her father was the head of the house but she would inherit when he died.

She did not think they really understood; they were happy to call her Elona tu-Gey Corlain. Even more upsetting to them was Chara's desire to make Elona her sister when she was matriarch of such a distinguished family. Without other sisters it would put Elona second in line, whether Chara had daughters or not. They had tried to persuade Chara to make Elona her daughter instead, but she would not change her mind.

The three wooden blocks were sounded and the noise in the room evaporated. Chara was commanded to come forward. In the Slissac tongue she was blessed by the power of the earth mother and her children the moons; Elona and Chara had been through it several times, so that she would understand each part and make no mistakes.

'Who do you choose as sister, Chara ar-Gey Aytrueth Aka Hanna?'

'I choose Elona tu-Gey Corlain Aka Corlain to be my sister and my blood.'

Every eye was turned on her; she felt as if her legs were part of the stone floor. She breathed deep and forced her body to walk towards them. She could feel the animosity building behind her. At first it felt as if all were against her, but as each step brought her closer the hate coalesced into a single point. A pattern of cold white light flecked with red flames. Someone hated her, someone wanted this to stop, someone wanted to cut her down so her blood spilled on the ancient stones. This abomination, this human, this slave that mocked them with its pretences.

There was a murmur of sound that brought Elona back to the real world; she had stopped walking before she had reached Chara. The moment was broken and she no longer felt the point of hate. Instead, she concentrated on walking and crossed the final distance to receive the blessings of nature. In an effort to understand, Elona had asked whether someone could be an heir to both houses, only if the original family had no other direct heir was the reply, so that made her heir to both Corlain and Aytrueth, though she and Chara were the sole constituents of a family that owned nothing.

The Slissac high priestess stepped forward. She lifted the ancient staff polished by so many generations of hands, holding it horizontally before them both. She murmured words of patterning.

Tek placed her hand on the staff, and Elona put her hand on top for the right binding. The priestess chanted more loudly, though her face was expressionless as she looked intently at the two hands, then at Elona alone.

Elona could feel it. The binding did not want to attach, something prevented it. Elona closed her eyes. More than anything, she had known before she wanted to be sister to Tek. In the dark behind her eyes there was a blaze. The same binding held her as a sister to the woman who planned her death.

Elona shrugged. Metrid's strand of power withered.

The new one took its place.

Elona opened her eyes and looked directly into those of the priestess, who backed away as fast as she dared without losing her dignity.

'I have to get married,' Tek said.

'Married?'

'Well, take a partner, hussband I ssuppose.'

'Why?'

'Because I—we have nothing. We are borrowing everything on my name, that we will be able to pay it back on way or another.'

'You never get anything for free in politics,' said Elona.

'Sso I learn,' sighed Chara. 'I have been approached by a small family with no heirs and their matriarch is dying. I marry her eldesst sson and the family becomes mine.'

'What's he like?'

'Who?'

'The eldest son!'

'I don't know. Does it matter?'

'But what if you don't like him?'

'Then I won't mate with him. Why?'

'Because...' but Elona knew it didn't matter, not here, not among the Slissac. It was position and power. Just like everywhere else, no difference between Slissac or Human. 'I can't wait any longer, Chara, I have to leave, I have to stop Metrid.'

'Please wait for the wedding ceremony, I need you.'

~

He was here. She knew it was the same one. Somewhere in this room his hate bubbled and burned. The chamber they were in occupied the whole upper floor of the family Chara was taking over. The males stood on the left and she sat with the women on the right. She could feel all eyes boring into her bare head. She wished she could have been veiled again. Chara was, as was the male. He was very tall but more than that she couldn't tell, neither she nor Chara had seen him before today.

Chara really didn't care. In the days since they had arrived here she had become increasingly ... Slissac. Less dependent on Elona, more confident in her dealings with her people. Elona told herself that it was good and right, but she felt the loss of a friend and she desperately wanted to be on her way. Spring was giving way to summer and Tirnia would be marching on Taltia, where the King and the Prince would be waiting. And Metrid would be hatching plots to destroy them.

A matriarch overseeing the ceremony was declaring the conditions of the marriage, especially complicated since Chara was absorbing the entire family. The old matriarch was there too, standing to the side and giving her authority over to the new. The wedding ceremony had come to an end but there was the final step as Chara gave a cup of water to the old woman in exchange for the family she received.

The woman raised the wooden cup to her lips and drank deeply. She tried to place the cup into the hands of one of her attendants as she slumped. The cup clattered to the floor and she fell into the arms of the girl behind her.

Chara gasped and Elona jumped to her feet. No one else moved.

The old woman's attendants carried the body away.

265

38

───────

Elona held the shaking form of Chara. They were in the guest apartments. The servants had tried to make them go to the matriarch's rooms, but one look at the bed and belongings still present had driven them away. The stark rooms mirrored Elona's empty heart.

'I killed her,' sobbed Chara.

'No, you didn't.'

'I gave her the cup.'

'You didn't know it was poisoned.'

'I thought we'd stay here until she died then we'd take over.'

Elona had no answer. To her it made sense, as if she understood the Slissac while Chara did not.

'You took her family. That was the contract, she had nothing left. You took it all.'

'But I didn't want to kill her—'

But that's what you do when you take someone's life away. 'I have to go.'

'What?'

'I have to go. I have to go now, today.'

'But how can you stop this woman?'

'I don't know but, Tek, I must try.'

'You called me—'

'Because that's what you are now. You are my sister but also my mistress and my mother. I ask you now, please let me go.'

'I–I'm not. Why do you have to asssk?'

'Because you are the head of the house, because you are the only one who can let me go. I love you, Chara, but I must do this thing. It is a blood feud between the matriarchs of two families. Would you deny me if I were Slissac?'

Chara turned away. 'I would not lose a daughter any more than a sister.'

They stood on the upper gallery of a quay. Below there was the bustling of traders and porters, while vessels large and small floated in the underground cavern; a huge tunnel lead off to the west. A Slissac patterner was moving around the edges of the gallery, tidying the glowing moss and increasing its glow as he passed.

Below them a set of stairs ran down to the edge of the quay where a large boat lay bumping against the quay. Elona was covered head to foot in white with a veil hiding her face and gloves on her hands.

Chara stood at her side. 'I have paid for the boat and the patterner. They will take you to Kasssarina and then on to Garhrana. They said that was as far west as the canals go before running into the human settlements. You will be my emissary seeking to expand my family lands. The money I have given you should pay for a guide from there. Once you are gone from here you must not let anyone see you. Toleg will speak for you.'

They embraced and Chara whispered, 'I love you. Please come back.'

'I will.' *I will try.*

Chara stayed in the gallery while Elona and Toleg descended the steps to the boat, watching as they stepped aboard and sat in the raised seats facing forward. Toleg gave a short command to the Patterner and the boat moved off from the quay. Elona twisted round and looked up at Chara, both remaining motionless as the water widened between them. Finally, the tunnel closed around her and Chara was lost to sight.

The darkness closed around her, and Elona became numb with the task she faced: on a boat with the Slissac, pretending to be one when one word would reveal her; to travel from this world back to that of humans, to stop a woman who had already made her daughter the consort of the future King. And to do all this when any Slissac would kill her and no human would believe her. It made no difference, prophecy or not it's what she must do. One step at a time.

Toleg interrupted her thoughts some time later to give her something to eat. Every now and then they passed way-stations where boats and barges were tied up. The air was thick with the smell of thousands of *Slissac*. If they wanted to retake the slaves, what would stop them? Only their fear, and that fear would drive them to kill them all given the right push.

Time passed inexorably, and before she expected it they were approaching another opening in the tunnel. This time fresh air and bright daylight flooded in, silhouetting other boats against the glare.

They disembarked and Elona allowed Toleg to lead her through the town on its upper walkway. The individual buildings were smaller than at Hanna but they were the same fortresses. They found a hostelry and Toleg arranged for a private room.

The next day they went on, though now her fears were tested by huge steps in the waterway. They sailed into gated areas. the water was let out and they descended to the next level. Sometimes she stared ahead, but at others she closed her eyes while the boat was buffeted against the sides. Once she looked up to the sky framed by a small rectangle high above, water dripping from the mossy walls as her stomach lurched.

While Hanna had been set in a deep valley within the mountains, Kasarina and Garhrana were on the mountainside. At first, she could see across the foothills, but to the north were dark areas of forest while a little to the west, in the direction they travelled, the forest gave way to grasslands. West again and there was more forest, but another range of mountains rose, and with the sight of them her heart rose too; it was the Gap of Dirdin once more. The twin peaks of Faordranil and Liniel marked the southern border of Taltia, still a great ways off yet it almost felt as if she were home. With that came the thought of Chara, and she wondered what was happening in her other home.

The long descent through a dozen great steps in the canal had hidden the view of her future, and in the late evening they entered Garhrana. It was a much smaller town, without double level roadways; the buildings were lower, though still crowded around the cliffside. The hostel Toleg found for them had fewer rooms but he managed to pay for one on the top floor, suiting her position as a tu-Gey. But where the larger towns provided anonymity, a matriarch travelling from the city attracted attention in this small place, and she was glad to reach the safety of the rooms Toleg had hired.

There was an awkward exchange between them, as Toleg tried to understand where she wanted to go. She eventually managed to acquire a stylus and clay tablet. She sketched a map of the twin peaks and the Gap of Dirdin. The capital of Taltia, Aris, was located further along the range at the end of a lake-filled valley. It was said to be impregnable unless an army could walk a path to its ley-circle. She did not know how far she could persuade the Slissac to take her, or how far they could travel.

Toleg took the tablet and, the next morning, left her alone in her room. He returned in a state of excitement but she could not understand a word. He kept pointing towards the sky and the north repeating the word *tekrak*. Yet it was not even midsummer and the marauding plants did not cross the sky until autumn. He gave up trying to explain and settled for miming another sleep and then indicating they would go.

Toleg woke her before dawn and she dressed quickly. They made their way from the hostel through the quiet town, towards the northern gate. The sun was tinting the sky pink as they emerged into a wide space beyond the gate. Huge, dark shapes like haystacks lay spaced out around the field and each had a tent at one end. As they passed close to one she saw the tent was a curious construction of wood and basketry topped with a canvas awning. Dwarfing the tent was one of the shapes; she could make out huge veined leaves and a blunt stalk at one end. She could not contain a gasp. '*Tekrasa*?'

Toleg glanced at her then walked on.

Elona's mind whirled; every few years the migrating *tekrasa* would fly over Corlain in the autumn and descend at night. The flames that drove them forward would set light to the fields when they took flight in the morning sun. So to protect the harvest in those years, everyone would take to the fields and puncture the great leaf bodies of the *tekrasa*, releasing the noxious smelling gas, then the farmers and armsmen would chop off their flame-makers and burn them all.

But the largest she had ever seen was as long as a man is tall; these were the size of a house, even bigger. She could see their massive roots, thicker than her arm, dug into the soil, and at each end ropes had been tied on to them and attached to metal rods driven into the ground.

They reached the far side of the field as the sun's light touched the snow-capped tips of the mountains and they lit up brilliant white. The air was cold but the day promised good warmth. All over the field Slissac were up and checking their ropes; behind them others were coming on to the fields, and some with carts and goods were being passed into the curious tents.

They reached a tent where a female Slissac was waiting for them. Toleg greeted her and gave Elona's title and family. She made an obeisance to Elona, who inclined her head in return. Toleg passed over some coins and she counted them. Then he guided the two into the tent. Elona looked around in confusion, but as instructed sat in a chair woven into the floor panels. The tent was divided into two sections: a smaller area that seemed to be the main living space, and another currently empty space. Two male Slissac appeared and made themselves busy rolling up the canvas that covered the upper part of the wall, revealing windows that looked out all around. The entire canvas was removed, opening the roof to the sky. An older female Slissac took another seat facing a window. The bulk of the *tekrak* lay dormant to the side.

The sun reached the field, and across from it the *tekrasa* rippled.

Their bodies ballooned and their roots wriggled free of the earth. But all were still attached to the ground by the ropes. Dozens of Slissac were active around the heaving bodies, and the Slissac seated before her began a chant. She felt the hair on her skin standing up with the power of a patterning.

The *tekrak* at their side slowly lifted from the ground while the Slissac held on tight to the ropes. She could see its roots dripping soil as it was carefully manhandled over the top of the tent. She felt the patterning change and its roots became alive again, entwining with the roof structure. The tent lurched to the side. One of the Slissac shouted orders and the crew piled into the tent as it lurched again and rose silently into the air.

39

Elona bit her lip in terror as the ground fell away and the whole tent swayed. She felt ill and her whole body shook. All around, other giant *tekrasa* were rising up in the sun's light; she felt the patterner modify her song and the *tekrak*'s flame tube roared into life. Elona fixed her eyes on the distant mountains to quell her vertigo as the creature turned in the air towards the sun.

There was little sense of movement. The crew around her laughed and joked. She kept her eyes shut as much as she could, but when they moved the whole floor swayed and her sickness returned. The nightmare journey continued through the day; at one point Toleg tried to offer her food but she could not face it. The sun moved round from in front of them to behind and they descended.

Elona woke from her fear-soaked daze as they hit the ground with a thud. She watched the *tekrak*'s roots unravel from the structure; then as it was manhandled across to land, next to them, where it rooted itself. The constant pressure of the Patterner's chant stopped and Elona staggered out on to solid ground.

A fire was started and food cooked. The flying room was converted back to a tent and Elona given a private area. Inside she lay down on a pallet, grateful that the floor no longer moved. Toleg brought her food and she slept like the dead.

She was woken again before dawn with a hot broth. Toleg held a clay tablet and stylus. They wanted to know where to go next. She wondered how far they had come but she saw a mark had been made below the Gap of Dirdin. The journey that had taken ten-days to make on the ground, the *tekrak* had covered in a single day, perhaps thirty or more leagues. If that were the distance they might reach Mt Liniel with another day's journey, and another day would take her to Aris. She marked a point by Liniel on her map and returned it to Toleg.

Ensuring no one was nearby, she made her ablutions in a nearby stream. By the time she returned the sun was rising over the ridge. She was cheered by their rate of progress and decided she would try to be less afraid.

When she returned to the *tekrak* it was being held in place by the crew and she hurried to her seat. The patterner's chanting grew louder and the creature took hold of the vessel and lifted it from the ground. The shock of movement made her stomach turn over, but she gripped the chair and kept her eyes open.

They turned northwest and the flame roared, pushing them ahead. The mountain slopes dropped away and she saw the plains of Taltia spreading out like a map into the blue distance, to her right were forests and directly ahead Mt Liniel, with Faordranil rising higher behind it. She had seen the mountains from here before, from her journey with the Kadralin and then the bandits.

She wanted to see more of the land across which she had walked. Steeling herself, she stood up. Toleg jumped up beside her and the crew stared. She turned to the left and walked slowly and carefully towards the side. The crew that lounged on that side moved swiftly away in deference and the whole vessel swung. Impulsively she reached out and grabbed Toleg's arm for balance, and her sleeve slid up her arm.

She dropped it again as fast she could and prayed to Taymalin that none had seen the colour and nature of her skin. She continued to the edge and gripped the vertical support, holding her entire body against it. She forced herself to look down.

It felt as if they hung motionless. Below her was the northern peninsula of the mountains. She thought she could see a track running across it, the track she had passed across. Further to the northwest she saw the sea of trees that filled the Gap and, on the far side, the green and purple base of the Mt Liniel emerging. She closed her eyes and breathed the clean, cold air deeply. Soon she would reach humanity, soon she would be able to face her enemy and bring her down. Somehow. Even if she had to strangle her with her bare hands.

As the day progressed she felt something change in the patterning that drove the *tekrak*. A wind had blown up and clouds were filling the sky from the west. It seemed as if the patterner drove the flying plant harder, and the sound from the flame tube grew louder.

When Toleg brought her food she was able to eat it, though the uncertain nature of the vessel still made her heart skip a beat each time it moved unexpectedly, and it was happening more often with the change in the weather.

They crossed the Gap in the late afternoon and with Mt Liniel growing on their left they crossed a large river and descended into a valley. The landing was rough. The crew leapt out as they were touching down and pulled hard on the ropes, but not before they were dragged across the ground and Elona and Toleg were thrown to the floor. The patterner forced the *tekrak* to release the vessel before they had completely stopped, and they came to a rest with a thud as the basket righted itself. The Slissac hanging on to the ropes were carried a short distance before the creature came to rest and dug in its roots.

Next morning there was a continuous drizzle; the wind did not seem strong but the patterner kept looking at the sky. The day was well advanced and the *tekrak* strained against its ropes before they took off. Elona could tell they were concerned; the crew did not chatter and laugh the way they had but concentrated their attention forward.

Despite the bulk of the *tekrak* above them, the rain came in sideways and soaked them all. Elona's clothes were saturated and she had trouble moving in them, cold seeping into her bones. The patterner kept the *tekrak* flying low and the buffeting from the wind kept them swinging. After three days she did not feel so ill but the closeness of the ground and the instability of the floor kept causing bursts of vertigo.

Cliffs and valleys slowly passed by as they made their way north-west on the leeward side of the mountains. As they flew through the huge valley between Liniel and Faordranil, the wind from the west became much stronger and continuous. The patterner's concentration and the volume of her chant increased as she drove to the plant to expel more flame and keep on the course she desired.

Looking out and down Elona saw, not far below, a caravan of traders, their faces toward her and some pointing directly at them. The crew seemed unhappy at this and only ceased complaining when they had crossed the valley and were back into the buffeting winds.

Dark was coming on them as they made it passed the high peaks of Faordranil; Elona could feel the *tekrak* resisting as the patterner's chant forced it to go higher, towards a ridge that they then passed over, dropping into a valley with a small lake at its centre.

Elona was as grateful as the rest to disembark at the end of the day's journey. The patterner seemed grey with exhaustion and the crew made up the tents sullenly, with the occasional sly look in her direction as if they blamed her for the bad weather. She retreated to her private area as soon as she could and peeled off the wet clothes. She hung them as best she could to dry but the air itself was cold and full of moisture.

She smiled as she dressed herself in the practical but restricting clothes Chara had left for her. She wished she could at least write something for Toleg to take back to her but Chara could not even read the Slissac writings, let alone human script. Elona ran her hand over her skull and felt the bristles scratch her palm. She took out the sharp little knife and carefully ran it across her scalp until it was smooth again.

Later, Toleg brought food and the clay tablet; she wiped away the existing map and drew what she remembered of the thin spit of a ridge, the Kichek's Back, joining the twin peaks to the next range with Taltia to the north and Dirdin to the south, and the valley where the city lay beside the lake.

When morning came she put her still-damp clothes over her dark leather to keep it from her skin and covered her head. In the pre-dawn light the crew was packing their gear. The sky was over-cast but the rain had stopped and the wind was lighter. She took her seat and the *tekrak* was wrestled into position, taking off and turning to the southeast.

Fear shot through her; they were going the wrong way.

40

———————

She did not know what to do. She could not order them to change their course; she could not ask Toleg what was happening. Slowly she got to her feet and walked forwards to where the patterner sat at the front. She knew all eyes were upon her. They had passed over the valley's ridge and the ground fell away precipitously. She grabbed the patterner by the shoulder and pointed back, but the patterner ignored her. Then she knew that, somehow, they had discovered her secret.

She pulled the hood and veil from her head. There were cries of surprise and she looked around at them staring at her.

'I am Elona tu-Gey Aytrueth,' she shouted above the noise of the flame. She looked at Toleg; he alone seemed uncertain. She continued to stare at him as if willing him to obey his true mistress's command. His resolve seemed to coalesce and he stumbled over to her, keeping his eyes down, then stood protectively in front of her.

Elona fumbled beneath her robes and pulled out the little dagger. One or two of the crew clicked in humour. Elona brought the knife to patterner's throat and the clicking stopped. Once more she pointed to the northwest and she felt the change in the pattern as the plant slowly turned.

She tried to think what she should do; some plan, but there was nothing, only to keep threatening the patterner until they reached the city. Then what? She did not wish them harm, and if her people discovered *Slissac* lived in the mountains there would be war, but once on the ground they would not hesitate to kill her.

As the day wore on she had Toleg bring her something to sit on and then a meal. Still, she could think of no way to resolve her problem. By late afternoon they had run the length of the Kichek's Back and seen patrols of armsmen riding its length. She could not see their insignia but guessed them to be Taltian, unless Tirnia had already penetrated this far and decided to bypass the city. An unlikely strategy, with the Valley Circle so close to the city, it could not be starved into submission by siege, and could be used as a staging post for thousands of troops to take any invader from behind.

She guided the patterner by pointing, and aimed to come to the city from across the mountains, as that would be least likely to be watched. They climbed across foothills, rivers and valleys heading north and northeast. Elona laughed at herself; there was no problem with the crew. She mimed for Toleg to tie up them, they would not be needed for the landing she had in mind. She watched carefully for the point at which the rivers and streams ran north and when they had reached a broad sweep of green that descended to the north she had the patterner descend.

The *tekrak*'s flame was off and they silently descended into the shadowed valley. Goats grazed on the grasslands and she knew there would a goatherd nearby, no doubt in some hiding place, watching in terror as the monster floated silently from the sky. It could not be helped.

As they touched down Elona turned to Toleg and thanked him, then jumped over the side and landed on the grass. Instantly she felt the pattern change and the *tekrak* rose again. Its flame roared into life and it curved round and up. In almost no time it had lifted over the ridge and was gone. Elona stripped the flowing cloth from her body and let it lie where it fell.

~

It was almost completely dark as she emerged from the valley above the city, the light of Colimar hanging low in the sky, reflecting from the calm waters of the lake. The city of Aris stood on its nearer shore; surrounding it were the lights of many campfires. Nearer and to the left another encampment ringed what she guessed to be the Valley Circle, and across the river to the right were other encampments and smaller lights from the villages. On each side, flanking the lake almost to its very shores, the mountains curved around.

Her enthusiasm evaporated like a drop of water falling into a fire. It was impregnable and untouchable. What could she do to get in, let alone find Metrid and stop her? And, given this, what could Metrid hope to achieve?

She sat on the grass.

Only four days ago she had been living in a Slissac town over a hundred leagues from here. She had come so far. She had promised herself one step at a time, that's all it would take. The clouds moved above her and the light of Lostimal broke through, silvering the land. She found a hollow in the ground, ate, and settled down to sleep.

The sun was lighting the sky and she felt a pattern she knew well: wolves. They were scared. Too many humans in the valley, too dangerous, and they felt the loss of a brother. They were not close and Elona did nothing to attract them. They passed by and went on their way up the valley. She hoped the goatherd would have the sense to avoid them.

She walked down the slope near the river. As the ground flattened she came to fields and turned left towards the Circle and the road. As she edged her way around the field she saw Brothers and Sisters of Taymalin working in the fields. She ran her hand across her head and smiled. She walked through an orchard and reached an out-building. She peered round into the Sanctuary; there were a few people about but, more importantly, there were robes drying on a line.

Elona stepped out on to the road from the avenue that led from the Sanctuary. She carried her food and clothes in the large pouch hanging from her shoulder and walked confidently towards the city. Human faces. Armsmen, farmers and children. Their familiar faces made her feel confident and happy, and though they glanced toward her there was no suspicion, no hate. She was just another person, a Sister of Taymalin; just human.

She walked through the main city gate, smiling at the guards and into the streets. After asking directions, she headed for a Sanctuary of the Sisterhood. The doorkeeper eyed her up and down, then admitted her.

'I am Edoline of Revor, a novice freshly come from Faerholme by request of the Revered Malea. I have some skill at healing and wish to offer my help.'

'Welcome, Novice,' said the Sister. 'The Revered Malea is known to us by name. We have little space but we will find a pallet for you no doubt.'

Elona prepared to follow the woman into the building when she pulled back to allow a Revered one to come through first. She was followed by an armsman, a captain of guard wearing the tree of Dirdin on his tabard. Elona dropped her head instantly, for it was Jalka. She cursed him silently for being there and interfering. With luck he would not see her, only the shaved head of a Sister.

'Thank you, Revered Tolin; my men will be grateful for a visit from the Sisters.'

'Captain, the Sisterhood is grateful for your contribution especially in these times.'

The doorkeeper went through and Elona followed unable to hear any further conversation. She was passed to another Sister and shown to her pallet.

Elona had delivered the alms to the hostel of elders and listened for what seemed hours to them talking about people and times long gone. She had to find Metrid, she needed news of Faerholme, of the

King and the Prince. Unless she knew what was happening there was nothing she could do.

She stood in the middle of the market. The hustle and bustle all around her. Among the townsfolk walked the richer, the well-to-do; they would surely know, but how did one approach? If she were not a Sister of Taymalin she could chance a tavern. If she were older and a full Sister she might find an excuse but it would be so inappropriate for a novice it would surely be noted. Besides, she had no money.

She turned again, the frustration building.

'Lost, Sister?' said a voice in her ear. She spun round; Jalka stood at her shoulder, grinning in that oddly familiar, oddly disagreeable way.

41

She turned to run and he grabbed her wrist and held it tightly, but she was more than she had been. With her free hand she plunged into her bag and allowed herself to be pulled close. The little blade inside pierced her bag, his tabard and his mail beneath.

'Ow!' He pulled back suddenly but still held her wrist. With his other hand, he touched his stomach and looked in surprise at the blood on his fingers.

'What did you do that for?' He looked about quickly but no one was paying attention. 'Come on, quickly.' He released her wrist and headed off into the crowd. She didn't move but felt the power of the Valley Circle and, without knowing why, built a reservoir of light. After a few steps he glanced behind and stopped. People flowed between them. He waited.

Elona could not understand the emotions within her. He had chased her but he had also freed her. Now he was here, though that was not so surprising. She did not move. He walked back slowly through the crowd.

'I am in need of a healer at this moment. I'm bleeding,' he said. 'My billet is this way, we can talk in private. I promise I'll leave a window open.'

'Very well.'

She released the power and followed behind him, through the crowd out of the market and through streets that got steadily narrower. At the end of one she stopped. He took a few more steps then turned.

'Where are you taking me?'

'There,' he said, pointing at a house a little further down. It was decrepit, though once it had been a home of quality. 'We did not arrive until recently. It's all they had, even for a captain of guard.'

'How do I know I can trust you?'

'I helped you escape at the Woodcircle, who do you think paid the Kadralin? And I didn't give you away at the Sanctuary.'

'You've been following me.'

'We need to talk.'

Elona sat opposite Jalka with the table between them. The dirty walls were damp and the room had an unpleasant acrid smell. Light forced its way through the grimy windows and made patterns on the floor. Jalka found two plain goblets and poured wine from a pewter jug. Elona lifted hers and took a long drink. She returned his gaze.

'You're different,' he said.

She gave a humourless smile. 'Yes.'

'The disguise is effective.'

'We're not here to discuss how I look.'

'No,' said Jalka. 'I think you want to tell me something.'

'I do? What's that?'

'Why you're here? If the powers from Faerholme catch you, you'll be imprisoned again. Yet you came. You were imprisoned for madness and murder—and you did kill someone, even if it was only a maid.'

Elona slammed her goblet down and leapt to her feet. 'You're the same as the rest of them! I killed someone I loved as a sister and I can never make it right. You have nothing to say to me.'

Jalka remained seated and leant over his drink. 'I am sorry. I didn't know.'

Elona wanted to leave, to spurn him, but he was listening as only Chara ever listened. She went and stood by the window. 'The Lady

Metrid of Betlain came to me in the guise of friendship. It was she who brought the madness on me with her gifts; they were patterned to make me believe that a poison destroyed my home, my family and my kingdom.'

'Why would she do that?'

'I stood between her and her daughter's marriage to the Prince. A marriage she has made happen. Tell me this: is there yet a future heir to the Faerholme throne?'

'I understand that the Princess Hope is heavy with child. The Dragonblade and his son are here in Aris.'

'Then her plan approaches fruition, she intends their death, and then if she cannot control her, her daughter too.'

'Hope? How can you be sure?'

'What has she not done? And it seems I am the only one who knows, and who would believe the mad girl who killed her friend?'

'I.'

'Why?' Elona went silent and her attention focussed on the window. A shadow passed in front of it. Then another. She jumped back, grabbing her little dagger from her bag. 'And you would betray me too.'

'No!'

There was a banging on the door. Jalka looked confused. 'I told no one. Out the back.'

Elona hurried through a second door behind and headed through a dingy kitchen; the sound of chinking mail and footsteps sounded from behind the door. Elona swung round and headed up the stairs two at a time with Jalka following.

'She found me.'

They rounded another flight as there was a crash from below and the sound of boots thudding across the floorboards.

'Keep going up. How can she? Round to the right.'

They arrived in a room containing a pallet. Jalka went to the window in the eaves and pulled it open. 'We've been here before.'

'When she did her patterns to confuse me she made a bond only recently broken. But she could know where I am when I draw power

—' she realised her mistake in the market and cursed her foolishness.

'You have to go now.' Jalka seemed not to have noticed what she was saying.

He held the window open as she slid past him. She smiled. 'Thank you for your kindness. What will you say to them?'

'You stabbed me and left a while ago.'

'Sorry—' she felt reluctant to leave and it was not only her fear of the height.

'Go. How will I speak with you again?'

She clambered awkwardly onto the frame. 'The market tomorrow,' She said quickly, and he shut the window.

She climbed out and above the window, then crawled away along the roof ridge focusing only on the mossy thatch directly in front of her. Feeling her stomach turning over and the weakness in her arms and legs, she managed a smile. She had flown higher than birds and now was scared to crawl on a rooftop.

At the end of the houses she let herself down the back of the building where it butted on to the new row. She landed on the roof of the kitchen and slid to the ground. She moved rapidly along the alley, then out onto the street and merged into the crowd. It seemed Metrid could only find her when she used power, which meant she could not have discovered where she was staying. So Elona made her way back to the Sanctuary and more menial tasks.

The next day began the same way, up early for devotions and then cleaning and delivering alms. She arrived in the market as many were taking their midday meals and looked at the goods on sale while she waited in the hot sun. By mid-afternoon she decided he was not coming, and returned to the Sanctuary to be chastised by an Elder Sister.

On the following day Elona walked towards the elders' hospice on the far side of the city. The townsfolk bustled around her but she felt isolated. She wondered whether her mother's condition had changed and what it would be like to have her awake, and to hold her. What had happened to Jalka? Why had he sent no message, at least? And Chara? How did she fare now in the land of her birth?

The hospice housed twelve Sisters who were now so frail that they could not work, and often their minds would wander. The hospice was clean and simple, each occupant shared with one other; they tried to balance their remaining skills so each might help the other.

They were ruled over by Sister Mathilde, who suffered from a disease that no healer could mend. Her bones had become thin and brittle though this did not seem to affect her strength of mind. It was strange for Elona, she had never been around the infirm, always the healers had been there to put right what nature, or man, made wrong. Yet it seemed some broken patterns were too complex to mend or even to patch.

She stayed with them, as she had been charged, until the midday meal, but as she half-listened to Mathilde she grew restless; she was trapped again. How could she find Metrid and defeat her if she did not know where she was or what she would do? She needed Jalka. She grew angry with the thought that she needed him.

The sun beat down as she stepped from the hospice and headed back towards the market in the hope that Jalka would rendezvous with her today. People brushed past her, townsfolk and armsmen going about their business. She could not be about hers.

She stopped abruptly as a large armsmen walked in front of her. Bodies closed in behind and to the sides, then the one in front turned and grinned down at her. 'Don't fuss, Sister, or we'll have to hurt you.'

42

––––––––––

An hour's journey by cart brought them back to the Valley Sanctuary. She could almost feel the throbbing power of the nearby ley-circle. The fields were empty of Brothers and Sisters and she wondered what had been done with them, until she saw a body lying in front of a barn; it was a mess of blood and a distorted travesty of humanity. The barn itself had guards, and from inside came the sound of gentle chanting. For all their ceremonial weapons, those who dedicated themselves to Taymar did not fight.

As they entered the precincts of the sanctuary itself she saw dozens of armsmen, all bearing the design of Raertane. But she had heard the accent of that land and these spoke with quite another. They were no allies of Taltia. Somehow Metrid had arranged for this Tirnian horde to walk the Patterner's Path as if from Raertane. She judged them to be at least a hundred strong, perhaps even more, insufficient for open battle but it may be that they could take the Circle for long enough to bring their own reinforcements. And the impregnable Aris would be taken by treachery.

It has hard to breathe through the gag. She lay on her side as comfortably as she could make herself, her hands and feet bound tightly; she was tied to the bed itself. There was no escape from this, Metrid had won.

Where was Jalka? Why hadn't he come? If only there were a way to contact him, a pattern she could make that would bring him to her. She knew that master patterners had the skill to speak with one another if they could draw on the power of a Circle. It was a power that the nobility in all lands distrusted and ever their messages were sent written and sealed, borne by a trusted messenger.

She had no skill in such clever patternings, yet she had the power to heal and to be with wolves. She laughed at herself inwardly, why not try? She had all the time she needed. She imagined Jalka as best she could, his face, his name, his clothing. And felt nothing. She could not achieve the detachment she had when she had manipulated the wolves' thoughts.

When Bejeren had been teaching her to write she had the stylus in a death grip and her movements jerked, producing awkward letters that could barely be deciphered. 'Stop trying so hard,' he had said.

She relaxed herself and her perceptions changed. Now she saw the patterns of the world around her, simple and complex: the half-asleep guard beyond her door, the armsmen throughout the compound, the tight concentration within the barn, creatures large and small, *kichesa* and *kikisa*, wolves. She directed her attention to Jalka and imagined him. The city was a confusion of patterns all moving. How could she find him in this? She recalled his face and looked deeper. And felt something. Passion, but it was not Jalka.

She woke with a muffled gasp. This was not what she intended.

A jangle of keys at the door drew her attention. The door opened and the guard stood there staring at her. She had seen that look in the eyes of men before but she did not tremble. Not this time. Instead she stared back and conjured her own feelings, her own passions, then after a moment slowly looked away. It was the trigger he needed. He stepped into the room, turned and locked the door behind him. He turned back and walked hesitantly to the bed.

His grimy hand ran across her scalp. She did not flinch and looked up into his eyes again. He caressed her without finesse. She made a choking noise as if trying to speak. He reached to his belt, pulled a knife from its sheath and sawed through bonds at her ankles then ran his hand up the inside of her leg. It was all she could do to prevent herself from kicking out. Again she tried to speak and this time he took the hint and pulled the gag from her mouth.

She smiled. She remembered the stories that Savi had told her of her loving of Kienan and swallowed the grief that came with it.

'Kiss me.'

The stench of him was almost overwhelming as he pressed his unshaven face against hers, scratching at her skin. He was an animal in his lust as he touched her and pressed her body to his.

'Let me hold you,' she said.

He knelt on the pallet and found the knife that now lay between them. He pulled her so she was face down and sliced through the bonds at her wrists. Her fingers throbbed as the blood returned to them. He pulled up her robe and touched her again. She rolled on to her back and could feel the dagger beneath her.

He pushed his weight between her legs and reared over her. Elona closed her eyes and arched her back to reach for the blade; she gripped it then brought her hands up and around him. She brought her hands up to his shoulders and pulled him down so her lips pressed against his. He could not see as she hefted the knife. She gripped the knife in both hands behind his head. She slammed the knife through his neck, severing blood vessels and wind pipe.

He looked surprised. Blood bubbled from his lips and dripped onto her face. He twitched and the life went from his eyes. She pulled the knife out, and with a huge effort rolled his weight from her. She stood and wiped her face with the hem of her robe.

Save for a few guards, the Tirnian armsmen were gone from the sanctuary. Elona crept through the kitchens, picking up a few small rolls of bread and meat on the way. She considered her options. She might be able to kill a guard that was not prepared for her but she was no warrior. The Brothers and Sisters of Taymalin would have to stay where they were for now. Even attackers from Tirnia would think twice before committing mass murder on those dedicated to Taymar's memory. He was sacred to them as well.

That left the troops that had departed. They either didn't think anyone would notice the Sanctuary was very quiet or they were not expecting to return here. Their trap must be ready to be sprung. She was certain she was right, that with even two hundred men the force would be far too weak to make a real difference to the defences of Aris. They must be planning to bring in more troops and the only way to achieve that would be through the ley-circle, and so they must take control of it.

Elona stood and left the kitchen by the door that led towards the fields. She made her way through the goats. They were displeased at not being fed and tried to chew her robe. She climbed a fence and was out into the fields.

There did not seem to be any armsmen guarding this side; another clue; they were not intending to return secretly, otherwise they would have left more protection from discovery. They might have guards at the gate to the main road, so she would have to be careful.

She turned to the right and made her way towards the main road on the side nearest the ley-circle, keeping clear of the gate itself. Though she could see no guards there.

What if they had another plan in mind? She could not travel both ways. She stared down at the road. She could not tell if they had gone past recently, as she was no tracker.

The sun was descending towards the mountains in the west.

A hand came over her mouth and pulled her backwards.

43

She bit into the fingers that covered her mouth and reached for the dagger.

'Ow! Taymar's teeth, woman!' hissed Jalka. She turned and looked at him sucking his fingers. His eyes widened. 'Elona, are you alright?'

'What?'

'The blood—'

'It's not mine.'

'Oh.'

She rounded on him. 'Where have you been? I waited for you twice.'

'I had duties I couldn't get out of.'

'You could have sent a message.'

'I didn't know what name you were using,' he said. 'Look, I'm here now.'

'They're on the move.'

'Yes, I know. I passed an ambush on the way here.'

'You idiot, why didn't you go back and warn the King? How many were there?'

'More than ten, but less than fifty I would guess. Unless there were any that were particularly skilled.'

'Then they are moving to the ley-circle as well.' She fell silent and thoughtful.

'What's going on, Elona?'

'Tirnians. They will take control of the ley-circle and bring in more.'

'We must warn the Circle guard.'

'Yes, you must do that, they will believe you.' She took a deep breath. 'The ambush will be for my King and Prince; she must have been waiting for them to return home before springing her trap. Then Tirnia will have the legal heir to Faerholme's throne as a puppet to their will.'

'Take my horse and ride fast. If they want to ambush they may not shoot at you. I will go to the Circle guards and alert them.'

Elona looked up at him. 'You'll need to hurry.'

Jalka fetched his horse, shortened the stirrups and gave Elona his cloak. 'Hide your head so they don't recognise you as you pass.'

She mounted, pushing her robe beneath her to pad the saddle, and wished momentarily for Chara's clothes. She turned to thank him but he was already moving quickly towards the circle. She kicked the horse into a trot and clattered along the road towards the city.

It all seemed so calm and tranquil; birds sang their evening songs from the trees by the sides of the lane. Flowers adorned the banks at the roadside, and in the fields the burgeoning crops grew. The sun had reached the mountains behind her, their shadows creeping towards the lake in the distance.

The road curved around a hillock that blocked the view of the city, and as she came around it she could see dust rising from a large party heading her way. She glanced left and right but could see no armsmen in hiding. She urged her horse into a canter.

Her fingers grew cold in apprehension. It had been nearly year and an entire lifetime since she had stood in the grand hall in Canvor and made her claim on the Prince. Now she was riding to her death, one way or another. From a Tirnian arrow or sword; or from being chained in a dungeon until she died—if they did not behead her for the death of Kienan and Nursey.

She could not let Metrid win, but how many more deaths would there be?

She clattered over a wooden bridge; they were only moments away now. Had she passed the ambush? Perhaps there was no ambush? Was Jalka wrong? Had the armsmen gone elsewhere? Had he scared them off? She watched as armsmen on *kichek*-back formed up in front of the nobles. She reined her horse in and stopped, as they did.

'Make way for the King of Faerholme.'

'You must go back!' she cried. 'There is an ambush, Tirnia is here!'

She felt a change in the patterning behind her, kicked her horse forward and lay flat against its body. An arrow passed by her head. The guards drew their swords as she pushed between them. The air was filled with the buzz of arrows from further up the road and then a roar of voices as men leapt from behind trees and bushes, and the banks and came charging up the road towards them.

Elona scanned the group ahead. She saw the King and the Prince together, behind a rank of armsmen; other nobles were grouped beyond them. The King had his hand on his sword and was drawing it as an arrow sprouted from his chest. Drahail looked confused at the arrow which had pierced his stomach. Elona cried out 'No!' and tried to force her horse through the milling bodies. It stumbled and its head went down; she flew over its head but came up short. Her foot caught in the stirrup, leaving her hanging upside down.

She cursed the Kisharuk, pulled her dagger from its sheath, and cut the strap. She rolled over and looked about. Feet danced and stumbled around her; cries of attack and cries of pain mixed in equal amounts. She saw the King slumped on his horse and Drahail desperately defending himself against a man on foot, the stump of the arrow still showing in his side.

She crawled forward to the Prince's horse and then stood up by its shoulder. She ducked beneath its neck and drove the dagger into the attacker's thigh. The blade was ripped from her hand as he pulled away and fell. She tried to turn the horse. Drahail gazed at her with a look of confusion, then his eyes unfocused and he fell forwards on to the ground. Quickly she rolled him onto his back and looked at the wound, the arrow barely filled the space that had been opened in his side and blood pumped from it. She closed her hand about the wound but the blood seeped between her fingers. It would not stop.

Elona closed her eyes and imagined the wound. The sounds of battle faded and the patterns of the armsmen and horses came in to focus. She could see the Prince's wound, it was deep, and he had been cut and torn inside by the barbs as he fought for his life. And in fighting he had condemned himself. There was nothing that could be done, what patterner could mend this? But she knew she had to try.

She saw the wound as it was and saw it as it must to be whole. She saw that she must heal from the inside, removing the arrow as she went. She pulled; the barbed arrow resisted and the Prince moaned in pain. Someone grabbed her wrist and she snapped back to reality.

'You will kill him, Sister!'

'He will die if I don't.'

The hand suddenly released her and her hood was pulled back.

'Elona?' She stared into the face of Bejeren; he had not changed. It seemed wrong that he was the same when she was so different. His eyes took in her face still smudged in blood, her shorn head. 'How can it be you?'

'I can do this, Bejeren. But I must do it now. You must let me.'

He glanced to his right and then back to her and nodded; he pulled her hood back over her head but stayed by her side.

She moved into the other world again and stopped. She had done this for herself but never for another; she knew nothing of patterning, nothing of healing. But she had done it. She took a firm grip of the arrow stump and concentrated on the Prince's lacerated body. Then opened herself to the Valley Circle, never had she felt such a power, it glowed like the sun, like a dozen suns, she allowed the power to flow and moulded it. She saw how each part should be and changed it, strengthened it, and as she did so she pulled the arrowhead slowly from his body. Drahail moaned and squirmed but she kept at it slowly, steadily, mending as she went until the arrowhead came free. She breathed deep as if she had not breathed before and sat back on her feet. She let the power go.

Bejeren's hands lifted her to her feet and she looked about. The road was littered with corpses from both sides. The King had been taken from his horse and lain at the roadside. She leant against Bejeren as a familiar figure walked towards her.

'Who are you?' demanded her father. Tiredly, she pulled the hood from her head and looked him in the eye. For a long moment he stared at her and she saw the same old emotions become fixed upon his face. 'Bind her!'

'My Lord, she saved the Prince,' cried Bejeren.

'She is a traitor; she brought these Tirnians to assassinate the King. She still thinks she can have him. Bind her fast, be sure she cannot escape.'

44

Two armsmen hurried over, pulling her arms behind her back and binding her wrists. Bejeren looked confused but Elona held her father's eye. 'Father, you are wrong in this. It is not me that betrays the King but the Lady Metrid.'

'I do not see her here,' he said. 'You are mad.'

Elona sighed and looked away. The Prince's horse shuffled and shook its head, its ears pinned back nervously. She looked at the other horses; they were the same, swinging their heads back and forth looking for something, looking for a threat. They backed away, then the *kichesa* turned and fled. At that the horses took flight, ripping their reins from those who held them.

Elona could feel the pattern.

'Wolves!' She shouted. 'Bejeren, lift the Prince. Armsmen, make a circle around your Prince!'

Bejeren hesitated for a moment before gathering the Prince in his arms; the remaining armsmen, only five able-bodied and four others, grouped themselves around the two. The Lord Corlain stared at her. 'How dare you—' he broke off as the first wolf trotted onto the road, sniffing at the bodies lying there but not eating them. Another and another came, and they kept on coming ten, twenty, until over fifty grey and brown wolves stood facing them with yellow eyes glowing. This cannot be a single pack, thought Elona, she has combined two or three. How can she wield such control over so many?

Then a figure detached itself from the trees and stepped out on to the road behind.

'So, Elona, murderess of Corlain, you have saved your Prince. The King is dead, long live the King.'

'You cannot win,' Elona said calmly and stepped forward, though inside she shivered with fear. She heard Bejeren mutter her name in terror.

'Cannot? I already have. In a moment I unleash the wolves and there will be nothing left of you and your precious Prince but gnawed bone. My armsmen are opening the circle for the Tirnian forces and once opened it will not be closed until Aris is under our control. And I shall rule in Faerholme as is my right and my due.' Metrid's voice carried more than a hint of mania. She walked between the wolves at the rear.

The wolves edged forwards.

'Wrong on two counts, Lady,' said Elona. 'I sent someone to warn the troops that surround the circle, yours will never survive long enough to get it open—and if they do it will become a killing field and the blood of the armsmen of Tirnia will spill 'ere they reach the circle.'

Metrid's swagger ceased into rigidity at Elona's words.

'You forget the prophecy, Lady. I am the one who saves Faerholme.'

'If you are not lying then you may stop Tirnia for now. But you will not stop me because you will be dead and only my tale will be told.'

A second figure stepped from the trees behind Metrid, with an arrow notched in a bow, and Elona heaved a sigh of relief.

'My tale is already told, Mother.'

Metrid cried out and span around. 'Jaymis!'

Elona's world spun around, Jalka son of Metrid? He had lied to her—but he was accused of the murder of his father. Yet only one person laid that accusation.

The wolves seemed to ripple and Elona felt the pattern change.

'You will die too, ungrateful son,' Metrid said.

'I can lose an arrow before the first of them reaches me.'

Elona felt Metrid concentrate again and two wolves split from the main group and approached him. 'You could not kill your father, what makes you think you can kill me?'

'I did not want to kill him. I don't feel the same about you.'

'Enough talking!' cried Metrid, and Elona felt the control change again. The lead wolf looked at her and she saw its muscles tense for a spring. Then she understood Metrid did not need to control all the wolves, only the leader. Elona closed her eyes.

Moments before it sprang the wolf changed its mind and turned; the others that had surged forward stopped as well. Elona opened her eyes, and she saw that Jaymis had been knocked to the ground but the wolves were no longer interested in him. Why should they be? Everyone here was a wolf, everyone except Metrid.

The wolves turned and moved towards her.

'What are you doing? No, you wouldn't, you couldn't; you're nothing but a pathetic little girl. You have no strength, you have no skill. You cannot kill!'

'Yes. I can,' Elona said. 'You have taught me.'

When the screaming stopped Elona drove the wolves into the hills and released them. Then collapsed. When she came to herself, she had her back to a tree and Jaymis was pressing a cup of wine to her mouth. She took a sip.

'Hello,' he said.

'I would really like to go home,' she said.

EPILOGUE

Elona watched her mother's pale body on the bed, her chest rising and falling gently. The chanting of the Sisters filled the high chamber with echoing, discordant sound. Cold draughts from the vaulted stone ceiling disturbed the torch flames, making shadows dance about her mother's thin face.

Jaymis stood at her side. 'She sleeps still.'

'Yes, she sleeps still,' Elona said. She is untouched by all that happens while I am torn apart and re-made.

'The prophecy is fulfilled,' said Bejeren.

Elona felt that perhaps she ought to be angry at him for mentioning it, but there was little point. He and all the others said it: the prophecy was fulfilled, she had saved Faerholme and brought down the evil that threatened to engulf it, everything was back to the way it was. Was that all? Stopping an invasion from Tirnia? Tirnia was not defeated. It had nothing to do with the prophecy; there had been no great battle, either with or without her. It was nothing more than a skirmish.

But my mother still sleeps and I am re-made. A sad, strange girl. She ran her hand across her head; the bristles of her hair had softened as they had lengthened. She wondered whether she would cut it again; she wanted to remember her only sister.

She looked around at her father, though she was invisible to him. He had not spoken to her since the fight at Aris. She looked at the child standing beside him. Barely two years old, Manvord—Savi's son, was now heir to Corlain. She did not begrudge the child; she had taken his parents from him, and the debt was repaid.

Jaymis and she were both pardoned but no one forgot. There was no question of the deaths she had engendered and she was shunned by all. There were those who would always believe that Jaymis had murdered his father—the lands of Betlain remained with his uncle.

She glanced at Bejeren and Master Florian at his side. She had forgiven Bejeren, he had acted on her behalf and without his teaching she would have been lost. But the Arch-Patterner, with his schemes and plans to make her the pawn of the prophecy, she would never forgive.

The Revered Malea guided the Sisters from the hall. Elona waited while her father kissed her mother and departed with the boy. The other visitors turned and filed from the room until she was alone, save for Jaymis standing hesitantly by her side. The servants entered and placed the brazier and screens around the bed then departed as silent as ghosts.

Elona looked up at Jaymis. 'There's no need to wait for me.'

He opened his mouth to speak, then nodded and turned away. Elona walked slowly past the screens to her mother's side and sat on the bed facing the sleeper. She took her mother's hand gently and kissed it.

'Let me tell you about Chara.'

~ END ~

READ THE NEXT BOOK IN THE SERIES:

Elona's tale is not over.

Back in Corlain she finds her life to be dull and that's when she isn't just lonely. She and Jaymis decide to travel, which is when the trouble really starts.

Go to https://taupress.com/jaymis?__src=PP-01

READ VEONA (PATTERNER'S PATH 0)

Discover the real beginning of this story…

Subscribe to my mailing list and download the prequel **VEONA** (Patterner's Path 0).

Go here: **taupress.com/vs-veona**

ABOUT THE AUTHOR

Steve Turnbull has been a geek and a nerd longer than those words have had their modern meaning.

Born in the heart of London to book-loving working class parents in 1958, he lived with his parents and two much older sisters in two rooms with gas lighting and no hot water (true!). In his fifth year, a change in his father's fortunes took them out to a detached house in the suburbs. That was the year Dr Who first aired on British TV and Steve watched it avidly from behind the sofa. It was the beginning of his love of science fiction.

Academically Steve always went for the science side but also had his imagination and that took him everywhere. He read through his local library's entire science fiction and fantasy selection, plus his father's 1950s *Astounding Science Fiction* magazines. As he got older he also ate his way through TV SF like *Star Trek*, *Dr Who* and *Blake's 7*.

However it was when he was 15 he discovered something new. Bored with a Maths lesson he noticed a book from the school library: *Cider with Rosie* by Laurie Lee. From the first page he was captivated by the beauty of the language. As a result he wrote a story longhand and then spent evenings at home on his father's electric typewriter pounding out a second draft, expanding it. Then he wrote a second book. Both were terrible but it was a start. After that he switched to poetry and turned out dozens, mostly not involving teenage angst.

After receiving excellent science and maths results he went on to study Computer Science. There he teamed up with another student and they wrote songs for their band - Steve writing the lyrics. Though they admit their best song was the other way around, with Steve writing the music.

After graduation Steve moved into contract programming but was snapped up a couple of years later by a computer magazine looking for someone with technical knowledge. It was in the magazine industry that Steve learned how to write to length, to deadline and to style. Within a couple of years he was editor and stayed there for many years.

During that time he married Pam (also a magazine editor) who he'd met at a student party.

Though he continued to write poetry all prose work stopped. He created his own magazine publishing company which at one point produced the glossy subscription magazine for the *Robot Wars* TV show. The company evolved into a design agency but after six years of working very hard and not seeing his family—now including a daughter and son—he gave it all up.

He spent a year working on miscellaneous projects including writing 300 pages for a website until he started back where he had begun, contract programming.

With security and success on the job front, the writing began again. This time it was scriptwriting: features scripts, TV scripts and radio scripts. During this time he met a director Chris Payne, who wanted to create steampunk stories and between them they created the Voidships universe, a place very similar to ours but with specific scientific changes.

But you can't keep a good writer restrained, so apart from the output of Steampunk stories Steve returned to his first love of Fantasy and Science Fiction.

Don't forget you can read VEONA by going to **taupress.com/vs-veona**

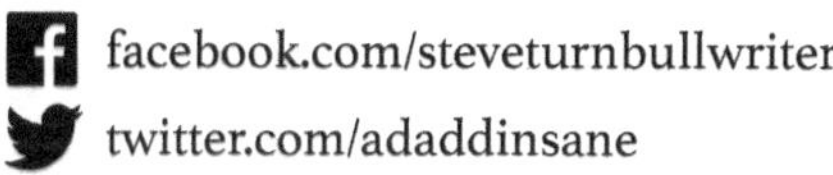

www.ingramcontent.com/pod-product-compliance
Lightning Source LLC
Chambersburg PA
CBHW051641180726
48284CB00006B/1812